Charred

A whipped and Sipped Mystery

G.P. Gottlieb

DX VAROS PUBLISHING

Published by:
DX Varos Publishing, Inc.
7665 E. Eastman Ave. #B101
Denver, CO 80231

Book cover design and layout by Ellie Bockert Augsburger of Creative Digital Studios.
www.CreativeDigitalStudios.com
Cover design features:
wooden spoon isolated on white background, clipping path, full depth of field By grey / Adobe Stock

ISBN: 978-1-955065-67-2 (paperback)
ISBN: 978-1-955065-68-9 (ebook)

Cast of Characters

The cops:
Frank Shaw, 43, homicide detective, dating Alene
Lee Bautista, 42, Frank's partner

Everyone Else:
Don Klavestedberg, 74, involved in the bank robbery
    with Finn Baron
Hugh Burgess, involved in the bank robbery with
    Finn Baron
Lester Crow, involved in the robbery with Finn
    Baron
Peter Berg, 38, Taryn's brother
Rhona Shaw, 22, Frank's daughter
Taryn Berg, 42, Peter's sister
Vincent Stevens, involved in the bank robbery with
    Finn Baron

Chapter 1

Normally, the Whipped and Sipped Café would have been bustling, the nearby sidewalks filled with people, and the streets packed with cars and bicycles. Now, the café was barely getting by. Yet that Friday morning, proprietor Alene Baron looked at the end-of-the-month accounts and saw that they'd sold more cookies in April and May 2020 than they'd sold in all of 2019. Everyone was craving cookies. They were anxious about catching the Covid-19 coronavirus, shocked that it was killing a multitude of people, and distraught at being stuck in their homes with nowhere to go.

"Maybe isolating people keeps the virus from sending more victims to the hospital, since they're already overcrowded," Alene told Ruthie, her best friend and pastry chef, "but I think closing all the public buildings and outdoor spaces is going too far."

Ruthie, who was kneading a bread dough, and usually saw the positive side to everything, said, "They're trying to keep people safe, Alene. I know you're upset that all our sales have to come from online or phone-in orders, but not having customers also protects us."

"I know," said Alene, "but I'm still frustrated. I miss people stopping by to grab a latte or indulge in your vegan baking." Ruthie acknowledged that everyone was frustrated. Alene went out to the café and made herself an almond latte before going back to her office to finish the accounts.

She'd woken up early that morning after another night of terrifying dreams about her children, her father, and her friends and employees catching the virus. Usually, she would have gone out for a run before the sun rose, but instead she'd gotten dressed, tied her hair in a ponytail, grabbed her purse, masked up, and gone to knock on the door across the hall.

Long-time neighbor Kacey Vanza and her boyfriend Kofi Lloyd were already standing in the hallway, ready for her to drive them to a burned-down building about ten minutes away. Alene had heard about the fire from Ruthie, and had told Kofi, but he'd already learned about it because he tracked fires with an illegal scanner.

Kofi, who created sculptures out of interesting cast-off materials and was constantly searching for pieces of burned wood that looked like they'd undergone trauma, couldn't afford a car. Usually, when he wanted a lift to the aftermath of a fire, he'd wait for a ride from his cousin Umar, who taught high school and was usually free on weekends, but Umar and his pickup truck were no longer available. Now that the schools were closed and Umar could only communicate with his teenage charges over the internet, he'd been going back and forth to Galesburg, Illinois, where he and Kofi had grown up.

Kofi was much different from Alene's neighbor Kacey. He was tall, she was short; he was an artist, she couldn't draw; his skin was the color of chocolate, hers was pale pink. Kacey's only family was her mother, who spent more time worrying about the purity and provenance of her food than the well-being of her daughter. She also had two stepbrothers, but never saw them. Kofi's parents, grandparents, aunts, and uncles lived within fifteen minutes of each other in Galesburg, and he and his cousin were the only ones in their family to ever leave western Illinois for college.

Alene was grateful that Kacey and Kofi had become a part of her "family pod," and could saunter across the hall with a carton of ice cream to share with her and her father and children. Their visits helped break the monotony of being stuck at home.

Kofi had graduated from the School of the Art Institute of Chicago with a focus on sculpture. When Alene first met him, he'd said he preferred salvaging and recycling materials, especially those that had gotten charred or twisted, and he was always on the lookout.

"I'm glad developers went back to wood frame construction," he told Alene that morning on the way to the fire site. Kacey sat next to her, and he'd sat in the back. "This could be a treasure trove." Kofi liked to get to fire sites before insurance adjusters or other scavengers arrived, but he also had to wait until the fire had cooled down. Alene had seen scrapes and scars on his arms and legs from previous expeditions. He'd brought thick, fireproof gloves this time.

Alene had bought one of his sculptures a few years before. He'd used discarded bicycle parts and shaped them into a rainbow. The Whipped and Sipped Café was in a neighborhood known as Boystown, although there'd been rumblings about changing it, and the "Rainbow Sculpture" had been an iconic fixture of the neighborhood since it went up. Alene had organized a neighborhood art walk that would start and end under Kofi's sculpture, but that could only happen if the sun came out and the pandemic was under control.

It was a ten-minute drive to the fire site through narrow streets, passing a mixture of magnificently built old apartment complexes, charmless "four-plus-ones," and various modern, visually unappealing rental properties. They drove by boarded-up storefronts, bars, and restaurants. When they reached the property, the darkness was dissipating, and Alene could vaguely see what looked like piles of garbage behind a chain-link fence. She parked on a side street next to the building site. Kofi and Kacey, both wearing windbreakers, pulled on the matching blue hats Alene had knitted for them and jumped out of the car.

Alene relished sitting alone with her thoughts. How much stress could a person handle before breaking down? First, there was the insidious pandemic killing people across the globe. Blanca, her father's caregiver was seriously ill, and Alene had driven her to the hospital three days before. They'd both worn masks and kept the windows open regardless of the rain. "Patients only," the guard had said. He'd worn protective gear, as if noxious gases were leaking from the hospital's old radiators.

Cal had hired Blanca—who spelled her name with a C, instead of the Polish way with a K, because she thought it looked more American—when Alene's mother got too sick to take care of herself nearly twenty years before. After Alene's mother died, Blanca had stayed on to cook and clean for Cal, even though he'd been younger, healthier, and didn't need as much help back then.

She'd also cleaned for other families in the building and saved for fifteen years until she was able to buy her own condo. Alene suspected that Cal had helped with the down payment. When Cal was diagnosed with myasthenia gravis a few years before, Blanca had started to spend more of her time taking care of him, like she'd taken care of Alene's mother. Cal enjoyed her company. They played chess, read books, did puzzles, took walks, and argued about politics. She also fed him, helped him stretch his muscles, and kept him hydrated.

Blanca was a vivacious woman in her late forties, with a sharp mind and a sharper tongue. Alene's father adored her and they'd been together on Thursday, before she fell ill the following Monday. Cal had not caught it from her, which seemed to Alene like a miracle. He was health-compromised with an autoimmune condition, and nobody knew if he could survive a bout of Covid.

Alene looked out the car window at the dripping trees, empty sidewalks, and foggy buildings. She contemplated the plethora of changes since March. Her business had shrunk, the Chicago Public Schools had closed, and her kids now learned remotely in front of a computer screen. They only had a few weeks of school left, but lately, getting them to focus on learning while sitting at the dining room table had been practically impossible. Since the pandemic began, she'd tried to spend time with each one, reviewing their plans for the day, making sure they finished some homework and had activities to fill the day, so they wouldn't resort to hours of playing video games and binge-watching cartoons, YouTube, or TikTok.

Alene planned to be back at home before anyone woke up that morning, but she'd left a note on the kitchen table just in case. Blanca, had she not been in the hospital, would have been happy to show up early. Cal had taken over with the kids all that week. Blanca was stricter but better organized than their grandfather, and they missed her. They also missed their friends, favorite teachers, and after-school activities.

Alene's boyfriend, Frank, pitched in too. He helped Noah with his reading, did math with both Noah and Quinn, and worked with Sierra on a project about city government. Alene and Frank had been dating since the previous summer, and she was eager to get married, but he still lived with and took care of his troubled adult daughter.

It was warming up inside the car. Alene searched for Kacey and Kofi through the car window and the construction fence, but there was a jungle of trees and bushes lining the sidewalk. The post-fire building site was probably soggy and disgusting. If only she'd thought to bring an old blanket to protect the back seat from burnt wood.

Alene also wished she could chat with Frank, but it was too early to call. He'd worked the previous night and had gone home to his own apartment. Was it crazy, at age thirty-nine, to be stealing moments together like when they were teenagers? Maybe she wouldn't be so impatient with everyone if he moved in, but Frank's grown daughter, who was a bit of a train wreck, needed him even more than Alene did.

Rhona Shaw had recently turned twenty-one. She hadn't finished college, had no career plan, and hadn't been able to hold a job. She seemed to spend most of her time worrying about her health. She was allergic to foods, nature, and animals, and suffered from debilitating headaches. Frank suspected she had a problem with prescription drugs, but hoped he was wrong. She'd moved in with him six months ago, after a final drawn-out battle with her mother, and often ordered vegetable-packed soups from the café.

Kacey startled Alene by opening the passenger door and jumping back in. "He doesn't need my help," Kacey said as she cleaned her glasses with her shirt. "We were looking for a way to get into the site and my glasses got too smudged for me to see. I'll stay in here with you."

Kofi had probably circled the tall fence surrounding piles of wet, muddy, and burned wood, trying to get inside. Moments later, they heard an owl hoot, and Kacey whispered it was Kofi letting them know that he'd gotten past the fence. What if tromping through the remains of the fire exposed Kofi to toxic materials? He wore gloves and a mask, but it wasn't an N95 with protection against particulates.

If paper masks didn't protect against airborne particulates, how could they protect against a cunning virus?

The sun had risen, but a scrim of humidity diffused the light. Alene thought she saw Kofi alternating between moving and crouching. She figured he was trying to be invisible. He was lanky, his legs bulging with muscles from years of riding his bicycle for miles through and around the city. They both lost sight of him for about ten minutes, but suddenly he rushed back to the car and jumped into the back seat. He hadn't taken a single piece of wood. "How was it?" Kacey asked.

Alene heard his jagged breathing and turned around to watch him pull off his gloves and hat. "It was, um, weird and chilly," he said, haltingly. "And there wasn't anything I could use." His focus was sideways, out the window, and he looked tense. Alene turned away, imagining one of Frank's police friends driving by and stopping to ask what she was doing. They drove home in silence and trudged to the elevators. Kofi, usually cheerful after an expedition to find materials, was unreadable and oddly stone-faced as he thanked Alene for the ride. Kacey mouthed her thanks as she unlocked her door, and Alene held her hand to her ear in a sign for Kacey to call later.

Alene unlocked her own door, wondering why Kofi hadn't found any usable wood. Before she could take off her jacket, her phone rang.

"Kofi wants you to promise not to tell Frank about this morning," Kacey said in a whisper. It seemed unnecessary—it wasn't as if Kofi had started the fire, and Frank was a homicide detective, not a cop on the lookout for arsonists.

"I can't promise that. We tell each other everything," said Alene, "But there's nothing to tell, because Kofi came up empty."

"He's worried that someone saw us there and the police will get him for trespassing," said Kacey. Alene could hear her sniffling.

Alene had already frittered away forty-five minutes driving them over there and waiting for Kofi to hunt for wood. "Come on, Kacey," she said. "We didn't see anyone, and no one saw us."

"But are you going to tell Frank that we were there?" Kacey asked.

"Kacey, Frank would never do anything to hurt me or the people I love." Being with Kacey had always required patience. "And I'm driving the getaway car, so if we were committing a crime, I'd be just as guilty."

Kacey said, "I hope you're right." She sounded more than a little paranoid.

Chapter 2

It was six in the morning and someone else was opening the café, so Alene had plenty of time to make breakfast for the kids. It was an oatmeal kind of day. Usually, Blanca would have shown up and tossed in a load of laundry before helping Alene's father get dressed, but she'd been diagnosed with the virus the week before. Then her oxygen level plunged, she couldn't breathe, and she'd been in the hospital for four days, since late on Monday. Cal was getting more and more apprehensive about her health, and texted inane comments, trying to provoke her with their usual joking. Blanca hadn't yet responded.

Noah, Alene's eight-year-old, came in rubbing his hands through his hair. She was grateful that he let her scoop him into a bear hug and inhale his musky scent, but he no longer allowed her to kiss him, except for the top of his head. She made him wash his hands, since he occasionally forgot, before she gave him breakfast. As she got him settled at the table with his chocolate chip oatmeal and a homemade smoothie, Quinn, who woke up enthusiastic about each new day, came in smiling as usual and squeezed her mother. Alene kissed her neck and blew a few raspberries against her skin, something that had made Quinn laugh as a baby.

Soon-to-be thirteen-year-old Sierra entered the kitchen, her pretty face marred by a constant scowl ever since school had closed. She spent as much time as Alene allowed texting with her friends, but that didn't make up for seeing them and being with them. She was already wearing a soft pink sweater with a matching ribbon in her ponytail and looked disdainfully at her younger sister. "As usual, you look like you just got out of bed," she said to Quinn. "Do you have to be a slob? Don't you have any self-respect?"

"Stop bugging me," said Quinn, pouting, "I did just get out of bed." She was almost eleven and didn't yet care what she wore or how she looked. Since the pandemic began and school went remote, she'd been showering before bed and putting on an outfit that she'd sleep in, and then she'd stay in all through the next day. "It doesn't matter," she added. "You're the only ones who see me."

Alene gave Sierra a look, but Sierra knew not to glance her way. "Good morning, sweetie, how'd you sleep?"

Not that Sierra was chirpy in normal times, but these days she seemed depressed and spoke sharply way too often. "It doesn't matter how I slept since we never go anywhere or do anything, ever," she said.

Cal looked up from where he was reading the paper and said, "Sorry, honey. It's a rough patch, I know, but these things pass."

"Nobody has ever seen a coronavirus that's this scary before, Grandpa," Sierra retorted, like a challenge. "What if it never goes away and I don't get to go to high school and college and everything? I'll just be here forever, and I'll never have a normal life."

Cal reached over to pat her hand, gave her a cryptic smile, and focused on his newspaper. Alene wished she had cheerful news to pass along. The three of them ate silently, until Quinn perked up enough to start talking about the book she was reading. "It's about a girl who spies on a drug-dealing neighbor." Quinn said.

"I hope you're not planning to sneak into any of our neighbors' apartments," Alene said, pointing to Quinn's bowl so she'd put it in the sink.

"Because you're not smart enough to get away with it," said Sierra, earning her another glare from Alene. Quinn had already run back to the bedroom.

When Cal and the children were settled at a desk, a table, the floor, or in her dad's case, his favorite chair, Alene headed to the café. She'd already had to let a few of her employees go despite the enormous uptick in cookie sales. Her budget had been strained since the pandemic started.

When Alene arrived, an Eddie Vedder ukulele song was playing softly. LaTonya James stirred fresh-squeezed lemon juice into a batch of almond pralines while Kacey, who'd opened the café with Ruthie that morning, was at the stove caramelizing onions. Ruthie was measuring ingredients for a version of her well-loved chocolate chip cookies; they sold hundreds of them every month, in every imaginable eggless, butter-less permutation, because Ruthie was a strict vegan.

Alene put on an apron, covered her hair with a scarf, washed her hands, and prepared to chop vegetables. They'd be used in salads, omelets, and stir-fries that would be carefully boxed and packed in bags for the delivery kids to transport around the city. Ruthie turned on the industrial mixer and, over the whirring noise, talked about her husband's building that had burned down. "We're sick about it," she said, "and that's all Benjie is going to focus on for the foreseeable future." Alene and Kacey exchanged glances across the kitchen.

"The fire department got there in minutes," Ruthie added, her forehead furrowed. She'd stopped the mixer and was scraping down the sides, speaking in a hushed voice even though there were only a few of them in the kitchen. "But it burned fast. By the time Benjie arrived at about ten last night, the fire had gotten out of control and only remnants of burned wood were left. He's devastated."

Alene said, "I hope they figure out what caused it."

"There were storms late yesterday afternoon," Ruthie said, "and the fire department thinks it could have been caused by anything from lightning to an

14

electrical short. Benjie and one of his employees are walking the property's perimeter looking for clues with an inspector this morning. I don't know if they are going to find anything."

Pieces of cookie dough shot out of the bowl, and Ruthie added, "They think it could have been arson, and Benjie worries that it'll turn into a fight with the insurance company." Ruthie always got more vigorous with kitchen tools whenever she was agitated. She slowed down to gently stir in the chocolate chips and chopped pistachios.

LaTonya, one of Alene's long-time employees, wiped her brow with the back of her arm and said, "I bet neighbors will start making claims about how the fire caused smoke damage in their own apartments. And insurance companies are great until it's time to pay up." LaTonya, who kept her nails perfectly shellacked and her hair stunningly braided, had just completed her master's degree in urban studies. She was supposed to have started her first full-time job, but the offer had been rescinded because of the pandemic. Alene told her she could work in the kitchen until she found another job.

"Was the fire just off of Diversey?" Kacey asked, looking nervously at Alene. She'd always spoken softly, but the mask, in addition to fogging up her glasses, made her almost impossible to understand.

"Yes, it was," Ruthie said. Benjie, her husband, developed and managed affordable housing, and shared Ruthie's passion for social justice. "They'd only gotten the skeleton up, but that building was going to provide a mix of fifty-two standard-priced and twenty-six affordable apartments in a relatively safe neighborhood."

"Last year I wrote a paper about Chicago's Affordable Requirements Ordinance," said LaTonya. "You would not believe these wealthy developers who fuss about including a small percentage of affordable places in their massive money-making projects."

Rashid Freeman, a slightly hearing-impaired, shy twenty-three-year-old who was one of Ruthie's assistants, said, "I'd believe it."

Kacey said, "There are probably some wealthy developers who are kind and considerate." Was she thinking about her late father, who'd amassed a small fortune? The bulk of what she'd inherited when Gary died was tied up in real estate.

"I sure hope Benjie, who is doing God's work," LaTonya continued, "isn't going to lose his shirt because of that fire."

"Me too," said Ruthie, an uncharacteristically glum look on her face. She'd decorated a cake for LaTonya's graduation in December and they'd toasted with sparkling wine. "It took a long time for him to get financing and permits. They were just about to start on the mechanicals."

"The important thing is that no one got hurt, right?" Kacey asked. She burst into tears and ran out of the kitchen. Kacey had been sensitive since she was a baby, but pandemic stress was causing almost daily outbursts. Maybe she fretted that Kofi would get in trouble for having trespassed at Benjie's building, or she was worried because he hadn't sold anything since March, now that nobody was thinking about art. Alene wished Kacey understood that she didn't have to worry about money. Long before he died, Kacey's father, Gary, had set up a trust to pay her bills. He'd feared that she'd relapse after all that work to overcome her former meth addiction and wanted to make sure she was comfortable.

Alene was glad Kacey was no longer alone in that apartment, and Kofi was constantly fixing and improving it, like her father had. Squeaking hinges, doors that didn't close, and backed-up drains no longer plagued Kacey or Alene. Alene's father, Cal, had tried his best after Gary died, but fixing things had never been Cal's forte, and these days, even though he wasn't that old, she preferred that he avoid anything requiring a ladder or a drill.

Cal and the kids liked Kofi too, especially Quinn and Noah, who were entranced with his ability to twist and turn a simple piece of metal into arresting and unusual shapes. He'd once brought over a box of discarded nuts, bolts, springs, and hanger pieces, and helped them make little metal sculptures. And since the pandemic began, he'd led them on bike riding expeditions north to the Montrose Point Bird Sanctuary and south to the Lincoln Park Zoo.

"Was Benjie the sole owner of that building?" LaTonya asked after a pause. Alene had thought they were done talking about the fire.

"No," said Ruthie. "He usually has investors on his projects." Ruthie folded candied orange bits, cardamom, and chocolate shavings into another version of her cookie dough as she explained how Benjie's business worked.

LaTonya, whose resting expression was either angry or mournful, said, "I think Benjie ought to get a medal. My guess is that his building was torched by some NIMBY nutcase who thought Benjie was going to rent apartments to convicted felons and drug dealers." Alene had been thinking along those lines. She was sickened by developers who only cared about property values.

"Maybe if people who need help with their rent stopped drowning their sorrows in drugs and alcohol, they wouldn't suffer as much," said Edith Vanza, who'd worked in the café since her brother, Kacey's father, bought it nearly forty years ago. When Alene turned sixteen in 1998 and Gary Vanza hired her as a kitchen assistant at his café, Edith Vanza was already wearing floral sweaters and had seemed just as old then as she did now.

She was supposed to be helping Dori Stevens, whom Alene had hired in November, but was instead wandering into the kitchen. In addition to floral sweaters, Edith wore a constantly bitter expression. "And there wouldn't be hundreds of filthy bums accosting people in the streets," she added. The staff looked up and gaped at her. Lately, there'd been a bedraggled homeless guy sitting outside the café a couple of times each week.

Alene looked out into the café and saw Dori sitting in front of her laptop, fingers flying. Dori coordinated the online orders that were keeping the café going. She had a compact body and pretty but overly made-up eyes. Before the pandemic began in March, Dori had scheduled events through the spring of 2020, but everything had been canceled. She'd also created the Whipped and Sipped logo, three tiny, colorful spatulas above the café's name, that was stamped onto their carryout bags, wrapping papers, plates, and cups. Her skills had been crucial.

"Can you go back out to the café, please, Edith?" Alene asked. "It looks like orders are coming in and you might be needed."

"Is it against the law to take an occasional break?" Edith asked. Alene just shook her head. Edith was supposed to deal with the phone orders, mostly from older customers who didn't like or understand online ordering. She should have been answering the phone that was now ringing on the other side of the door, and Dori hadn't stopped her from walking away.

Alene pointed to the door and asked Edith to leave the kitchen and get to work. Edith, glowering at Alene over her floral mask as if she'd been wounded, slouched out the door. As soon as Edith was out of hearing, LaTonya said, "She should be fired, Alene. Did you hear how she talked about homeless people? I had to stop myself from smacking her."

Alene was relatively sure that LaTonya would never actually strike a fellow employee, especially one who was over sixty.

"Alene is not going to fire Edith," said Ruthie. Alene had promised Edith's brother, Gary, when he sold her the café, that Edith could stay on as long as she wanted to. LaTonya shrugged as if she'd said her piece and it was up to Alene to follow through.

"LaTonya, wasn't your thesis about homelessness?" Ruthie asked. "Maybe you could explain what you learned."

"I'll make copies," said LaTonya with a twinge of sarcasm and a toss of her head. "But I think the only way to make people understand is by taking away their privileged educations and forcing them to walk nine blocks to a bus stop and two miles to a grocery store that doesn't have any fresh fruit or vegetables."

Ruthie blinked at her without speaking until LaTonya cleared her throat and added, "I mean I hope everyone learns something from reading my thesis."

Ruthie waited another moment, until LaTonya said, "I just meant that I'd have given Edith a figurative smack, Ruthie, not a real one." Ruthie pretended to wipe her brow with the back of her hand, and the lines on LaTonya's forehead relaxed. Ruthie had a way of making people care about her opinions.

Everyone focused on their tasks for a while, but Kacey hadn't returned from the restroom. Alene walked over, knocked, and asked if everything was okay. Kacey opened the door. Although she wore glasses, Alene could see that her sea green eyes were red and teary.

"What's wrong, sweetie?" Alene asked. "Can I get you some soda water?"

"No, thanks," Kacey said. "It's bad, but I promised Kofi I wouldn't tell you."

"You already asked me not to tell Frank about the fire site." Alene hustled her over to the office, ushered her inside, and closed the door. "Is it still about that? Nothing we can't solve if we put our minds to it, right?" she asked. Her mother used to repeat that constantly, until her cancer metastasized.

"Alene, you have to promise you won't say a word to anyone, especially Frank." Kacey sank onto the office couch.

Alene sat next to her and reached over to gently rub her neck. She'd known Kacey since her parents brought her home from the hospital as a baby. Kacey had always loved having her back scratched and her neck rubbed. "I promise," said Alene.

Kacey didn't look convinced. "You're going to want to tell Frank, but you can't. This is important for Kofi."

Alene said, "I already promised, Kacey."

"It's just that Kofi saw something this morning at the fire site," Kacey said. "It was yellow fabric, the type they use in windbreakers."

"Okay," said Alene, flashing back to Kofi jumping into the car saying that he hadn't found a single thing. She'd noticed that he was tense.

"He didn't touch it, Kacey said, trembling, "because it was a jacket, and someone was wearing it. And then he got closer and saw that it was a dead body."

Chapter 3

Alene's pulse raised and her hands sweated. Who was it? Why was it there? If someone had been squatting in the unfinished building, why didn't they run when the fire started? She jumped up to bring Kacey a drink and consider what to do next. Did she know anyone at the fire department who could tell her what caused the fire?

Sometimes she wanted to kick herself. Why had she promised not to say anything to Frank before she knew what Kofi had seen? It might not have been a homicide, but someone should know about it, and Frank would know what to do. Maybe it wasn't a dead body at all, just someone sleeping on an uncomfortable bed of burned timber. Maybe not. A few minutes later, she returned with a cup of peppermint tea and sat next to Kacey again.

"So," she said, slightly calmer, "you're telling me that Kofi saw a person this morning while he was searching for materials on the site of Benjie's burned-down building. How could he be sure it was a dead person?"

"He said it was," Kacey sounded unsure. "But even if it wasn't, you promised not to tell Frank."

"You know, Kacey," said Alene, giving Kacey's knee a squeeze, "I think we've got to say something. I can't keep a secret like that from him. Finding a dead body is serious, and it involves his job. Also, he'll be able to coach Kofi about what to do next."

"Traveling Alone" by Passenger came through the speakers, reminding Alene of the pre-pandemic days when people could get on a plane and fly far away from their troubles. Kacey started crying. "I promised Kofi I wouldn't say anything, and you promised you wouldn't tell Frank."

But that was before she knew what Kofi has seen. Alene stroked Kacey's hair and said, "We can talk about it later, but anyone might have seen Kofi there. That block is lined with apartment buildings, and we have no idea who might have been looking out their windows. Also, this isn't just a personal secret, Kacey. We're talking about a human being who might have died in the fire. Can you just think about it for a while? Telling Frank is the right thing to do."

Kacey looked rattled. "Please, Alene. You can't tell anyone." She lowered the mask to sip her tea but pulled it back on between swallows.

"Then Kofi should tell Frank himself," said Alene. "This isn't a secret I can keep, Kacey." Her ex-husband had kept a boatload of secrets, some minor, some major. She didn't want that to happen again. "That's not how healthy relationships work."

Kacey rose from the couch. "That's the thing, Alene," she said. "What if Kofi's keeping secrets from me?"

"Like what?" Alene asked.

"Like what if he knew that body was going to be there?"

Alene pulled her into another hug. "You know he's not that kind of person, Kacey, and if he was, he'd never have let you come with him to the fire site," said Alene. "Kofi loves you. He might ride that bike of his all over the city and go garbage-picking in all sorts of unsavory places, but he'd never do anything to put you at risk."

Kacey sighed, a sign that Alene had worn her down. "Will you please just give me some time to think, then?" Kacey asked.

Alene agreed. "But not long," she added.

They left her snug office and were quickly swept into the rhythm of the kitchen. LaTonya was holding forth as she bent to place a tray in the oven. "It's pretty clear, in spite of what Edith thinks, which groups of people are hardest hit by this pandemic and everything else that's going on," she said. "And who is taking advantage of the chaos? Thieves, politicians, and small-minded people like Edith, who blame the poor because they're not working hard enough. That's an exact quote."

Dori had come into the kitchen and had picked up a shapeless empanada that she now wrapped in the café's sandwich paper. Alene allowed her employees to eat whatever they wanted, but asked that they take the ugliest, least sellable products.

As she wrapped, Dori said, "LaTonya's got a point." Alene wondered how Dori managed to live in a posh high-rise in River North. Maybe she came from money. She didn't brag about it, but Alene had recognized the address Dori gave when she first applied for the job. "But Edith also has a point, and I don't think she's completely heartless."

Ruthie said. "I agree. I don't think Edith is trying to be heartless at all." Dori had already taken the empanada and left the kitchen.

"Maybe not," said Alene, "but who knows what her opinion is based on." Ruthie was Alene's best friend and they often agreed with each other, but Alene thought that Edith was cunning and mean-spirited. Ruthie thought she was just sad and lonely.

"It doesn't matter, because Edith's invitation led to something positive," Ruthie said. That was her impossible dream, getting everything to lead to something positive. "Dori has said she lives in River North, and that neighborhood has been besieged during the protests and riots. I think it's wonderful when employees take care of each other."

LaTonya, waiting for the timer to ding so she could remove trays from the oven, said, "I thought Dori lived with some guy in a plush condo."

"She hasn't shared details of her personal life," said Alene, who'd been surprised that Dori's plunging necklines hadn't stopped Edith from issuing the invitation. Edith had loved when Jocelyn DeVale, who used to be one of Alene's employees, had temporarily moved in with her the previous summer. Alene knew that Edith was dying to have another roommate.

"I'm sure Dori would rather move into Edith's dilapidated four-flat than live with a man in a swanky high rise," said LaTonya as she pulled on oven gloves.

"How can you be sure that she's living with a man?" Kacey asked. She looked less chalky than earlier. "Also, my father bought his kid sister a beautiful condo," she said. "I was there once with my dad. It's not dilapidated at all." How sad, thought Alene, that Edith had never invited her only niece for dinner, or just to visit.

LaTonya half-heartedly raised her shoulders.

Alene said, "We don't know that Dori's living with anyone because she doesn't talk about herself. Anyway, the question is how to convince Edith to stop blaming the victim for society's ills."

Ruthie said, "How about we just don't discuss politics in the Whipped and Sipped kitchen."

LaTonya objected with a toss of her head, "Edith doesn't think what she said was political."

Alene stifled a laugh. She recalled how Edith had ranted about uneducated immigrants in front of Zuleyka, who came from Panama, and Manny, whose parents had brought him to the States from Mexico when he was six. Edith also expressed her disgust for radical Islamic terrorism, Iran, and

27

Afghanistan to Rashid, who kept trying to tell her that he was from the northwest suburbs and had no connection to radical Islam. Edith continued to lump him with terrorists anyway.

Alene was trying to raise her own children to be aware of how privileged they were. Just the week before, she'd explained how some of the problems homeless people face could be solved if they were given a clean room of their own with access to a bathroom. Nearly nine-year-old Noah, her most sensitive child, had been concerned about children who had no bathrooms, and asked Alene if he should save his allowance and buy a Porta-Potty to put somewhere that could help homeless people. She'd wanted to simultaneously laugh and cry.

"It's none of my business what Edith cares about," said LaTonya. "Not all human beings were created with the capacity to be kindhearted."

"And that's where we disagree," Ruthie said with her usual sweetness. She'd started rolling the cookie dough into perfect balls during the conversation, and Kacey flattened them using the tines of a fork. They talked about kindness as they covered the dough with reusable plastic wrap and set the pan in the refrigerator. Kindness was one of Ruthie's favorite subjects. She also liked talking about how the entire planet and its inhabitants would be better off if humans stopped eating animal products.

Olly Burns, another of Alene's former full-time employees, abruptly danced into the kitchen from the café, his orange curls bouncing. He knew Alene was anxious about the café surviving and had been trying to help her with marketing. He'd designed posters to put in the windows, with cheerful sayings like, "Cookies against COVID." He also suggested baking pandemic cookies in the shape of the virus with spikes and "Destroy Me," written in icing. He had an idea regarding the November elections, but Alene thought it would be too politically charged and too difficult to keep a tally of how many cookies in the shape of fat red elephants or sparkly blue donkeys they sold.

The pandemic had begun months after Olly quit the café to start his own carpentry business. During the lockdown, Olly couldn't meet with prospective clients in their homes, and couldn't make enough money to pay his rent, so Alene had hired him to fix the café's wobbly tables and chairs. She'd also asked him to repair and repaint the windowsills and frames. Kacey's dad had done a great job of making the café functional in his years as proprietor but had never found time to do much-needed updating.

"What are you so cheerful about, Olly?" LaTonya asked. "The world is a mess, climate change is destroying the planet, and people are sick and dying from this virus." LaTonya distrusted anyone who was too enthusiastic about anything, and Olly upped his antics just to get a reaction from her.

Olly said, "Can't say it out loud, but I've got a few things up my sleeve." He loved creating intrigue. He'd had his heart broken in January when his latest boyfriend moved out, but he'd bounced back as usual. Now, Olly stopped fidgeting and caught

Alene's attention with a laser-eyed look. "Any discarded cookies or crumbles from a cake needing attention? A person can build up a sweat out there."

Kacey asked if he wanted anything to drink as she passed him the platter of malformed empanadas and cookies. He thanked her and held a cookie aloft like a prize as he exited the kitchen door. He and Kacey had been good friends for years.

Alene caught Ruthie's eye. They'd been going outside whenever possible, except when the snow was too deep, the sidewalks were too icy, or the rain was coming down too hard and fast. "All right with the rest of you if Ruthie and I go out for a stroll?" she asked.

"Have fun," said LaTonya.

Kacey added, "Take your time."

Alene removed her apron and followed Ruthie out of the kitchen. As they passed through the café, Dori handed over a cup of hot tea and the wrapped empanada. "This is for Vincent," she said. Vincent was the frazzled, bony old guy who'd been sitting on the ground outside the café once or twice a week for months.

"Tell him that it's a spinach and pistachio hand pie," said Dori. "He'll understand that better than 'empanada.'" Alene thanked her, pleased at Dori's thoughtfulness.

"That's very kind of you, Dori," said Ruthie. "I thought that was for your own lunch." Dori shook her head. Edith was busy taking an order over the phone and Olly sat texting on his cellphone, his tool bag on the floor.

Most of the other homeless people in the neighborhood had been relocated by the police, but Vincent kept showing up. He sometimes brought a piece of cardboard, or he sat on the sturdy rubber bin filled with used clothes and shoes donated by people in the neighborhood. It had a sign on it that read, "Please take what you need." Vincent had probably taken a discarded rain slicker and the dirty turquoise cap now pulled low over his ears.

On their walks, Alene and Ruthie explored the neighborhood whenever possible, checking out who was in business and who been forced to close. If not for the pickups and deliveries, Whipped and Sipped would have gone under. Thankfully, Alene had employees who could speed around the city on their bicycles, delivering full meals, savory hand pies, single-serve fruit tarts, and muffins. Not a single significant cake had been ordered since the pandemic began; people weren't gathering anymore. Instead, they ordered cupcakes, or small desserts that served, at most, a family.

Ruthie and Alene stopped to give Vincent the empanada and hot tea. "Hope you're having a good day," Ruthie said.

Vincent took the cup without responding, and Alene explained that it was a hand pie as she gave it to him. He squinted up at her and grumbled something unintelligible as he unwrapped and started gnawing at it. They walked up the block, and Ruthie whispered that everyone had challenges to overcome.

"Or they're just miserable people," said Alene, earning a disappointed look from Ruthie.

It was another overcast day that made it feel like spring had decided not to turn up at all. Alene had loved walking with Ruthie ever since college, when they'd meander across Northwestern's sprawling campus and follow the lakefront north or south, depending on their mood.

As they turned the corner, Ruthie asked about Blanca. Alene lamented how long she'd already been in the hospital and how much Cal missed her caregiving. "I just want her to get well," Alene added.

"She's strong," Ruthie replied. "Almost as strong as you."

If only Alene felt that way about herself or the people around her. Blanca, her father, the café, the employees whose hours she'd had to cut ... add all that to having three school-age children stuck at home learning over the internet, and it was a humongous effort for Alene to stay positive.

"Blanca's one of the toughest women I know," Alene said.

Ruthie put a hand on her arm and said, "I know she'll be okay, Six"— Alene's nickname since college, when they'd discovered that their birthdays were August sixth and ninth. Alene was frightened. She'd seen stories all over the internet about people who struggled to breathe and then abruptly died. Not a single doctor or researcher in the entire world understood what was going on with the disease, but Ruthie, eternally optimistic, was sure that scientists would soon discover either a cure or a vaccine. Alene worried that the virus would mutate, as viruses do, and become more contagious and more devastating, before scientists figured out how it worked.

Blanca, before she got sick, had thought of herself as almost impervious. Nothing could make her sick, she told Alene before the pandemic began. She could run a marathon, go grocery shopping, take care of Cal, and make a marvelous dinner from scratch later the same day. How could someone so strong and hearty end up in the hospital?

Blanca had saved for fifteen years to buy her own apartment and was now the proud owner of a two-bedroom, small but spotless third-floor walk-up.

Recently, she'd rented her extra bedroom to two young men she met at a church program, Marek and Ziggy, who were both from the town in Poland where her grandmother lived. They were short on cash, they told her, but skilled at renovating houses, so she bartered several months of rent for painted walls, repaired fixtures, and updated plumbing. Marek and Ziggy, who were looking for day jobs and worked on the condo in the evenings, had already snaked the lines, replaced pipes, and installed new faucets, but after just a few weeks in Chicago, both caught the virus.

Blanca didn't understand how they'd passed it to her, she'd told Alene. They had their own bathroom, and she always waited until they'd finished eating before she went into the kitchen. The only time they passed each other was walking up or down the stairs, and she'd always worn a mask.

Alene wasn't surprised. She'd been hearing similar stories about people getting sick after a trip to the grocery store, or a single conversation with a neighbor. Thankfully, her household had held strong. And Frank was hale and hearty even though he had to work with Lee Bautista, his partner, driving around the city investigating homicides. Frank insisted that people mask up before he interviewed them, he'd reported to Alene.

"I don't have time to walk that far today," said Ruthie as they strode north down the mostly empty sidewalk. Ruthie went home early on Friday afternoons to prepare for the Sabbath, and took Saturdays off, so she'd leave as soon as they got back to the café. "How about if we try to focus on anything we see that's positive."

Alene had been focused on what was missing— the museums, theaters, restaurants, schools, and parks. "You take the lead on that, Nine," she said. "I'm more drawn to negativity."

"What about how lucky you are to live in a four-bedroom apartment overlooking the lake," said Ruthie, "with your father and his caregiver available to help with the kids?"

"But that caregiver is currently in the hospital, and we just passed three closed businesses," Alene said.

Ruthie's laughter filled Alene with sweet memories. "You're doing an exceptional job on that negative thing." Alene turned to search Ruthie's golden-brown irises, grateful there wasn't a raging pandemic that required everyone to cover their eyes.

34

"Someone's got to do it," Alene said with a smile under her mask that Ruthie couldn't see. They discussed Frank's daughter, Rhona, who blamed her father for everything that was wrong in her life. Alene had seen her throw tantrums and scream at Frank like a teenager, even though she was already in her twenties. She didn't know which of the young woman's issues was most challenging, but Rhona didn't seem to have life goals, hobbies, or friends. Did anything make her happy? Frank had brought her to the café a few times before the pandemic, and she'd said that she liked the gluten-free food and friendly atmosphere, but she'd been overwhelmed by the number of people.

Frank said Rhona had been leaving the house more often than usual during the month of May. She wouldn't tell him where she went, even if it was just to the Whipped and Sipped Café to pick up something healthy for dinner. Alene wondered aloud if she was seeing someone, or just searching for her dealer.

"She's never dated," Frank had argued, "so how is she going to start now, during a global pandemic?" They were alone in Alene's bedroom long after everyone else was asleep. She knew it was old-fashioned, but she didn't think it was good for her children to see him coming and going.

"She's not unattractive," Alene told him, though she privately thought that when Rhona scowled and grumbled, which was often, she looked like one of the fierce painted aluminum owls on the roof of the Harold Washington Library. "Her hair is shiny, she has lovely deep-set gray eyes, like yours, and she has a cute, husky laugh. For all you know, she could be the life of the party when you're not around. Also, she's been wearing mascara. That means she cares about her appearance. I'm going to bet that there's a man. Or a woman."

Frank had stroked her arm absently, saying, "I thought she was allergic to cosmetics. Also, what kind of person would go out with her right now? There's nowhere to go, and she's only twenty-one but spends an inordinate amount of time focused on her health."

"That's what she talks about with you," Alene said, although she thought Frank could have been referring to Edith. "I hear Sierra on the phone gabbing with her friends for hours. With me she mostly tells on her siblings, complains about having to be stuck at home, and only occasionally drops a hint about what's going on in her head."

Frank was worried that Rhona was making bad choices. "When she was a kid, she used to tell me more than I ever wanted to know," he'd said. "I know she's got some health issues, but I don't know when or why she started overdoing the medicines."

Alene hadn't responded. There was a difference between taking medicine and abusing prescription drugs, wasn't there? Was Rhona a hypochondriac or an addict? All he wanted, Frank said, was for Rhona to be happy and flourishing. He'd admitted that she'd seemed somewhat cheerier the past few weeks, smiling more than usual, and less critical.

"My guess is that she's seeing someone," Alene told Ruthie now, as they walked past closed storefronts on sidewalks that used to bustle with people. "But she's being secretive about it, so Frank assumes that something is off-kilter."

"Like what?" Ruthie asked.

"He doesn't know," said Alene. "He's just got an uncertain feeling about it, and he trusts his intuition."

"There's a difference between hunting criminals and raising children. Maybe she's growing up," said Ruthie, "but he has to stop trying to make everything right for her."

Ruthie was intuitive, but Alene wasn't sure she was right about Rhona. What if Rhona was like Kacey's stepbrother Sandy, who couldn't take care of himself? He lived in a highly supervised facility for challenged adults, and preferred plants to people. Frank's daughter might be better off in a place where she was managed and cared for. But if she was addicted to painkillers, that was a different problem.

They walked quietly for a bit, the air still damp and cool for the end of May, until Ruthie asked if they had enough work to keep Olly busy. Alene said, "Yes, but we're paying him less than he deserves. He says he's grateful and excited about revitalizing the café. Also, he invited Kofi Lloyd to help and is splitting whatever he earns from us."

"Sounds on brand," Ruthie said with a laugh. She asked Alene about the café's finances, and Alene assured her that everything was fine. Alene didn't like to talk about it, but her father had made sure that she had enough money to raise her children, send them to college, and retire one day. Knowing that she and her kids would be all right made a huge difference for Alene. She worried about the café's success, but not inordinately. She agonized about her employees who had no such cushion.

A couple holding hands strolled by, and Alene thought about how Frank always reached for her hand when they went walking. Ruthie said, "Benjie is depressed and preparing for a battle with the insurance company about that burned-down building."

Alene said, "It seems like a cut-and-dried situation, doesn't it? The fire burned down Benjie's building and the insurance will have to pay to rebuild it."

"Nothing is ever cut-and-dried in the world of insurance," said Ruthie. "He's also afraid that the federal eviction moratorium is going to drain the business. He won't be able to get rid of tenants who refuse to pay their rent."

"Oh," said Alene. "But he'll still have to pay the bank, won't he?"

Ruthie bobbed her head. "Exactly."

"If anyone can battle a bureaucracy," Alene said, "it's your husband." She admired Benjie's discipline and passion—he loved buildings the way Ruthie loved food.

Ruthie said, "But it's not just up to him."

Alene stopped abruptly. "Who gets to decide?" she asked.

"It all boils down to money," Ruthie said. "I have no idea why anyone would put that before human dignity, but there are apparently people and corporations that can't think past their own pockets."

She continued in that vein, but Alene knew how Ruthie felt about selfish people, and started thinking about the body that Kofi had seen. Someone must have dumped it after the fire ended, or it would have burned up. Maybe Kofi had stumbled upon it right after it was placed there. What if Alene had driven faster, and they'd run into the murderer? And what if that evil person had watched Kofi run back to Alene's car?

"Did you hear anything I just said, Alene?" Ruthie asked. "I was telling you about buildings that were waiting to be started or had been started but not finished because of the pandemic."

Alene shook her head to get rid of the thoughts that had started to plague her and apologized. They heard Vincent yelling as they turned the corner and saw two people standing in front of the café, probably customers waiting outside for their order. The woman had spiky, highlighted blond hair, and was holding the hand of the tall, dark-haired man at her side.

Alene had seen them before—they were regulars. She and Ruthie stepped around the man and woman and then around Vincent, who spat on the ground. He'd moved closer to the door and Alene had to stop herself from admonishing him. The tall man, who was large and floppy, wore a sweet, childlike expression. The woman, who was short and trim, wore an unzipped bright red raincoat over a shirtdress the color of orange sorbet. Her expression was terse and irritated.

"Do you understand what six feet means?" she snapped at Alene and Ruthie. Alene briefly considered falling to the ground so she could take the woman down with her.

Chapter 4

"If you're concerned about someone getting too close to you," Alene said to the woman in what she hoped was a chilly tone, "you shouldn't stand within six feet of the door to my business." Wasn't it true that UV light from the sun destroyed virus cells if you were outside?

Ruthie looked dismayed. "I know it might be inconvenient," she told the woman in her calming voice, "but we're just taking online orders right now and only employees are allowed inside. We've set up a display of our baked goods that you can see through the front window, and you're welcome to browse at your convenience, but it'll be safer for you both if you stand away from the door."

Alene was always impressed by Ruthie's ability to maintain her composure in the face of rudeness. "Please move away from the entrance so you don't get in anyone's way," she added in as friendly a voice as she could muster. "If you wait there," Alene gestured toward the designated waiting area, "someone will come outside with your order soon."

The woman said, "We've already ordered, thank you, and it's taking a very long time."

"I like waiting here," said the man, who spoke slowly while wriggling the zipper on his jacket. Something was different about him, and it made Alene feel awkward about having snapped at the woman. He turned his head to look at Ruthie. "I like to come here every day. Do you like the Whipped and Sipped Café too?"

The woman interrupted to say, "This lady just told us that she's the owner, Peter."

Ruthie said, "I'm the pastry chef, and Alene," she pointed, "is the owner, but the answer is that we absolutely like the Whipped and Sipped Café."

His eyes widened and he shook his hands in the air like he was trying to dry them. "She's the owner, Taryn," he said as if Alene had discovered a cure for cancer. "You said I could come here every day, right Taryn? They have cakes and cookies and pies and coffee. I like coffee, right Taryn?"

He was gangly, with massive hands and a broad nose jutting out over the top of his mask. "I'm Peter Berg," he said to Ruthie, "and this is my sister, Taryn Berg. What's your name?" He stepped away from Taryn, who'd tried to pull him closer, and offered a handshake.

Taryn said, "Put your hand down, Peter. We can't touch people because of the scary virus, remember?" She sounded weary, as if she'd reminded him several times already. Peter brought his hand up to his face and looked down, embarrassed. "Peter has special needs," she told Alene and Ruthie in a flat, expressionless voice. "And he loves talking to people. We've been coming here ever since we moved to Chicago a few months ago, and your café is one of his favorite places."

"Hi Peter, I'm Ruthie," she said, "Alene and I are glad to meet you, and we're happy you like coming here."

"I do. I love to eat everything they have," Peter said, sidling closer to Ruthie until his sister pulled him back to her side. He tried to shake away, but then stopped to count on his fingers, "I love the breads and muffins and cupcakes and cookies. Taryn hardly eats anything." He looked at his sister as if she were at fault. "She just likes coffee, but I like coffee too."

"You like milk and sugar with a tiny drop of coffee," Taryn said. Her chin jutted out like Peter's, and they had similarly shaped, gigantic hands. She looked at her watch, as if she had somewhere important to be, and again pulled Peter away from where he'd inched closer to Alene and Ruthie. "Remember what I told you about not getting too close to anyone," she said.

"Also, I like coffee ice cream," Peter added.

Now that customers weren't allowed inside, Alene felt bad about not being able to make them feel welcome. She waved at Peter, who waved back enthusiastically. "We don't have ice cream, but I hope you love everything you try," she said. They tapped elbows in what had become an acceptable pandemic replacement for handshakes, and Peter seemed to enjoy it. He tapped his sister's elbow too.

"Also, I always leave a tip, right Taryn? Here it is," said Peter as he pulled a dollar bill out of his pocket. "It's for the person who gives us our bags. That's what you're supposed to do when someone gives you a bag of food."

Ruthie said, "That's a lovely thing to do."

"I know," said Peter, using his hands to emphasize whatever he was saying. "And this building looks just like our building, except we don't have a rainbow over the door, and we don't have cakes and cookies and everything." He looked at his sister as if she was at fault.

Taryn's glance swept over the front of Whipped and Sipped. "They're similar," she said. "Maybe designed by the same architect." Alene had always thought of it as a nondescript building that just sprang up without any thought to design. The café's windows were large though, and Alene liked the reddish color of the bricks.

Taryn was also nondescript, except for her very pale skin and the jutting chin, but her eyes were an interesting shade of blue that reminded Alene of a frightening movie involving children with eerie-looking irises.

"This neighborhood is filled with buildings that went up in the 1910s and '20s," said Alene. "Some have courtyards, and the ones on the main streets have tall windows in first-floor storefronts, with apartments above. I grew up a few blocks east of here," she added.

Peter kept nodding. His cornflower blue eyes were like his sister's, but innocent and wide open. His hair was thick and dark, and he looked to be in his late thirties, but it was hard to tell. "I especially love the lemon-poppyseed cookies because they're soft and chewy."

Taryn said, "He loves whatever he ate the previous day." She sounded surly and bored.

"I love when my customers are happy," Ruthie said. "So, you recently moved to the building where you now live?" She changed the subject whenever people started praising her or her baked goods. Alene kept meaning to ask if that was a religious thing, or just her way.

"Our father bought our building as an investment around thirty years ago, and someone else managed it until Peter and I moved here in April," said Taryn.

"And our dad too moved here too," Peter said, "but he has a different bedroom. He didn't want to go back to our other house. He's very old and it's my job to help him eat his dinner and take his bath. When I was a little boy, he took care of us, and now we're taking care of him, right Taryn?"

Taryn said, "That's enough, Peter. We don't tell everyone everything about us, do we?"

Peter shook his head although it wasn't clear what he understood. "But it's a very important job, taking care of our daddy, right Taryn?" he said, taking a deep, noisy breath. "And there's a window so I can watch people walking by, and I saw a fire that burned down a whole building. It wasn't a real building, but it was going to be a real building."

Alene froze.

Peter's forehead was creased with worry. "That fire is going to be a mess to clean up, right Taryn? That's what you said." Taryn moved her head up and down. All Alene could think about was that Peter might have seen Kofi running to or from the fire site, but it was crazy to think he was talking about the same fire.

"I already met the man who owns the building that burned down," Peter continued, reminding Alene of Noah, who got enthusiastic about his stories and bounced on his heels like Peter was doing now. "Because I like making friends, and he was looking at it, same as me. And I went outside to say hello. His name is Benjie, and he's my new friend."

He was talking about the same fire.

"You know what, Peter?" said Ruthie. "Benjie is my husband."

Peter opened his mouth wide, impressed. "Benjie! When you see him, you should tell him that I said hello. Peter says hello."

"I will do that," said Ruthie, turning to Taryn. "So, is your family in real estate?" She'd never have asked that question before Benjie started his real estate business. "Are you doing a lot of managing?"

Peter said, "I'm just managing bath time and eating, which is very important because Daddy is in a wheelchair. Taryn takes care of buildings, right?"

He looked at her for verification. "Tell them about the beach, Taryn."

Peter put his face up against the café window to look inside and waved at Edith and Dori. Only Dori waved back. Taryn struck up a conversation with Ruthie about real estate while Peter continued looking through the window. Alene wished she could just dash back in but knew that Ruthie would think it was rude. Her thoughts turned to getting out of the city with Frank and the kids. They'd have to wait until Blanca was recovered and strong enough to help Cal before they did anything of the sort. Was she fantasizing about vacations, so she didn't have to think about not reporting the dead body to Frank?

Alene imagined a rugged cabin surrounded by trees and looking out at the water. They could take walks, ride bikes, maybe go fishing. They'd be able to go to bed and wake up without Frank having to rush out, like the married couple they should have been by now. Frank would have to make sure Rhona had somewhere decent to live and a way to make a living. It would be excellent if she was seeing someone.

Another idea sprang to mind; she and Frank and the kids could take her father on a birthday outing. Cal would love to visit a place with history, like Springfield, or maybe Galena, since he'd just finished reading an outstanding biography of Ulysses S. Grant. Alene peeked at her watch; they'd been standing outside the café for five minutes. She imagined how it would feel to be alone with Frank in a cabin up north, surrounded by trees and hiking trails, away from the city and the raging virus.

"Anyway," Taryn said, pulling Alene out of her daydream, "I'm going to let Peter walk over here by himself now that he knows how, but we both came today because I want him to try new things. Otherwise, he gets in a rut. What would you recommend that he order next time? What's best?"

Alene and Ruthie answered simultaneously with their stock phrase, "It's all best."

"But we have to get back to work," Ruthie added. "Nice talking to you both, and sorry to make you wait outside for your order."

"That's okay," said Taryn, "and thanks for talking with us."

"You're welcome," Alene said, still annoyed by Taryn's "six feet" remark. Ruthie was probably already over it. Alene smiled, making sure to involve her eyes, since they couldn't see her mouth. She leaned closer to Ruthie once they got back to the kitchen, and said, "She reminds me of a seventh-grade mean girl."

"Six feet, Alene," said Ruthie, joking although it was true. Just before she left for the day, she added, "That woman, Taryn, is probably faced with constant challenges. She's taking care of both her father and her brother, and I think she's just doing the best she can." Sometimes Ruthie was too sweet.

Kofi came into the café to wait for Kacey when they were nearly finished closing. Alene pulled him aside and told him he had to tell Frank about the body he'd seen at the fire site. It was a potential crime scene and for all she knew, firefighters and cops were already investigating.

"It's not fair to make me keep it a secret from Frank," she said. Kofi bowed his head, as if she'd wounded him. He quietly begged her to give him some time. He seemed resigned and let his head fall forward when she said, "One week." She knew it was wrong to wait, but she understood that Kofi was terrified of the police. Still, what if not telling Frank somehow impeded the investigation?

That evening Frank couldn't come over, so just her children and father enjoyed Alene's vegetable fried rice. After dinner, Alene washed the dishes, and as Cal picked up a towel to dry them, he said, "My brother texted me today, out of the blue."

Cal's brother, Finn, had been involved in a bank robbery in Galesburg, Illinois years before. Alene had heard the story a million times. Finn had served six years at the state prison in Joliet, and when he got out, Cal helped set him up his own business. Finn had been a skilled electrician and plumber. Six weeks after he left prison, without saying a word to anyone, he'd packed a bag, left the house, and disappeared. When he first got out of prison, Cal had helped him plant four flowering cherry trees in his backyard, and always suspected that his brother had buried and then unburied the stolen money, because Finn left four hastily filled, empty holes, one under each tree.

The stolen money was never recovered, and Cal used to go on about it all the time. Alene remembered her mother asking him to give it a rest at one point when he wouldn't stop speculating about it. Everyone in Galesburg was wrapped up in the discussion for a while, but as the years passed and new problems arose in their lives, the bank robbery, missing money, and empty holes faded into a legend from the past.

Cal had never stopped thinking about it. Sometimes, he'd recall Winnie, Finn's wife, saying that her husband had seemed happy, and had spent those weeks after he got out of prison working around the house. He'd repaired and replaced squeaky floorboards and steps, snaked the pipes, and painted faded walls. When he'd finished inside the house, he worked outside weeding, dividing clumps of hydrangea, planting sod and rosebushes. She'd loved those cherry trees and cried every spring when they bloomed. Winnie said she didn't know what made Finn pick up and leave, but everyone agreed that he must have taken a train, because he left their Chevy station wagon parked in front of the house.

Cal always said that it wasn't the first time Finn had run away. As a teenager, he'd gotten caught hotwiring cars, and instead of facing the consequences, he'd left town. Cal told different stories about why he'd gone, and where, depending on the message he was trying to convey to Alene and Lydia, and later to his grandchildren. Finn had returned when school started, and never told Cal, who was just a boy, or their parents where he'd been or what he'd been doing that summer.

Whenever Cal told the story of his brother leaving a second time, he said, "I never saw it coming." Alene wondered why it had been such a surprise. People show you who they are, don't they? She thought that had been one of her parents' messages about how the world worked, but her dad made it sound as if Finn running away a second time had been a weird anomaly.

Alene remembered driving with her parents and sister nearly every month to visit Winnie, and her son, Jimmy. Lydia would always get carsick and change places with their mother, but Alene suspected that Lydia had just wanted to sit in the front seat. Cal thought of Galesburg as a pretty place filled with history. He loved announcing that his hometown had been a stop on the Underground Railroad and had hosted the fifth Lincoln-Douglas debate at Knox College in 1858.

Alene remembered little about the town itself, but she recalled Finn's wife, Aunt Winnie, teaching her and Lydia how to make an olive oil cake. Winnie told them that women, like her own mother, had baked cakes using olive oil during World War II. It was one of the first recipes Alene saved into a scrapbook, and a few years later, she created a modified version, her Meyer lemon-rosemary olive oil cake. She liked cake with a history.

She'd sat at Aunt Winnie's kitchen table with Lydia, cutting pictures out of magazines or putting together a puzzle while the parents drank coffee and nattered. Their cousin Jimmy had joined them, until he turned twelve or so. During the winter, Alene and Lydia had loved sledding and skating on the pond in Winnie's backyard. They could ice skate in Chicago, but in Galesburg, they'd been surrounded by trees and fields. And there'd been chatty neighbors stopping by endlessly, which used to annoy their mother.

"We had an idyllic childhood," Cal liked to say. Any childhood without a global pandemic sounded idyllic to Alene. She and Lydia had enjoyed a relatively normal childhood, although there were occasional setbacks, a few heartbreaks, and challenges that seemed insurmountable at the time. Then, their mother had been diagnosed with breast cancer.

Alene shook herself out of her reverie at the sound of her father's voice. "So, Finn is still alive," Cal said as he returned plates to the cabinet while Alene wiped down the sink and counters. "Unless someone is pretending to be Phineas Morton Baron. He had my cell number, but maybe the pretender got it from Finn."

"If you talk to him, you'll know soon enough, Dad," said Alene. They hadn't spoken about Finn in a long time.

"If it's him, I don't have that much to say anymore," said Cal. It always took time for his bitterness to dissipate. "He missed his son's, your mother's, and his wife's funerals."

Alene said, "Maybe he wants to apologize for disappearing." Noah wandered back into the kitchen to ask for dessert, and Alene offered to slice an apple. His shoulders slumped, and he made a face.

"Finn asked if I'd be willing to meet," said Cal. "That's what he texted."

52

Alene asked, "What did you tell him?" Just then, Quinn and Sierra also came in, so Alene set out three plates of apple slices with a small bowl of softened peanut butter for each of them.

Cal made a disgruntled face exactly like Noah's before shuffling back into the living room. He sat back in his comfy chair to read a book about the history of humanity. Alene finished up in the kitchen and lay down on the couch next to her father's chair, to read an intriguing British mystery about a troubled detective, set in 1860s London. She had thirty minutes before it was time to remind the kids about bedtime.

Cal's phone pinged then, and she heard some cheer in his voice as he read the message out loud. "Blanca just texted to say that she's leaving the hospital tomorrow."

Alene looked up from her book, "That's great, Dad. We needed some happy news," she said.

"She also writes that she's irritated," Cal added. "The two guys who rent her extra bedroom, the ones who got her sick, never got as sick as she was."

"I'd be irritated too," said Alene. "Send her my love." Alene called her sister to bring her up to date about their long-missing uncle. Lydia, as usual, wasn't that interested in anything aside from her pregnancy.

"Did you hear that dad hates Theo's idea of Phineas as a possible boy's name?" Lydia asked. "He's okay with Fiona if it's a girl. What do you think?"

Alene had learned not to express strong feelings about anything having to do with Lydia's baby. "They're both cute names."

"I understand how Dad might have feelings about the name Phineas," Lydia said, chewing something noisily while she talked. "We're also considering Algernon." Alene had to turn her giggle into a coughing attack. She got the update on how big the fetus was, the size of a bell pepper, and then offered to bring food over the weekend. Lydia never turned down food, especially if it came from the café.

Later, before bed, Alene had one rushed phone conversation with Frank, who was still working. She didn't know how or why he worked so many hours each week. Didn't a city the size of Chicago employ enough homicide detectives so that people like Frank didn't have to break their backs? He said he only put in long hours when he absolutely had to, but that seemed to be nearly every week. After saying goodnight, Alene read until she couldn't keep her eyes open.

On Saturday morning, Alene set out breakfast, got her father and kids organized, and walked to the café with Kacey. She'd made sure the kids were ready for her ex-husband to pick them up, since he'd decided Saturdays were better than Sundays, now that nobody was coming in to buy cars of any kind. Alene preferred to have them on Sundays, which she usually took off.

Zuleyka, who was chopping vegetables, and Rashid, who was at the grill, had opened the café earlier. They were trying to communicate—he had

54

trouble understanding her thick accent and had started teaching her sign language. Two weeks before, Ruthie had watched them and suggested that the entire staff learn along with Zuleyka. So far, they'd learned several signs that were useful in the kitchen, like yes and no, stop and go, and cookie. Now he was teaching them the signs for sugar, salt, less, and more.

Alene greeted them and went to get her apron. Zuleyka had come from Panama to work as Alene's au pair when Noah was born. She'd been endlessly patient and amiable with the kids but had let them make noise, which sometimes aggravated Cal. When Noah started going to preschool, she'd come to work at the café. Both Zuleyka and Rashid were still trying to figure out what to do with their lives and were grateful to Alene for letting them stay on at the café through the pandemic.

While Kacey started working on the doughs that had been refrigerated overnight, Alene studied the detailed instructions that Ruthie always left for Saturdays. Then she headed out to the café area to confirm the number of orders Dori and Edith had already taken. Olly came to the front door, and Alene let him in. He reported that his plan that morning was to get rid of several un-reparable, rickety chairs.

"You're taking them to the dump, right?" Alene asked, wishing she didn't need to keep reminding him. "We don't have room for furniture in our garbage bins."

Olly laughed, "Of course not," he said, "but we were thinking about building a bonfire in the alley. It won't cost you anything."

"Olly!" He loved nettling her. He started taping off a section of the café next to the crimson-colored wall, and by the time Kofi showed up, Olly had set aside the chairs they'd save. Kofi got to work breaking down the rejects. Alene thought Kofi seemed back to normal.

Her ex-husband called to cancel about fifteen minutes before he was supposed to pick up the kids, and Alene simmered with anger. She called home and spoke to each of them, promised that she'd leave work early, and told her father that she owed him.

"That was always the case, my dear Alene," Cal replied, "but it's my pleasure to be with my grandchildren. We're going to be doing some science experiments. Hope you don't mind." Alene stopped herself from warning her father to be careful.

Just as lunchtime was coming to an end and online orders were dwindling, Olly asked Alene to come back out to the café. "We're done with the chairs, and I've got something interesting to show you," he said with a hint of mystery. Alene told him she'd come when she finished a batch of her radish-top pesto.

"Up to you," he said. "FYI, this is enormous." With Olly, everything was enormous, but Alene didn't like stopping in the middle of a recipe. That's when she made mistakes, like adding too much lemon or salt, which could ruin the whole batch.

"I'll check my schedule," she said, waving him out of the kitchen as she picked up a clean teaspoon to scoop a taste of the dip. Then she gestured to Zuleyka, who'd spent the past hour preparing jars and now stood at Alene's side, ready with a small spatula. The Whipped and Sipped Café was known for sauces and dips. Customers smeared them on thick slices of Ruthie's bread, used them for dipping vegetables, or added broth to thin them into soups. Those jars deserved almost as much credit as cookies for getting the café through the pandemic so far.

By the time Alene left the kitchen, Olly was nowhere to be seen. She assumed he was squatting behind the counter, eating something, but next thing she knew, Kacey came running from the kitchen and said, "Follow me for a second. Olly said he wants to set the stage."

"Seriously?" Alene asked. The last thing she needed from him was an entrance, but she followed Kacey back to the kitchen. Thirty seconds later, Kacey pivoted back to the café, Alene at her heels. Olly was posing next to the counter, ready to perform. She assumed his discovery would be that the café's sewage pipes had been leaking into the wall for thirty years, or something along those lines. "I'd like to preface my remarks today," he said, "by explaining that unearthing a buried treasure has long been my dream." His voice carried into the kitchen, and the employees hurried out. Ruthie didn't allow breaks before bakers completed whatever they were working on, but rules were often broken on her day off.

As she waited— Olly loved wasting her time— Alene browsed through her texts, emails, and the local news, in case there was anything about the fire on Diversey where Kofi had seen the dead body. Why hadn't anyone else found it yet? It had been twenty-four hours! What if the person didn't have any family in Chicago? What if it was a troubled person who'd lost a long battle with addiction or mental illness?

Now Olly signaled Kacey, and she removed one of the posters taped to the crimson wall. Ever since Alene had purchased the café nearly nine years before, that wall had been painted a deep crimson color and covered with art. While he was working for Alene, Olly had curated a rotating collection, some local and for sale, but since the pandemic began, only employees could enter the café, and no one had taken Olly's place. The poster Kacey took down was the only thing that had changed since March.

Zuleyka had gone to wash her hands behind the counter, and now joined the others near the crimson wall. "What Kacey is doing?" she asked.

"I'm taking down a poster of the actor who played God in that movie," Kacey said. She swept by holding up the *Bruce Almighty* poster she'd removed. "I can't remember his name."

Kofi said, "Morgan Freeman. A *Shawshank Redemption* poster would have been more fitting, but this one was cheaper."

"That's just sad," said Olly, standing in front of the crimson wall. "You can rattle off the names of sixteen actors from crummy sitcoms, Kacey. I'm starting to lose hope in my quest to teach you the difference between art and popular culture."

"You lost hope long ago," Kofi said. They high fived each other, and from across the room, Edith yelled that they were standing too close together.

Olly stepped aside and revealed an opening in the wall where the poster of Morgan Freeman had hung. He reached up to a dangling piece of the wall and pulled it down. "Kofi and I have spent the last few weeks pulling out drywall so that you can see how it was once a door that led to a staircase."

Alene saw a gaping hole. "You're planning to close that up, aren't you?"

"That's not a mistake, Alene," said Kofi. "It's a door that someone plastered over a long time ago. Behind it there's a staircase leading to a basement."

"We have a basement?" Alene could only think about the cost of fixing the wall before the pandemic ended and customers started coming in again. "How did you find the door?" she asked.

"I ran my hands over it," Kofi continued, "and realized that there weren't any studs on the right side of the wall, so we decided to check it out."

"I don't know what you mean." Alene rubbed her forehead. "Why did you look for studs?" It was the wrong question—she didn't care about that.

Olly said, "There are crumbling old steps that you can see from here. They go both down to the basement and up to the second floor." He pulled up a chair for Alene and plopped himself down on one nearby. "We've already cleared the descending steps." He paused to build drama. "I think the basement might have been an entertainment space. There's a raised area, possibly a stage, and a few rooms off to the side. One of them is a bathroom with a rudimentary shower."

"The wallpaper is racy," Kofi added.

How racy could old wallpaper be? Alene hoped Olly wasn't going to say that her floor was structurally unsound or that the café was at risk of being sucked in when the basement ceiling fell.

"Didn't you see the blueprints for this building?" Kofi asked. "I mean, like when you bought the café from Kacey's father?"

Alene tried to remember the papers Gary Vanza had given her nine years before, when she used part of her divorce settlement to buy the café. "Maybe, but I'm pretty sure I'd have noticed a blocked-off doorway and a basement with a stage and a bathroom."

"I'm glad you asked," said Olly, even though she hadn't asked anything. "We found lots of broken glass and a treasure trove of old tables and chairs. Also, a bar."

Zuleyka interrupted, "What if no people ever again come to the café? As we say, from the plate to the mouth, the soup sometimes spills." They all stared at her until she said, "It sounds better in Spanish."

"I think this place was a speakeasy where they sold liquor during Prohibition," Olly said, pausing to make a gesture resembling that of a circus ringmaster. "And I think we're going to find a tunnel to the alley or something equally intriguing. That's how patrons would have escaped during police raids."

Kofi said, "I've seen a few of the old Chicago speakeasies converted back into regular basements."

"Why did they hide the basements?" Zuleyka asked.

"There was a ban on alcohol," said Kofi, "from 1920 to 1933."

Alene didn't remember seeing the blueprints, but she'd had a lot on her mind back when she bought the café: a new baby, Neal telling her that he wanted an open marriage, their subsequent divorce. "Before Kacey's dad, our neighbors Brianne and Dennis Flynn owned this building," she said. "And Brianne's parents owned it before that, so maybe they knew about its history, but they're dead. Brianne might know. I only know that it was built in the early nineteen-twenties."

Kofi said, "Imagine mobsters escaping up the secret staircase just as the Prohibition police came running in waving their guns."

"Or they'd flee through the tunnel with the dolls who sold the booze and cigarettes," said Olly with what he imagined to be an accent from that period. He must have gotten it from watching old movies.

"Dolls, Olly?" LaTonya asked, looking up. She'd been studying her nails during Olly's presentation.

Olly said, in his own accent, "I've read about tunnels between buildings that had something to do with coal delivery from earlier years, but I won't be surprised if we find a few bodies buried in the rubble."

"Hah," said Zuleyka. "Funny joke."

What if it wasn't a joke? There it was again, the fatigue that enveloped her whenever she confronted death. She hadn't told Frank about the body Kofi had seen on Benjie's property. Wouldn't he know about it by now? And if he knew about it, why would she need to mention anything about Kofi? Alene had to admit that she was intrigued by the basement, but it wasn't the first time Olly had found a way to distract her from running the café.

"As lovely as it was to have a chat with you and hear about your new discovery," she told Olly and Kofi, "we need to get back to work."

"We're obviously also hoping to find a vault filled with money," said Kofi, "and we noticed bricked-up windows along the perimeter of the building. If we unearthed some of those window wells, you might be able to have some natural light down there."

"Isn't there any light at all?" asked Alene.

"Just electric lights," Kofi answered.

Kacey said, "In the movies, mobsters always stash their loot in vaults."

"That was one of my favorite decades," said Olly with a dreamy expression. Edith piped up again to say were standing too close to one another.

Alene thought that the café very well might have once provided cover for a speakeasy. An old high school friend had lived in a nearby building in which the speakeasy had been converted into a parking garage. And Cal used to take Alene and her sister to hear jazz at the Green Mill, where Al Capone had had a special table that allowed him to keep an eye on the entrances. Maybe there was a way to monetize the connection, perhaps a "Prohibition cake" filled with liquor.

They started cleaning up for the day. Final orders came in and the bicyclists headed out with their last deliveries. By two o'clock, Alene was ready to go home to relieve her father, and asked Olly and Kofi to join her in the kitchen while she made a package for her sister. "You two are responsible for locking up," she said. "Also, please let's keep this secret door to ourselves for now."

Olly flashed her an okay with his thumb and forefinger. Then he and Kofi thumped back down the stairs, and she could hear Kofi warning him to watch out because the stairs weren't strong enough to take that kind of pounding.

Chapter 5

The sky was hazier later in the afternoon, and it was warmer outside when Alene returned with the kids after dropping off food at her sister's. They'd had fun doing experiments using food coloring with Cal, but now she wanted to get them outside, and enticed them with stories of a surge of puppies in the neighborhood.

That plan didn't turn out as well as Alene had expected. Too many people feared that animals also carried the coronavirus, and the children weren't allowed to touch any of the dogs they passed. They were crestfallen not to see any of their classmates and complained that most of the kids were younger. After twenty minutes, they turned around and went back to the apartment, where Alene engaged Quinn and Noah in baking an orange-cardamom cake while Sierra watched a movie on her iPad.

That evening, Frank came over. In the before times, they'd have gone out to dinner and a movie or a show on Saturday night, but restaurants and theaters had been closed since March. Alene had also invited Rhona, but she'd gone out, and Frank had no idea where she was. She refused to share anything about her personal life with him.

Alene made a salad and rice while Frank used her countertop grill to cook the marinated vegetable kabobs. Every time they passed each other, he caressed her shoulder or squeezed her arm. The children behaved slightly better when Frank was over; either they were intimidated because he was a homicide detective who carried a gun, or they liked him.

They each had two pieces of cake, and Alene was delighted that no one seemed to have noticed how she'd slowly decreased the amount of sugar she used in her frosting. Cal, after just one rambling tale about his brother while the children were still finishing their dessert, told a funny story about a woman who saw a famous movie star at an ice cream parlor. The woman decided to act normal and was about to get into her car when the famous movie star tapped her shoulder and told her that she had put the ice cream cone in her purse. He always laughed at his own jokes, which sent the kids into a round of giggling. Cal had been somewhat tense since he'd heard from his brother, so Alene was pleased that he could relax enough to laugh.

After the kids and Cal went to their rooms, and it seemed like they'd all fallen asleep, Alene and

Frank snuggled, and she told him about the Morgan Freeman poster, and the basement. Frank begged her not to go down the stairs until they'd cleared away the broken glass and garbage. "Let Olly and Kofi do the exploring," he suggested.

He told her about one of several cases he'd worked on that day. "The frame of a building burnt to the ground and two young boys managed to sneak under the construction fence yesterday," Frank said. Alene didn't trust herself to speak. "Turns out it was one of Benjie Rosin's properties."

Frank liked Benjie. Before the pandemic they'd met up a few times to visit new microbreweries, and they'd made plans to go boating when the pandemic ended, and boats were allowed back in the harbor.

"Their mother called it in today, and when I spoke to her, she was bubbling with excitement that her sons had found a dead body," Frank said, disapproving. "She didn't seem at all troubled that a person had died and thought it was just a piece of news to spread."

Alene was relieved. At least the person would get buried, and their family would know what had happened. It was a horrible thing to hear, but what if the person's husband or wife had waited up all night? Or worse, what if nobody noticed the person was missing because he or she didn't have anyone to care?

She didn't tell Frank that unless two different bodies had been found in the rubble of fires close to Diversey, they were discussing the one that Kofi had seen the previous day. After everything she told

Kacey about relationships, here she was doing the exact opposite. But if she said something, he'd ask a zillion questions, and that would be the end of their night together. She wasn't feeling very amorous, though.

"And we won't get identification or autopsy results until the coroner's office gets caught up with a backlog of weeks, if not months," Frank continued. "It's aggravating for relatives of the victims, but there's nothing I can do to speed things up."

They talked about how critical it was to convey the fragility of life to children, but Alene was thinking about the fragility of relationships, and wondering if she'd just made an enormous mistake by not telling Frank about the body Kofi saw.

"Don't worry about the rest of the world, Frank," she said. "I'm committed to sleeping through the night, and to that end, I'm going to get up and get myself a tiny edible." She knew he wouldn't partake, even though marijuana was now legal in Illinois, so she just grabbed one for herself. Frank didn't like taking drugs of any kind. He left to go home after they'd tired each other out in the best way possible, and she got five hours of uninterrupted sleep. But her dreams were wacky and troubled.

Alene always woke up early to go running on Sundays, her day off. Few people were out, but she ran into her old trainer, Michael, who said he was doing his training via Zoom. Alene told him she'd come back after someone found a cure for Covid-19 and they could meet in person again. A mile or so later, she passed Peter Berg, the brother of the woman who'd provoked her with the six-feet comment. He was pushing an old man, probably their father, in a wheelchair. Alene waved, but Peter was looking off to the side, and didn't respond.

Ruthie called. Frank had told her husband about the dead body. Alene's stomach flipped. That poor person's family had no idea what had happened. Why was it taking so long for it to be in the newspaper? Maybe they needed to identify who it was before they announced it to the public.

"Now it's a murder site," Ruthie told Alene. She was justifiably shaken, but at the café, so she couldn't talk. Alene promised they'd discuss it later. She'd have to tell Ruthie everything. She'd only promised Kofi that she wouldn't say anything to Frank.

After her shower, she made waffles with berries and vanilla yogurt. Quinn and Noah ate with gusto; Sierra picked at her food the way she'd been doing lately. Cal ate slowly as he turned the pages of the *Chicago Tribune.* He was crankier than usual--he'd gotten three more texts from his brother. "He hasn't picked up the phone to call me in years," said Cal, "and now he's Mr. High-Tech, sending me texts every fifteen minutes."

Alene asked, "What does he say?"

Cal swatted the air. "Mostly nonsense. He keeps telling me not to tell anyone where he is, as if I know. And he says that I shouldn't believe anything anyone says about him, but who's going to tell me anything, and why? Also, he wants us to meet, but he's making it seem like an undercover operation for the C.I.A."

"Dad," she said, "what if he had a stroke, or got bashed on the head and didn't know who he was all these years?" She'd seen movies like that. "I think you should reserve judgment until he gets a chance to explain." She wasn't sure she'd even recognize her uncle if she passed him on the sidewalk. "Do you want to meet him in the park?"

Cal said, "I don't know. What are we going to talk about after twenty-two years? The only thing I want is an apology. It's not just that he missed the funerals. And now that Blanca's getting out of the hospital, I don't want to subject her to him."

"She'll be in quarantine for ten days, Dad, so don't worry about that," Alene said. He'd been anxious about Blanca from the moment she got sick. "And I'll go with you to meet your brother."

"Unless Finn decides to hang around until Blanca gets out of quarantine," Cal grumbled as he folded the *Trib* and picked up another of his newspapers. The kids, who weren't paying attention to the conversation, finished their breakfasts, put their dishes in the sink, and ran back to whatever screens they'd been watching. Alene fretted that they'd need glasses, or their brains would be altered by so much screen time. After she'd washed the dishes, she coaxed them through their Sunday cleaning, caught up with her emails, and prepared veggie balls and garlic bread to serve with fettucine for dinner. In the past, she'd occasionally made real meatballs, but Ruthie had gotten under her skin about the meat industry.

Frank called that afternoon. He was worried about Rhona because she'd stayed out until nearly two in the morning. She'd woken him up needing a hot pad for one of her terrible headaches. She'd also wanted painkillers, the legal kind. Frank was afraid that she'd already taken the illegal kind and it wouldn't be safe, but she said she'd just get up and get it herself if he wasn't going to be helpful. "She's still sleeping," he added, sounding grumpy.

"That would make sense," Alene said, "if I'm correct about her having a boyfriend."

"I think her numerous issues make it difficult to be in a relationship," Frank said. He hated when Rhona was out all night, but it also worried him that she spent hours alone in her room.

"Can't you just imagine her having some normal fun, Frank?" Alene asked. "She's a grown-up. Also, I used to love sleeping in on Sundays. You can't be upset with her for that."

"I don't think she has a normal grown-up life, Alene," Frank said "No degree, no job, no prospects. I wouldn't be as worried if she had some direction."

"I know," said Alene, trying to sound sympathetic. Frank hadn't asked for her advice. He'd just wanted her to listen. She confirmed that he'd come for dinner before hanging up.

While Cal was in his room having his usual siesta, Alene took Quinn and Noah outside to roller skate on the sidewalk. There was hardly anyone out, so she didn't have to worry about one of them accidentally skating into the street. They were disappointed that none of the other kids in the neighborhood were playing outside.

After about an hour, they went back in. Alene and the girls worked on making bracelets from a kit and Noah worked on one of his complicated Lego sets. Frank made it over at about five and stayed for pasta and veggie-ball night. Because he was there, Sierra made more of an effort to be a part of everything, and even giggled at a story Frank told about falling off his boat. Then Quinn annoyed her, and the moment passed.

After dinner, Alene offered popsicles she'd made by blending frozen fruit with peeled zucchini. Nobody suspected that the popsicles were healthy, and the kids scarfed them up while watching a documentary about an octopus. Then Frank went home, and Cal and the children went to their bedrooms. Alene longed for the day when Frank could move in. Their phone calls could be about when he was coming home each day. Alone again in her bed, Alene started reading a new mystery, this one set in Chicago just after the Civil War, about a female detective and her crusty partner.

Monday morning dawned dreary but warmer. Alene opted for a long walk because her knees couldn't take running more than three times a week. It would have been more fun for her if one of the lake paths had been open, but she had to stay on sidewalks. She passed Peter Berg, again pushing an old man in a wheelchair. This time, Peter stopped and waved, clearly delighted to see Alene. The old man barked out an order for him to keep going, and

Peter lowered his head, fiddling with his mask until the old man reached up and smacked his hand.

Peter seemed to be happy except when he was being scolded. Alene wondered about the trade-off. He might not ever be able to live on his own, but he'd also never be pressured to get a job. And he wouldn't be thwarted by life because he didn't have big expectations. Either way, if there was one thing Alene admired, it was people being kind to their parents. She also liked seeing parents express love to their children. It broke her heart when her ex-husband sniped at the kids. And it made her sick when he was rude to his mother, making a fuss every time he was asked to do something simple, like pick up her dry-cleaning or fill a prescription at the drugstore.

Alene's sister, Lydia, also carped whenever Alene asked her to help with their dad, to take him to a doctor's appointment or to buy new orthopedic shoes. Lydia, who'd struggled for several years with frustrating infertility treatments, hadn't seen Cal in person since March. She was being extremely careful, now that she was at long last pregnant, and wouldn't go into anyone's home or allow anyone to enter her apartment. Alene stopped to text her—she hadn't said anything about the bread, muffins, and protein-packed frittata that Alene had dropped off.

She turned around to go home and woke the kids up so she could give them breakfast before she left. It was Memorial Day, when they usually went the cemetery to visit those Cal had fought with who hadn't survived, followed by a picnic with the ones who had. Since all gatherings were canceled, the children were going to spend the day with their father, Alene's ex, who'd promised them a ride in a convertible with the top down.

"They're not even holding any events this year," Cal said, "and the kids are going with Neal, so I guess I'll just read through the old letters and call a few of the guys."

She knew he meant other guys who'd survived Vietnam, like him, the ones who still had their wits about them. Cal had been in one of the final groups of draftees sent over, in early 1972. At least now he and his fellow vets were finally appreciated for the sacrifices they'd made, unlike when they first returned and were stunned to be confronted by mockery and derision.

Neal arrived closer to the expected time than was his usual custom. Now that the children were old enough to demand to be fed when they were hungry, her only worry was that they'd get bored sitting in the car, even with the top down, and he wouldn't know what to do with them. After some thought, Alene realized that it wasn't her problem. If they weren't having fun, they'd let him know, and he'd have to deal with them.

When she finally arrived at the café, Alene breathed in the smells of cinnamon and yeast. Employees seemed to be moving at a leisurely pace. Normally, Whipped and Sipped would be packed with gatherings of people enjoying a Memorial Day breakfast or brunch. The kitchen would be filled with the sounds of scraping, stirring, chopping, and oven doors opening and shutting. Today, the kitchen was relatively quiet. Alene kept hoping business would pick up with summer, but here it was, virtually June, and the coronavirus pandemic was killing perfectly healthy people. Even if the sun started shining and the air warmed up, the city would still be on lockdown.

Ruthie, who had a witchy sense about Alene, must have noticed that she was already feeling put-upon. "The first batches are in the oven," she said in a lighthearted voice, "so I have some time to walk if you're up to taking a break."

"I just got here," said Alene, "and I've already walked this morning."

"Have you forgotten that 'taking a break' is code for wanting to talk?" Ruthie asked. They'd invented a code in college, but that was getting close to twenty years ago.

"Oops," said Alene. "I wasn't paying attention." She and Ruthie put their jackets back on and headed out. Dori said that she'd already brought a sandwich out for Vincent, so Ruthie just gave him one of her cheery greetings and asked if he needed more to eat. He spat on the ground, as usual, and mumbled something into his coat as they passed by. Alene didn't understand a single word and hoped he didn't start showing up more than once or twice a week.

"I try to be welcoming when he appears," said Ruthie, after they'd walked a block, "but he keeps yelling about how I've ruined everything. Does he do that to you?"

Alene said, "I'm not sure what he's yelling, but maybe he's sad because so few people pass by on the sidewalk these days, and those who do cross to the other side."

Alene had read that the city was serious about getting homeless people off the streets before they overwhelmed the hospitals. Why was Vincent sitting there, scaring the delivery kids and the few customers who came to pick up their orders? She said, "I can't imagine getting to that age and not having anyone to care about me."

Ruthie gave her a quick, one-armed hug and said, "I'll always care about you, Six."

That was another thing that made Alene's eyes tear up. "Do you want to talk about the dead body they found on Benjie's property?" she asked, sickened again that there hadn't been a blurb describing who the person was and what had happened. They were walking one of their usual routes, and Alene again counted the businesses that had shut down since the pandemic began. It temporarily distracted her from thinking about the dead body.

Ruthie didn't answer. Alene tried again. "Is there any new information about the fire?"

Ruthie said Benjie was still dealing with insurance forms and adjustors. He was trying to put his energy into other buildings. "Did Frank tell you about the dead body?" Ruthie asked.

"I knew about it before he told me," Alene said. She felt sick about how she'd kept that secret from Frank, but it felt good to tell Ruthie about taking Kofi to the destroyed building at dawn on Friday morning. "I wanted to tell Frank, but it was never the right time."

Ruthie stopped. "Alene, aside from building trust between you, how can you keep a secret like that from Frank? He's a homicide detective. Don't you think he deserved a heads up about a dead body?" They walked without speaking for a while.

"I wasn't trying to keep it secret," Alene said. She knew how hard Chicago police officers worked, especially now, trying to maintain calm in a city of people who were agitated about the virus, frustrated by government chaos, and distraught about having their school-age children at home. Added to that were the protests around the country following the videotaped murder of George Floyd in Minneapolis. Either some of those protests had devolved into riots or some of those rioters had used the protests as an excuse to go wild.

Ruthie was breathing audibly, the way she did when she was upset. She said, "Then you know what to do to make things right." They walked a block before Ruthie's breathing returned to normal. She never stayed angry very long. They were crossing what was usually a busy street, but there were few cars out these days.

"Let's change the subject," Ruthie said finally. "Is it worth spending money to rebuild the stairs and renovate the basement? Will we get some use out of it?"

"It depends," said Alene, relieved that Ruthie had let it go. "Are we going to inform all the other tenants in the building?" They hardly knew any of the other tenants, but Ruthie was a stickler for rules and regulations. "And do you think we have to report it to the city?"

Ruthie chuckled. "What do we say? That we unearthed an old basement, and we'd like to offer to pay taxes on it?"

Alene imagined dollars flying away like birds. "No," she said, "Let's pretend it doesn't exist."

They turned on Diversey and walked towards the empty lot where the fire had been. It was longer than their usual walks. Just across the street they could see the building that looked like the one that housed both Whipped and Sipped and the neighborhood bar, Tipped. Same herringboned red brick around the windows, same large storefronts, except these were boarded up and empty. Alene wondered if they also had four floors of apartments and an alley in back. Were the old coal chutes also filled in from the outside? And was there a basement? Maybe they had customer parking in the back, unlike Whipped and Sipped. Parking would have been a game changer in the days when they had customers going in and out.

Ruthie cleared her throat. "Whoever lives here might have watched the fire," she said. "Do you think that the police interviewed the neighbors? Maybe someone saw what happened. Didn't Peter say that he watched it? Maybe that's where he and his sister live."

"I hope they find a reliable witness," said Alene. If someone saw the fire, they might also know something about the dead body. She didn't need to add that Peter wouldn't be considered reliable. They started walking back, and Alene told Ruthie about Cal's brother. Then she shared her hunch that Frank's daughter had a beau.

"One," Ruthie said in response, "people have lots of reasons for cutting ties with their families. I hope your dad lets his brother back into his heart. Two, it's not that mysterious that a young woman wants to keep her relationship secret from her father, who happens to be a detective."

When they were getting closer to the café, Alene went back to the first discussion. "Frank knows that I respect him and what he does, Ruthie," she said. It sounded like she was trying to convince herself. Frank had a track record and lots of people who respected him. He'd agreed that there were some bad apples at CPD, just like everywhere else, but thought most of his department was top-notch. He knew that his partner was so socially gawky he couldn't even look Alene in the eye. Alene wondered how the guy had gotten himself into the homicide department in the first place. And why had some higher-up thought he'd be the right partner for Frank Shaw?

Ruthie said, "I'm sure he does, Alene, because he respects you and what you do."

Frank's ringtone started up on Alene's phone. She changed it every month or so, and now it was Ed Sheeran's "Thinking Out Loud," a song that made her want to drop everything to be in Frank's arms. He was calling to say that he and Lee were heading over, and he asked if she'd bring some coffee out to their car. This time, it was police business. They wanted to talk to Ruthie also.

"How close are you?" Alene asked.

"See you in fifteen," he said.

Dori was squatting next to Vincent as they approached the café, conversing, and Ruthie lingered to wave at him again. Aside from Ruthie, Dori was the only one of Alene's employees who talked to Vincent. Maybe she was an angel like Ruthie, except that she could be aloof, and cagey when anyone asked a personal question. That was fine with Alene. She didn't need to be best buddies with everyone who worked for her.

Dori seemed friendly with Kacey, who tended not to ask personal questions, and with Jocelyn, who'd left the café to open her own Krav Maga studio next door, just months before the pandemic began. That had been unfortunate timing, but Jocelyn was starting to make some money doing online classes in the military-style self-defense discipline. Especially this past week, when some alleged protesters around the city had started breaking windows and stealing from stores. Cal said they were opportunists who just pretended to be protesters. Jocelyn said that she didn't care, because the chaos had inspired twelve more customers to register for her classes.

The kitchen staff continued doing their usual assignments, and a few of them shot the breeze as they chopped vegetables and stirred batters. Alene and Ruthie washed their hands and put their aprons back on. "We're talking about tips," said Kacey.

"Remember when people used to come into the café and leave money for the servers?"

Edith, again in the kitchen even though she was supposed to be working out in the café, said, "I never understand why people need tips for doing their job."

Kacey, Zuleyka, and LaTonya glared at her. Edith didn't need an income. Her brother, Gary, had left Edith enough to live on even if she chose to quit working, order in every night, take luxurious vacations, and get her hair done by an actual stylist. She did none of those things. Zuleyka said, "I need tips so I pay my rent."

LaTonya removed a mound of dough from the kneading machine and said, "Alene, would you let us put up a sign outside so customers know that if everyone left a little something, we could possibly earn enough to make up for a fraction of our lost hours?"

Alene tried to pay her employees a fair wage, but the margins on coffee and pastries were relatively low. Tips made a sizable difference. Ruthie said, "We aren't going to do that, are we, Alene?" She held firm views about what was appropriate. "We're not going to demand tips from our customers. They get to decide what to do."

Alene was checking the list of tasks. She'd been forced to cut hours. They closed after the final lunch deliveries now that no one came in to sit and eat or drink through the afternoon. "But you all deserve more than I can pay."

LaTonya said, "I think that if people in this neighborhood can afford to spend over four dollars for an espresso, they can afford to tip eighty cents. You know that tall white dude who comes nearly every day with his sister holding his hand? He leaves one dollar no matter what they buy."

"Are you complaining about it, LaTonya?" Alene asked. "That's Peter Berg, and his sister gives him money to leave that tip. I think it's sweet." Alene wondered if she was becoming more like Ruthie, who saw most people as compassionate. That wouldn't be so terrible.

Ruthie would have had more to say, but just then, Dori came back to the kitchen and asked if they'd learned anything new about the burned-out building on Diversey. "There was something about it in the online Tribune yesterday morning." Dori hadn't yet figured out that even if Ruthie knew, she wouldn't say anything if it smacked of gossip.

"They don't know for sure what caused it, but they think it might have been arson," Edith said as she slouched in after Dori. "I'm guessing it was another one of those homeless people."

Dori said, "You have to be cautious about getting your news from Facebook and Instagram, Edith." Jocelyn had taught Edith how to enjoy countless video of cats, and she posted weekly pictures of her own. "From what I understand, they haven't ruled out an electrical malfunction, or lightning." Maybe Dori had more common sense than Edith. "But it could have been caused by someone who had something against your husband, Ruthie."

Ruthie said, "Nobody has anything against Benjie. Everybody loves him."

Dori quickly added, "Or it could have been any number of things."

Alene thought it was an odd save. Frank called then to say that they were pulling up in front of the café. Unlike Neal, her ex-husband, who'd inherited his father's successful car dealership, Frank had worked hard to get where he was. She and Neal had made three wonderful children, but Neal had never looked at her like she was the most stunning woman in the world, the way Frank looked at her. As it turned out, he hadn't called just to hear her voice. "We're here to see Ruthie, but would you mind coming out with her?" he asked. "I think that'll make it easier."

Outside was better. It felt like there was less risk no matter how many people were around. Frank was conscientious about the coronavirus, but she didn't trust Lee. Also, the sun was shining, and the sky was tinted blue after months of gray. Alene gave Ruthie the message and ran to the counter to prepare drinks. Was it more ghastly news? They both removed their aprons before heading outside.

Alene carried out two black coffees and Ruthie brought several wrapped cookies. As usual, Lee's mask was below his nose, but Ruthie pointed it out and he adjusted it. He shook his head when she offered the cookie. "I don't eat desserts," he said, as if she'd presented him with a dead animal. He could have just said, "No, thanks."

Their car was double-parked. Alene handed them coffees, reaching over Frank, and Lee mumbled something unintelligible, blinking madly and looking down at the cup as if he couldn't turn his head and speak directly to her. Alene would never say it out loud, but she suspected that Lee was on the autism spectrum.

Why couldn't Frank have a partner who smiled and acknowledged her as a human being? Frank told her that even though Lee wasn't great with people, he was a solid detective and often noticed tiny things that Frank had passed over: a missing button, a slight tear in fabric, a miniscule smear of mud on the bottom of a shoe.

"As you're aware," Lee said to Ruthie without any preamble, "a building owned your husband burned to the ground on Thursday, and some children found a body in the rubble at 11:14 on Friday morning. What can you tell us about that?"

How would they know such a specific time? Maybe those kids found the body beforehand and the mother only called it in at 11:14. Lee was always so abrupt. Also, Alene hadn't known that Ruthie co-owned the business with Benjie. She'd thought the building was owned by a group of investors, or a nonprofit. Did Lee always have to speak like he was being filmed for a television show?

"We're just getting all the information, Ruthie," said Frank. "We have to ask what you know about the fire."

Lee mumbled something that sounded directed at Frank. "Not your problem, Lee," Frank said, stiffly. Alene wondered if he'd suggested that Frank bow out of the case and wished that Frank would use stronger language to tell Lee where to go.

Frank continued speaking to Ruthie. "Benjie's not a suspect, but we need you to verify where he was before the fire began late Wednesday night or early Thursday morning." He handed her a tablet to read. "We're trying not to bring people into the station."

Lee said, "We have two issues, Mrs. Rosin. One, your husband has been seen at that property every day by different neighbors. We have signed statements. He was also seen there on Wednesday night, sometime before the fire started."

It made Alene bristle to think anyone would accuse Benjie Rosin of starting a fire. There was no way he had anything to do with it. Ruthie read through the document and said sweetly, "This is all correct. Should I sign it?

"Yes, thank you, Ruthie," said Frank, taking the tablet after she'd finished. "We're just verifying information, as I said. Sorry we're doing it outside like this, but we need to be extra careful right now. And we're grateful for the coffee and cookies."

"What's the second issue?" Alene asked abruptly. "Lee said there were two issues, but he only named one, about neighbors seeing Benjie at his property."

Frank's shoulders fell and she knew that the second issue was going to be a challenge. He looked at Alene and said almost in a whisper, "The name

Rosin is written in indelible ink on the inside collar of the victim's yellow jacket."

Alene gasped.

"That was my son's," said Ruthie. "It was an adult-sized small rain jacket that he tore while climbing a tree. He only tore one pocket so I thought someone could still make use of it."

"You've got to be kidding," said Alene.

Ruthie blinked quickly for a moment, the way she did when she was thinking something through. She shook her head. "It's nothing, Frank. We have a giveaway bin right there on the sidewalk." She pointed to it. "The neighbors donate used clothes and small household goods, and people take whatever they need."

Lee said, "Interesting explanation," in a way that made it clear he was sure he'd uncovered a conspiracy. "But that's not all we found."

Frank said, "I'm sure we'll sort it all out. Thanks for your time, Ruthie." Lee looked annoyed at having been cut off, but Frank held up a hand and shook his head. He turned to Alene, made the sign of his pinky facing down and thumb up next to his ear, and drove away.

Chapter 6

"What are you going to say to Frank," Ruthie asked Alene after they were back in the kitchen, "when he learns that Kofi saw the body?" That very question had been roiling Alene's stomach. "And you knew, but never said a word," Ruthie added as she put her apron back on.

"Seeing a body isn't a crime," said Alene, even though she knew that wasn't the issue. Keeping that kind of secret from Frank was as bad as having told him an outright lie. She'd hoped that once the body was reported to the police, that would be the end of it.

"But, Ruthie," she asked, because it was easier to think about anything other than her dishonesty with Frank, "why do you put your names in your coats, and why don't you remove name tags before you donate them?"

"I put name tags in the kids' clothes because they kept losing everything," Ruthie said with a shrug. "Even Shaily, although she's old enough to keep track of her clothes. And I never think about removing the name tags later. We don't have control over who takes clothes out of the bin, so I'm not going to agonize about it."

Ruthie was too trusting, but Alene knew not to argue. She spent the rest of the day turning over and over in her mind the question about telling Frank. She tried to focus on work. Orders came in and were filled and everyone did their jobs. They closed early again—why keep the place open hoping for stragglers who never came, especially after the pumpernickel sold out?

Just before three, after most of her employees had gone home, Alene sat alone in her office reading about coffee roasters. Olly and Kofi came in with their bags of tools—she'd left the kitchen door open for them. Olly said, "I'd think you'd be more prudent, Alene, seeing as how fires are burning down buildings and some of the protestors are causing serious damage around the city."

"I don't think those are protestors who are causing the damage," she said. How did Olly always manage to sound like he was quoting an old movie? "I think those are people taking advantage of chaos from the protests to steal stuff. It's a crime of opportunity," she said. "Otherwise, they're the ones who'd be busy trying to scam everyone while people are stuck at home. You don't have to worry about the café, because the smash and grabs aren't happening at cafés."

"So, this pandemic essentially put regular burglars out of business," said Olly. "Thank you, Covid."

Kofi slouched in behind Olly. "Did you tell Frank?" he asked Alene. She shook her head, and he perked up. "I know how you feel about it, Alene. I owe you one." He gave her a bear hug.

Even hugs from a friend felt potentially dangerous. "You owe me more than one, Kofi Lloyd, but you didn't do anything wrong, so please just tell Frank. And I mean tell him now." She knew he spent hours scouring the city for materials. He'd run across tons of peculiar things, but that was probably the first time he'd stumbled upon a dead body.

Olly jumped in because he couldn't stand not knowing. "What happened, Kofi?" he asked, "and what'd Alene do for you?"

She gave him a disapproving look, the kind Ruthie would have given, and a moment to understand that he shouldn't have asked. Olly was rarely troubled by reprimands or subtle suggestions. He started to push Kofi for an answer and Alene interrupted.

"I've got to go because it's a school holiday and the kids are going to be bouncing off the walls by the time I get home, but will you guys please call me if you find anything? Like cash, for example."

That distracted Olly for the moment. "Maybe, after we take our eighty percent share of the loot," he said with a maniacal laugh. "But don't worry, we promise to clean up and lock the door on our way out."

"And set the alarm?" she asked.

He gave her a thumbs up as she left. Maybe there were some antique chairs tucked away down there that could be renovated, or old books that weren't too moldy after a century in an almost certainly damp basement.

On her way home, Alene stopped at the store for veggie burgers, buns, and sweet potatoes that she'd make into oven fries. While choosing a watermelon, she saw Peter across the aisle, playing with a piece of string while Taryn scrutinized fruit trays. It was nice that Taryn took her brother to the grocery store. He probably enjoyed being out and about, and there were a lot of things, colors, and people to look at. They must have left their father at home, maybe because it was hard to push a wheelchair around a busy store. Thank goodness her own father was ambulatory. Alene waved, and Peter's eyes lit up with recognition. He started to walk towards her, but Taryn pulled him back.

Frank called as she trudged home, the watermelon heavy in her backpack. He'd searched through Rhona's stuff, something he'd told Alene he hated to do, and had found a nearly empty bottle of Oxycontin prescribed to someone else. He'd confiscated the bottle and demanded to know where she got it. She told him to stay out of her business because she was now officially an adult, and he reminded her that he worked for the Chicago Police Department.

"She laughed," Frank told Alene. "If she wasn't my daughter, I'd have cuffed her and thrown her in the back seat of the car. I've started calling treatment centers, but they're closed for the holiday. I contacted her mother, who thinks I'm making something out of nothing, so that's a dead end. I also did some research, but I already knew that she'd have to check herself in since she's over twenty-one. She'd have to want to get well."

"I'm sorry," Alene said, wondering if Oxycontin was a better or worse addiction than meth, which had been Kacey's drug of choice. She'd told Alene that she'd gotten hooked after the first hit. Frank said he wished he could have Rhona locked up every time she swallowed a potentially deadly pill, but apparently they didn't keep cells available just for scaring the wayward young adult children of city employees. "Anyway," he added, "addicts don't generally get the help they need in jails."

"Isn't it illegal to buy and sell prescription drugs?" she asked. "Couldn't you follow her and nab whoever sells her the stuff? That's who belongs in jail, right?"

Frank said, "I could, but she'd never speak to me again."

Alene wished she could keep him from getting caught up in Rhona's drama. She'd been through it with Kacey. All those times when Kacey was snorting, smoking, or shooting up between her toes thinking that nobody would be able to tell. She'd never known if the meth had been laced, or if one of her so-called friends might turn on her, or if her heart might give out during an accidental overdose. Alene felt nauseous remembering how frightening it had been, never knowing if Kacey's father would get a phone call from the hospital.

Shouldn't Frank, a homicide detective with connections, be able to get Rhona the help she needed? He could ask one of his colleagues to bust her, with the provision that she'd be sent to one of the places that treat addictions. Or he could just send his partner to threaten to lock her up, and badger her into getting treatment. Frank would never agree to that, but until Rhona got clean, Alene would only get to see him during drive-by sightings like earlier that day, with Lee sitting next to him.

He'd agreed to come for dinner that night, at least for a short time. Alene sliced the watermelon and cooked the veggie burgers and sweet potato fries. When Frank arrived, they sat at the table, and her dad immediately launched into another memory, about the time his brother chipped a tooth. He was offended that the texts from Finn had dried up.

"I don't know what he's thinking, but I'm not interested in an on-again, off-again brother," Cal said.

"It sounds great to me," said Sierra, grabbing the bowl of fries from Noah, who'd taken a generous portion. Alene gave her a disapproving look and turned to encourage Noah to put a piece of lettuce back on his burger.

Quinn told a story about one of the boys in her online class tipping his chair and falling backwards.

"Everyone heard him bash his head on the floor, and he cried, which anyone would do, including me."

"I wouldn't cry," said Sierra. Alene and Frank exchanged glances.

Quinn continued unfazed, "But his mom came on the camera and talked to him like he was in kindergarten, and she called him "Pookie" instead of Paxton, and the whole class giggled. I tried not to," Quinn said, her eyes on Alene, "but I know the boys are going to call him "Pookie" all year long. It was sad and I feel sorry for him." Quinn liked to sum up her stories with how they made her feel.

Quinn's story reminded Noah of the time he'd fallen out of his chair at school a few months before the pandemic. Sierra and Quinn stopped him right there because they'd already heard it. Alene told them both to let their brother speak. Noah said, "Teachers can't tell us what to do in our own houses, so what Paxton did wasn't against the law. And Quinn, Paxton's brother Grayson is in my grade. He's the kid who learned how to surf. That's what I want for my birthday, Mom, surfing lessons."

Sierra looked up with her usual bored expression and said, "Where are you going to find waves in Chicago, genius? Also, teachers don't make laws, they only make rules."

Alene looked forward to Sierra getting past her sardonic phase. "When the pandemic is over, how about if we go on a vacation someplace where you can take surfing lessons, like California?" she asked. It was another place she dreamed about traveling to with Frank and the kids.

"I used to surf when I was younger," Frank said, "and I love California. Maybe we'll all go out there together sometime." Noah was open-mouthed with admiration.

"I'm pretty sure my brother was in California for years," said Cal.

He wasn't going to let it go. "Are you aware of anyone who's in touch with Uncle Finn, Dad?" Alene asked. "Maybe someone from Galesburg?"

"I heard that he cut ties with most of his old pals," Cal said, making his trademark gesture that resembled swatting flies, with a displeased expression. "Someone I used to work with had a cousin whose wife knew Aunt Winnie, but that was a long time ago. Finn used to send money orders to her every month. He supported his wife and son financially, even though they had no idea where he was."

She hadn't told Frank all the details, and he looked confused, so Alene mouthed the word "later" to him. One after the other, Sierra, Quinn, and Noah asked to be excused, and Alene set out the watermelon before they could leave. "Is this all there is for dessert?" Sierra asked. Alene smiled and passed her a plate, exactly the way her mother had smiled when Lydia complained about dessert.

After the kids left the table, Alene sat with Frank and her father talking about Finn and his son, Jimmy. She hadn't known Jimmy well because they'd lived over three hours away. "Do you remember that I was traveling with Ruthie, Dad? I was sorry to have missed Jimmy's funeral."

"I remember," he said, sighing, "but Finn missed the funeral too."

"Where was the money sent from?" she asked. "Finn must have had a job—couldn't someone trace the checks?"

"He wired money from all over the country," Cal said. "You don't have to report transfers under ten thousand, and Winnie told me that the money cleared every time. She was able to pay the mortgage, the bills, send Jimmy to school and everything. Including paying for his funeral." He explained that he'd traced some of the wires, but the only thing he learned was where the money originated. He'd gone to towns where Finn had been and would show his picture around, asking if anyone recognized him. It had all been a waste of time.

"People would point to me," said Cal, still needled. "Finn and I are similar-looking, and they often thought I was off my rocker, you know? As if I was searching for myself."

"Where'd your brother get the money?" Frank asked.

Alene tapped her dad's hand and asked, "Was it stolen?"

"Maybe, but he never told me anything. I know he never had a problem getting jobs. He knew how to do electrical work and plumbing," Cal explained to Frank. He'd already told Alene all about his brother.

Alene didn't ask how Finn would have earned money without paying taxes. Maybe the Internal Revenue Service was searching for him. There were probably plenty of people who paid for home improvements in cash, so maybe he did everything under the table. He also might have used a fake Social Security number.

Frank had to get back home then, and they only got a few minutes to kiss each other goodbye. After cleaning up dinner, Alene sat down in front of her laptop and googled Cal and his brother. She'd never thought to do it before. It looked like Cal and a few of his buddies occasionally used Facebook to share pictures of grandchildren or rant about politics. There were a couple of Finn Barons listed on the different platforms, but none of them was a seventy-one-year-old guy from Galesburg, Illinois, who was skilled at plumbing and electrical work. She offered Frank's detective skills, but Cal thought that was overkill.

"I don't understand why he texted me all these years later," said Cal, as Alene was washing the dinner dishes. The kids had all gone back to their rooms. "And then why did he stop texting? Maybe he already got rid of the number he texted me from, so now he's unreachable. I feel like he enjoys being the one in control but that doesn't mean I want to see him again. It's sad how you can push a person out of your thoughts when they stop treating you like family."

Frank called to ask if he could vent for a minute, and Alene was relieved to put her father's situation on hold. Rhona had already left the house by the time he returned, Frank said, agitated. She wouldn't assure him that she was being cautious about the virus when she went out, so he was justifiably worried.

"Maybe she's with someone who loves her and takes care of her," Alene said. Even better, she thought, if Rhona developed the capacity to love and care for that someone.

"Don't I wish, but she couldn't have picked a worse time to be running around the city," Frank said. Before she'd turned twenty-one, he used to ask colleagues at the police department to keep an eye out for her.

Alene repeated what her father usually said, "Everyone has to learn about consequences."

"I know," Frank said, "but she's my daughter and there's a virulent disease galloping around the world. What if the consequences are deadly?"

Kacey used to stay out until all hours, and her father always worried that she'd gone to find drugs. Alene knew that she had several dealers. The fear was that she was lying in some filthy alley.

"Maybe Rhona will find her own way, Frank," Alene said. "You can keep a close watch or ask colleagues to look out for her, but she's young and she needs freedom to make her own mistakes." Would she say that if Sierra acted out and risked her health like that? Probably not.

"But what if she catches the coronavirus and passes it to me," Frank asked, "and then I pass it to you or your dad? What if the person she's with turns out to the one who's selling those illegal prescription drugs?"

Frank had been through this too often to need her advice. "You can ask her to wear a mask at home and tell her how upset you are that she's not being extremely careful right now. The message is that you love and care about her. But I admit that if Sierra ran off like that, I'd have her followed."

"I can't," Frank said. "She'd never forgive me." Alene knew he wanted to move on with their lives too.

Rhona's nineteen-year-old brother, Trey, who was still in college, had seemed normal. Alene had met him when he came home for Christmas. He looked like Frank, with his olive complexion and cleft chin, and he had a thoughtful way of listening when anyone was speaking. Rhona had been polite to Alene that night, but she'd sniped at Frank and had been sarcastic to her brother. Frank said she'd learned that from her mother.

They said goodnight to each other, and Alene hoped she'd managed to make him feel, if not better, then at least listened to. She turned off her light and tried to sleep, but Frank was still on her mind.

When he was married, his ex-wife, Yvette, had frittered away her days, he said, with shopping, lunches, and spas. His marriage had ended when he infuriated Yvette by quitting his job. He went back to school to earn a degree in forensics, got into the police academy, and after graduation, was hired by the CPD, where he had to prove himself again and again before he reached his current position in the homicide department. It had taken a decade, and

Frank loved the job despite being partnered with the annoying Lee Bautista.

He had no idea what Yvette's life was like now or if she was happy, but she refused to deal with Rhona, even after it became clear that their daughter had serious issues. And even after Rhona threatened to kill herself if Frank didn't let her move in.

Alene thought back to when Frank first told her about Rhona. He wanted her to know in case she preferred to get out of the relationship before it went any further. That had seemed odd--she knew plenty of people with troubled kids. Aside from agonizing about his daughter, Frank had been considerate and good-natured, easy to talk to, and enchanting in bed. He never yelled, behaved irresponsibly, or made negative asides like her ex-husband. But she'd never dated anyone in law enforcement, and she'd been concerned about how little they might have in common.

She'd also wondered if they'd like each other's friends, but Frank turned out to be easygoing. He told good jokes, they laughed together, and when they played cards or other games, he was gracious about both winning and losing. Alene's employees liked his interest in their lives, her sister liked that unlike Alene, he never interrupted her, and Ruthie and Benjie thought he was a good, thoughtful partner for Alene. He was also an excellent detective.

He'd told Alene he was sorry it had taken him so long to figure that out. During college at the University of Illinois at Chicago, he'd met Yvette, and her father had offered him a position in investor relations at his company as soon as he and Yvette were engaged. Frank hadn't found the work to be challenging or satisfying.

Yvette had worked for her father for a few years and become a stay-at-home mom after Rhona was born. Two years later they had Trey, and their lives were filled with kid activities, dinners out, annual vacations, and a boat docked at Montrose Harbor. Frank had been content spending evenings out on the lake but grew increasingly bored and unhappy in his marriage.

He'd never thought of himself as the kind of person who'd get divorced, but neither had Alene. They'd talked about their failed marriages, and what they would do differently this time. They'd talk everything through, never take each other for granted, try their best to make the other happy. Alene understood there'd be days when they couldn't see each other for any significant amount of time, but if they were married, it wouldn't matter. They'd decided not to get engaged until Rhona was healthy enough to move out. Because of Alene's children, they'd have to be married, not just living together.

Alene realized why she hadn't been able to fall asleep. Something had been gnawing at the back of her mind, and she'd realized what it was. She turned on her light and wrote it down on a notepad so she wouldn't forget. Frank needed to have a boat at Montrose Harbor.

Chapter 7

Frank called on Tuesday morning when Alene was sitting in her office, sipping an almond latte, and scrolling through the June schedule. He'd been doing his office work from home since the pandemic began; he could research cases, submit reports, and follow leads from his computer. He often told Alene that being a detective wasn't as glamorous as it looked on television.

Working at the kitchen table made it easier for him to grapple with Rhona's needs. "You were right, Alene," he said. "When she got home last night, we talked for a bit, and she admitted that she's been seeing someone, but wouldn't say anything else about it, so that's all I know."

"That's absolutely what you want for her, Frank," she said. "It's terrific news!" But what sort of person would be interested in a prescription drug–

addicted hypochondriac like Rhona? And what had made Rhona turn into such a problematic challenge? Frank was a skilled detective, but he hadn't grasped that his daughter might be in a romance until Alene told him.

Cal called, and she had to say goodbye to Frank. Apparently the kids were acting up. They were cranky about having to go back to internet classes after the long weekend, and they bickered constantly. It would have been nice if their father was available to take them for a day, but since nobody was buying cars, he and his latest girlfriend had been holed up at his new lake house near the Indiana Dunes. At least somebody was enjoying the pandemic. Alene had a conversation with each of her children, and they all promised to let Cal get some rest.

Maybe they'd tried, but the minute Alene walked in the door that afternoon, Cal went to his room to lie down. She spent some time with Sierra, asking about school and engaging in an ongoing discussion about when she'd be allowed to wear mascara. All her friends got to wear make-up, Sierra said, which made a huge difference between looking nice or looking revolting during online classes. Alene promised to consider allowing it after she turned thirteen.

Next, Alene went into Noah's room. They played a board game involving geometric shapes while Noah shared facts about bears and other animals that hibernate. From there, she invited Quinn to join her in the kitchen and help her make a vegetable lasagna with a quinoa sweet potato salad and garlic bread. Quinn liked cooking with Alene all by herself, only allowing Sierra and Noah to come out of their rooms when dinner was ready. By the time Frank came over, the kids seemed less tense and more relaxed.

The children scarfed the food as if they hadn't been fed in days. Alene reminded them to finish their homework before watching television, and on their way out, they all gave a sign that they'd heard her. Cal picked at his food for a while, saying he was too tired to eat. Then he went back to his room. How could she expect him to supervise all three children on his own all day? Everything would be easier when Blanca came back to work.

Alene cleaned up dinner while Frank helped Noah with his math homework. Quinn and Noah watched a show about aliens while Sierra played on her iPad in her room. Frank and Alene sat at the kitchen table drinking wine, and Frank griped about the city being behind on autopsies. He was upset that they hadn't yet identified the body from that fire at the Rosins' property, but at least they'd gotten fingerprints, so it was possible that they'd know soon. Alene was about to come clean about Kofi, but Sierra screamed for her, and she jumped up from the table.

Sierra was upset that Quinn had left her dirty clothes on the floor of their shared room. Alene resolved the crisis and reminded Sierra of the story of the boy who cried wolf, suggesting that she reserve screaming for when it was truly necessary. Later, after Frank left for the night, Alene watched the news and fell asleep deliberating about what she'd say to the kids regarding the ongoing protests.

She was disheartened to wake up alone on Wednesday morning, and uneasy because she still hadn't told Frank about Kofi—five days had passed! She could apologize and say that she'd been about to tell him, but after dealing with the girls, it had just flown out of her head. Frank was a detective. He'd know if she was being less than truthful, even if he hadn't figured out that Rhona was seeing someone.

Alene dragged herself out of bed and got dressed for her run. It was overcast but not raining. Lilacs were in bloom, and she loved being surrounded by myriad shades of green. Unfortunately, the city's slatted fencing still blocked anyone from getting near the beach or onto the lake path. That must have cost a tidy sum they could have used to help all those people who couldn't afford to live anywhere. At least it was early enough that she was mostly alone and didn't have to weave around walkers, dodge bicyclists, or risk running through clouds of exhaled virus.

She passed a police car blocking access to Lake Shore Drive. What an abysmal assignment, to block cars from heading south toward the city. They were trying to prevent more of the window-bashing and out-of-control protests that had been going on. Two young officers were leaning against their cars, gesturing and talking over the noise of traffic. She wished Frank had a partner he could talk to.

She turned and ran for a few miles before heading home, where she showered, dressed, woke the children, and made peanut butter oatmeal, a breakfast they loved. Frank called again while she was brushing her hair. Rhona had come home late again. She wouldn't tell him where she'd gone with this guy about whom he knew nothing, or if they'd worn masks.

"Even if they did," Alene said, "they certainly didn't wear them in bed."

Frank groaned. "I can't think about that," he said.

"My dad used to get sick to his stomach when my sister and I went on dates," said Alene, "and he always thought there was something terribly wrong with the boys we chose."

"You didn't get home at three in the morning, you didn't have a problem with prescription drugs," Frank said, "and there wasn't a pandemic."

"She's young," Alene said. "If she gets sick, it'll just be like a regular flu."

"She has a slew of allergies, gets those terrible headaches, and abuses prescription drugs," he responded. "Also, people die of regular flu."

"Come on, Frank," said Alene. "We can't live our lives focused on worst-case scenarios. Do you expect her to sit at home day and night? Don't you want her to have some fun?"

Frank grumbled but said "I love you" before hanging up. He was so confident, except when it came to his daughter.

When she got to the café, she put on her apron, washed her hands, and greeted each of her employees. The kitchen was a fragrant cloud of fruity steam. Three oversized pots bubbled on the stove. "Apricot, strawberry, and fig jam, in case you were wondering," said Ruthie in a sing-song voice from across the kitchen. "Good morning, Six."

"How you doing, Nine?" Alene said. "Everyone okay today?" Ruthie gave her a thumbs-up.

Zuleyka stood behind a pile of dried fruits, dicing them to be used in a variety of muffins, and waved her chef's knife in response. Kacey looked up from where she was stirring one of the bubbling pots and said, "Hey Alene, have I told that I love poaching figs?"

Edith came through the open door from the café. "What you are doing is simmering the figs," she said. She fiddled with the buttons on her floral cardigan and repeated, "That's not poaching, it's simmering."

"Oh, Edith," said Alene, resigned to a tedious start to the day. "Please fix your mask and let's go over your schedule so you don't keep coming in when we already have enough staff." She headed to her office to hang up her coat and put on an apron. All her employees were supposed to wear an apron over their clothes, a bandana on their heads, and something over their mouths and noses. What did it matter if the fruit was poached or simmered?

There could only be six people working in the kitchen, few enough so that there was space between them. Alene wished there was a window they could open. Unless it was too cold or too hot outside, they tried to leave the back door ajar for extra circulation. At least the café was up and running, regardless of all the restrictions.

"I'm talking to you, Kacey," said Edith. "And you stop that, Zuleyka. I can see that you're making a face even with the mask. When did it become acceptable for people to make faces when someone is speaking?" Alene and Kacey exchanged glances. It was typically Edith who conveyed her displeasure by squinting and scowling.

"You're on the schedule for tomorrow, Edith," Alene said.

LaTonya made a crack about how there were other employees who needed the hours way more than Edith, and Alene gave her a zipping-the-mouth sign to hush. No need to ruffle Edith any more than usual. "You and I are both going to leave the kitchen, Edith, because only six people can be in here at the same time. Come sit in my office and tell me what's bothering you." It had taken Alene a few years to understand that the only way to calm Edith down was to let her vent.

Edith followed behind, making a huffing sound to make sure Alene understood her frustration. Alene at her desk and asked again. Edith stood in the doorway. "Dori is fine, even though her clothes could be a bit less revealing," she said. It was the fiftieth time she'd said something about Dori's cleavage. "But I don't know why she gets to do the scheduling. Kacey and LaTonya both got four days, but she only gave me three this week. It's not enough. What am I supposed to do every day? Can you please talk to her?"

How had Edith reached her seventh decade without finding a community? She liked Jocelyn, Alene's former employee, who'd taken over the gym next door but used to pop in all day before the pandemic started. It was an unlikely friendship, but Jocelyn was extremely considerate of people who were, like herself, different. It seemed like nearly every one of Alene's employees was a little different in some way.

"I know it doesn't make things easier for you, Edith," Alene said, "but Dori is doing the schedule so that I don't have to—have you read about the schools being closed?" It was the wrong question because Edith had no reason to follow news about schools. Alene started over. "Listen, Edith, I'm swamped and had to give up some café responsibilities, so I asked Dori to help me out." Edith needed to hear that part emphasized.

"Everything is not about you, Alene," Edith said. "Also, you said you'd talk to Dori about the way she dresses."

Did it matter when there weren't any customers? "No, I never said that. It's not necessary, and I thought you liked Dori," Alene spoke slowly for emphasis. "In any case, she's on the schedule and you aren't. Can you please go home for now and come in tomorrow when you're scheduled?"

Edith wore the utterly unsubtle expression that indicated she had news to share. She'd broadcast her news even though Ruthie was clear about not allowing negative hearsay. "I think Dori is having an affair with that tall, skinny guy who's here almost every day," Edith said.

The only surprise was how long Edith had waited before coming up with the accusation. "He's outside right now," she continued. "Every time he comes by, she goes out there and flirts with him. I've seen him with another woman too."

Alene rose from behind her desk and followed Edith out to the café. "That's Peter, and the other woman is his sister," she told Edith. "I'm glad that Dori takes the time to make them feel welcome. It would be great if the rest of my staff treated customers that way." Edith grumbled unintelligibly.

Outside, Dori handed Peter his order and came back in to return to her laptop. Edith should have been grateful to her: Dori had admired pictures of Edith's cats, they'd taken walks in the neighborhood, and they'd gossiped over a cup of tea, no doubt about the rest of the staff. Dori was one of few employees who even tolerated Edith. "Nothing you say changes the fact that you have to leave, Edith," said Alene.

Edith narrowed her eyes. "Everyone's against me." She strode out of the office, stopped, and pointed to Kacey. "The water has to be under 180 Fahrenheit for poaching. If it's over 180, you are simmering. And if it's over 212 degrees, then you are boiling."

"Hold on, Edith, you sound upset," said Ruthie, while the kitchen staff looked around with a sense of shared irritation. It was just like Ruthie to be concerned about Edith's feelings while all Alene could think of was how to get her out the door.

"I don't have anything to do," said Edith. The forced quarantine had to be hard for people who didn't have hobbies, friends, or family. It had been especially difficult for those who had underlying health problems and lived precariously or were homeless. Every day, there were stories in the paper about someone who was fine in the morning, and that evening was hooked up to a ventilator, struggling to breathe.

Kacey stood ten feet away from Ruthie, wearing a home-sewn, bright pink cotton mask. She pulled on vinyl gloves to chop vegetables. It wasn't the usual amount since they weren't serving anyone in the café, but she'd prepare a respectable mound of yams, parsnips, turnips, and rutabagas. "You could read a book," Kacey said. "Or you could watch some television and learn how the world works these days."

Edith looked at her with a blank expression. She was just so lonely—Alene saw it in every word, every movement. How do you help someone who's spent a lifetime alienating the people around her? How could Frank get that message to his daughter before it was too late? She wondered if it was time to get to know Rhona on her own. Maybe she could be helpful.

"I needed to get out of my apartment," Edith said. "I walked over."

Alene said, "Put your coat back on, Edith. You can't stay here." The city had been locked down since mid-March, and now it was June. People were tense. How could they not be?

Edith looked like she was about to cry. Ruthie started pouring batter into a muffin tray, and said, "It's just dangerous to congregate, Edith. Did I already tell you that three of Benjie's employees are in the hospital? You have to take care of yourself and stay home unless you need to be here." It was an empathetic Ruthie move.

"I'm praying for a coronavirus cure," said LaTonya.

"The common cold is a coronavirus and they've never figured out a cure or a vaccine for that," Edith said.

"I don't think people die from colds," said Kacey, not looking up.

At that moment, Dori came into the kitchen and reported that someone was knocking on the front door. "I pointed to the sign that says only employees could enter," she said, "and the directions for texting in an order, but the guy wouldn't leave. He's old, so I opened the door a crack, and he told me that he needs to talk to you, Alene."

Alene followed Dori back out of the kitchen. The man was bald, and his ears stuck out from his round head. His eyes were the same sparkling blue as her father's. His clothes were baggy, like Vincent's, but he looked clean and presentable, and Alene recognized him despite his paper mask. She wondered how she was going to explain this visit to her dad as she opened the door and welcomed Finn Baron into the café.

Chapter 8

"You look like my dad," said Alene. He was holding himself upright, his left fist pushed against his stomach. Maybe he was hungry.

Finn shuffled his feet and cleared his throat the way a shy person might do when they have trouble starting a conversation. "You look like your mother," he said. His voice was raspy like Cal's. "Thank you for letting me in. I've wanted to see your place. I heard about it and never understood how you bake without eggs or butter, although that's what our mother did during the war."

She knew he meant the Second World War. If he'd wanted to see the café, why hadn't he come before? And how much did he know about it? She'd owned Whipped and Sipped for nearly nine years, but he'd been gone far longer. "That's because my pastry chef is a genius. She's also vegan," Alene said.

"Does my father know that you're in Chicago?" The last thing she needed now was to get in the middle of a long-simmering squabble between brothers. Obviously, she'd be on her dad's side; she hardly knew Finn. Was she supposed to be polite just because he was related?

Finn lifted the bottom of his mask and took a few deep breaths, which made Alene nervous. She stepped back and gestured for him to sit down, while she sat on the other side of the table.

"I want to explain everything," he said, gratefully sinking into a chair. He scanned the café as if to check for cops, people out to get him, or anyone he knew. "I especially need to explain everything to your father. I never wanted to hurt anyone. He told you that I provided for my family, didn't he?"

So, the elusive Uncle Finn wanted her to think well of him. "My father told us that your wife received sporadic bank drafts from around the country." she said. "He worried about you. Your disappearance just about broke his heart."

Finn said, "I tried to keep in touch whenever I could."

Edith, who'd followed Alene from the kitchen, hovered near the table. Dori came and offered drinks, for which Alene was grateful, but Edith stood too close to Finn. Alene gave her a look and Edith responded by asking if Finn wanted anything to eat. It was almost enough of a shock to make Alene fall off her chair.

"Black coffee would be nice," said Finn. They'd never offered table service, even before the pandemic, and if they had, Edith would have been the last person to wait tables. She didn't understand how to be gracious. Even Dori seemed alarmed and edged closer with Finn's coffee a few minutes later, in case she had to rescue the old guy from Edith. Alene signaled that everything was fine, and Dori went back to her laptop.

Finn asked what Edith thought would go well with the coffee.

"Maybe something sweet," she said. "Our pastry chef makes heavenly hand pies, if you like fruit, and a tray of cookies just came out of the oven if you're interested." Did Edith just say the word "heavenly"?

Finn was older than Cal and seemed more hunched over and fragile. Finn said. "I'd like to try whatever's best."

Alene had to stop her jaw from dropping when Edith repeated Alene and Ruthie's phrase, "It's all best." Was it possible that Kacey's old Aunt Edith was interested in Alene's old Uncle Finn?

"I'm not asking for a handout." Finn said. He pulled two twenty-dollar bills from his wallet and set them on the table.

"I didn't think you were," Alene replied, moving to another table when he began sipping the coffee. Dori was quietly taking a phone order to cover for Edith, but she was watching closely.

"I wasn't able to get to Chicago until now," he said. "I would have come to see you if I could have. And it won't be safe for me to stay long."

"I'll just bring you a selection," said Edith, excusing herself to go back to the kitchen.

Alene didn't know what he meant about not being safe in Chicago. Was he afraid of someone he met in prison or was he worried about Chicago's high crime rate? She wasn't sure she cared. She shook her head and held up her hand as a stop sign. "My father is the one who needs to hear about it, Uncle Finn. He's been stewing about you all these years." She was curious, yes, but she didn't want to hear that he was a fugitive, or that he had a second family, a wife and children in another state.

Finn looked away. "I wish it hadn't turned out this way," he said after a few moments.

Alene wasn't interested in his apologies. "Dad felt like you cut him out of your life," she said. "For the past few years, he's taken my son to the aquarium on your birthday every year, because it reminds him of how you used to go fishing together."

He got a wistful look on his face. "Those were the good old days," he said. "I'd like to tell you how it all came about, if you have time." He admired the tray Edith now set in front of him and chose an apple hand pie. He stopped mid-chew to savor it while Alene sat there watching him, trying not to look judgmental or irritated, but it wasn't as if she had nothing else to do. Finn sipped his coffee, picked up a chocolate pretzel cookie and sighed with pleasure after taking a bite.

"My father's the one who wants to hear about it," said Alene. "He never understood what happened to you. Did you even know when your son died?" She was twisting the dagger, but what else did he deserve?

"I knew about Jimmy," he said. He sat hunched over as if his back couldn't hold him up anymore. "It wasn't easy. And there was more to his death that never came out."

She tried to marshal some compassion. "Dad's not in great shape, Uncle Finn. He was diagnosed with an inherited autoimmune disease called myasthenia gravis. There's no cure." She hoped he was anxious about getting it himself and remorseful about neglecting her dad. Hadn't he ever considered how his absence affected the people who'd loved him? What possible excuse could there be for a twenty-two-year disappearance?

"I'm sorry to hear that he's not well. Do you think you could arrange for him and me to talk?" asked Finn, not meeting her eyes. He was pale and clammy and didn't look so good himself. Ruthie would have said something about being empathetic.

Alene said, "He said he hadn't heard from you in all these years and doesn't know what you want now."

"I just want to see him before I die," said Finn. He gritted his teeth and exhaled as if that small movement had caused some pain.

"Listen, we sometimes take walks after dinner, and we can meet you tonight," said Alene, "if my father is up to walking. Let's say the east side of North Lake Shore Drive at Briar at seven-thirty. There's a bench. Can you find your way there?" He could look it up if he needed more explicit directions.

"Please don't say you'll come and then let my dad down again."

She wasn't going to start feeling sorry for him no matter how many painful expressions he'd mastered. He looked shriveled, like a sun-dried, wrinkled version of her father. Would Cal be disappointed to hear that she hadn't been as warm and friendly as possible, or would he understand that she was incensed on his behalf? Maybe Finn would have meant something to her if she'd known him better, but now he existed only in her dad's stories as an adventurous boy out of a Mark Twain novel. And an older brother who stopped being a brother.

"Why don't you give me your phone number?" Alene asked, "unless it's the same one you've been using with my dad since you got to Chicago."

"It's the same number," he said, and held his phone out to show her.

"All right," said Alene, pulling out her phone and copying it. "I'm calling you right now, so you have my number too. I can contact you later to confirm if Dad feels up to a walk after dinner." She heard his phone ring and rose from the table to excuse herself. If Finn wanted to stay and finish his coffee and pastries, Alene thought as she hurried back into the kitchen, maybe he'd distract Edith. Even if Alene couldn't get her to leave, at least she'd stay out of the kitchen. She'd already been hovering close enough to hear the conversation.

Fifteen minutes passed before Dori came back to the kitchen, this time to tell Alene that Frank's partner was standing outside the door. He wanted to see both Alene and Ruthie, but Ruthie was in the middle of a recipe and said she'd join them when she was finished. Great, thought Alene, because she wasn't tense enough already, now she had to talk to Lee by herself. She took her time getting there. She passed Edith and Finn, who were sitting closer than six feet, talking. If Edith caught the virus, she'd pass it to the entire café staff. Alene unlocked the door and stepped outside. There was no law that required her to let people in, not even if they were from the police department.

Vincent was sitting outside, although he hadn't been there earlier and didn't usually show up this late in the afternoon. Now he gathered up his cardboard and bolted as quickly as he could away from the café. Maybe he wanted to avoid being rounded up like most of the other homeless people in the neighborhood. He didn't realize that Lee Bautista only noticed people when he needed them.

Alene asked him to get back in his car. At least the mask covered his habitual scowl. "I don't want to inadvertently get closer than recommended," she said, surprised at how quickly he complied. It would have been funny, she thought, if a marked police car drove up and asked him to move, since he was double-parked. If Frank had been there, she'd have brought out coffee, but Lee reminded her of a tough kid who used to bully her younger sister at school. And the other day, he'd been rude about the cookie Ruthie had offered him.

119

What if he told her that there'd been a camera at Benjie's building site, and that she'd been seen sitting in the car outside the fence? His posture and expression made it clear that he was there to make her life harder.

"Why are you here by yourself?" Alene asked, her mouth dry. Lee never started conversations with a pleasant exchange, so she wouldn't bother either. "Where's Frank?"

Lee turned on the ignition, opened the window, and turned the car off again. "Frank's working on something else," he said. "And I asked to speak to both you and Ruth Rosin."

Alene had to admit that she was scared of Lee without Ruthie or Frank there. "He didn't tell me that you were coming or that he was unavailable," she said, as straightforward as she could. "And Ruthie will come out when she's finished with her recipe. She can't leave in the middle."

"I have nothing to say about what Frank tells you," Lee said with the swagger of a person who loves being in control. He'd always seemed tactless, but since the pandemic began, he'd become more aggressive. She was glad he was sitting in his car, because if he was still standing, she'd have had to fight the urge to push him off the curb. "I have questions for both you and your pastry chef," he added.

Alene pulled out her phone to send Frank a text. Lee probably wished he could slap some handcuffs on her wrists and toss her into a cell. "Frank usually warns me before you show up." Lee was always repeating himself, so why shouldn't she?

He said, "I'd like you to look at something." He pulled a plastic bag from his pocket. Inside the bag was a piece of the paper the kitchen used to wrap pastries both for serving on plates like in the old days, and to stuff into carry-out bags.

"That's obviously from one of our deliveries," said Alene. The logo of tiny silicone spatulas that Dori had designed always made Alene smile. It was printed on all the café's paper goods. She checked her phone, but Frank hadn't texted back yet. "I'm busy right now, Lee, so if this is something that can wait ..."

Lee cleared his throat. Her goal was to show him that she had nothing to hide, and he was not going to intimidate her. "This Whipped and Sipped carry-out bag was in a murder victim's jacket pocket," he said.

"Oh," said Alene, disconcerted. "But we sell lots of cookies, cakes, and breads, all wrapped in this exact paper, Lee. I hope it was helpful for you to confirm that the wrapping paper came from here. Of course, it's floating all over the city. Do you need anything else, or can I get back to work?"

As she turned away from him to return to the café, he said, "This is a picture of the victim." He reached into a second envelope on the car seat next to him, removed an eight-by-ten black-and-white photo, and held it out to her. "And that's the jacket with the name Rosin stamped on the collar. We want to know if she was a regular customer. Do you recognize her?"

That was a punch to Alene's gut. She hadn't realized it had been a woman—another lost daughter, mother, or sister, most likely at the hands of a man. She took the picture and saw a petite woman, small enough to fit into Avi Rosin's jacket and young enough to make Alene choke back tears. The woman's face was caked with filth and streaming mascara, and her messy black curls were matted or flying in all directions.

"Who is she?" Alene asked. "And how did she die?"

Lee said, "That's not your problem. Can I show this to your employees now?" He took the picture back from her.

Sometimes anger was the only thing that could pull Alene out of despair. "It's all of our problem when a young woman is murdered in the neighborhood, Lee," she nearly spat. "And we don't allow customers inside anymore, only employees," Alene said. "You're aware, aren't you, that we're in the middle of a pandemic and those are the mayor's orders?"

He looked through the café's front window. "Why do I see two old people sitting at a table drinking and eating?"

He knew who Edith was, so he was just being obnoxious. Alene let loose a stream of curses, but only in her head. She said, "That's my employee sitting with my uncle. I believe family members are excluded from the mayor's order about customers."

Alene watched Lee's gaze turn towards Dori, who'd come to the door to hand a bag to a waiting customer. He was always ogling her. The customer scurried away from the door. Something about Lee made everyone nervous. Peter Berg approached at that moment and waved at Alene. She waved back. He bent over his phone to text the number that would let Dori know he was there to pick up. Taryn must have had him do it again and again until he could do it by himself. He peeked in the window and Alene wondered what he thought about seeing Finn and Edith sitting there looking like normal customers. His face was pressed up against the window again.

Alene jumped when Lee said, "I asked if you recognized the woman in the picture." She tried to focus—it was strange to be standing on the sidewalk, talking to a detective sitting in his unmarked car. Or maybe the pale, bloated face in the picture turned her stomach. The woman had clearly once been striking, with her high cheekbones and long eyelashes. She had a heart-shaped face and a wide mouth—like Alene's employee Zuleyka. Maybe she was from someplace in Central America, or Puerto Rico.

Lee must have known that thrusting the picture at Alene would be disconcerting, but it was more than that. Either Kofi hadn't noticed or had neglected to mention that the dead body he'd seen had been a woman.

She had to unlock the front door again, this time to run to the restroom, gagging. Ruthie was waiting outside the door when Alene emerged and led her to a table across the café from Finn and Edith.

"Are you all right?" Ruthie asked.

Alene filled her in while Ruthie brought over a cup of peppermint tea and a glass of sparkling water. Before Alene could warn her, Ruthie opened the door to let Lee inside. He was holding a tablet along with the folder Alene had already seen. With his disapproving expression and blinking, reptilian eyes, he reminded her of a vampire, and she recalled that you're never supposed to invite them in because afterwards, they can enter freely, anytime. Lee set the tablet on a table. The staff filed out one at a time to look, followed by Dori and Edith, Cal's brother, and two delivery kids who'd come in to pick up more boxes and bags.

Alene glanced at her texts. Frank hadn't responded. Wednesdays were always busy for him for some reason. One of the delivery kids, a wiry twenty-year-old with troubled skin, said that he thought the face in the picture looked familiar but couldn't offer any further information. Alene looked again. The woman's skin looked blueish white, her forehead was high, and her left ear was pierced at least seven times. She'd been in her late thirties or early forties and could have been any number of women who'd once swirled in front of their mirrors, smiling with the promise of a future.

Ruthie, standing far from Lee, also asked why Frank hadn't come. Alene could barely look at Lee, but Ruthie was fearless.

Lee said, "He's busy." He looked pointedly at Alene, as if it was her fault that Frank was working on something else. "I have some questions for you, Mrs. Rosin."

Lee probably expected her to walk away, but Alene had no intention of leaving Ruthie alone with him standing there as if he were the judge and jury in a criminal case.

Ruthie, unceasingly polite, smiled like she was at a tea party, and said, "I've already told you everything I know, Lee, but I'm sure my husband will be happy to answer any other questions."

"We've got new information," Lee said slowly, pausing until he was ready to explain. Alene noticed that the windows could use a deep cleaning. Making people wait was no doubt an anxiety-provoking technique that Lee had learned at the police academy. She was pretty sure that Frank, in contrast, usually tried to assuage people's general fear of cops.

Lee passed Ruthie the electronic notebook and said, "This is a video of your husband hovering near the building several days leading up to the fire." He kept his attention focused on Ruthie's face as she watched the video. What if he'd planted the idea that Benjie was at the scene just before the fire, but it wasn't true? "What can you tell me about it?" Lee asked when the video ended.

Ruthie explained, as she'd done numerous times, that Benjie had pulled together the financing, and the building included some affordable units, but Lee interrupted to ask, "What was your husband doing there?" He had an irritating habit of clicking his fingernails against the tablet.

Ruthie's eyes flashed, but she was used to explaining Benjie's work to people who didn't understand real estate development. "The video shows my husband at work, Lee. He's doing what he's supposed to be doing."

Alene admired how Ruthie repeated his name as if he'd been sent to the principal's office for mouthing off. She didn't think anyone would ever have a reason to question Benjie's integrity. On the other hand, Frank once speculated out loud that Lee might have joined the police force so he could strut around with a weapon.

It made Alene happy that Benjie, whom she adored, and Frank, whom she loved, were becoming good friends. Frank admitted that it had been a long time since he'd found someone to hang out with. Alene imagined the four of them growing old together, celebrating each other's lives and holidays, taking vacations, learning to play bridge when their hair turned gray.

"Benjamin Rosin pulled together the entire deal," Alene said, trying to mimic Ruthie's slow and careful delivery. "As Ruthie just told you, it's his job to check the progress of his projects." Exasperation made her more obstinate. "Who took the videotape of him walking around the building, Lee? Or maybe a better question would be, who gave you the video?"

Lee blinked at her the way he always did as he slid a couple of photos showing Benjie's profile against the backdrop of the building's frame before it burned down. "Apparently," he said, "some of the neighbors don't like him."

Edith still sat at a table on the other side, yakking with Cal's brother as if they were old acquaintances, but she had her eyes on Alene and Ruthie. Finn was turned away from the door so only his profile was visible. What right did he have to waltz into her café and start gabbing with Edith, of all people? The first thing he should have done was to go straight to Cal and start explaining himself. He should have apologized for causing all that pain to so many people. She'd heard the stories about Finn being involved in a bank robbery, getting sent to prison, and disappearing hundreds of times. How often had Cal mentioned that the money had never been recovered?

Alene pulled her thoughts back to dealing with Frank's partner. She wished she could ask him to leave. Didn't business owners have the right to kick out anyone who was wasting their time? "They don't like Benjie because they're obsessed about their property values," she said, adapting Ruthie's school principal voice. "Why don't you talk to all the neighbors who tried to stop the building from being erected? They're busy drinking toasts to its destruction. And why don't you figure out who this poor woman was so her family can be notified?"

Lee barely glanced at her. "It's not my job to keep busybodies informed."

"Was there something specific you needed from me, Lee," Ruthie asked in her honeyed way, "or is this just about my husband?"

"As I said," Lee went on with no expression, "a piece of The Whipped and Sipped Café's wrapping paper was found in the victim's pocket."

"And I reminded you that this is a café," Alene snapped, "as you can tell from the name. We send out dozens of orders every day." She stopped to breathe so her pulse would slow down. "I think we're done here." But she still felt queasy. The important questions were, who was that poor dead woman? Why had she been murdered? And by whom?

"We've answered your questions, Lee," Ruthie said, as kindly as possible, "and now we both have work to do, so thank you for stopping by, and have a nice day." She stood and walked back to the kitchen without turning her head.

Alene hoped Lee was miffed. He shook his head and left without thanking her. Not long after, as she headed home from the café, Alene called Frank and was relieved when he answered. "I'm sorry I couldn't be there when Lee showed up earlier," he said. "I know he rubs you the wrong way."

Alene said, "Ruthie and I handled him, Frank. I understand that your work sometimes gets in the way of me having my own personal police protection."

"I'll try harder in the future," he said. "If anyone asks me to handle another homicide, I'll tell them that you're my top priority."

Alene laughed and told him about watching Finn and Edith walk out together. She reminded Frank that because her uncle had a habit of vanishing, she wasn't concerned about acquiring

Edith as an aunt. Then she described Lee's visit, trying not to complain again. It was baffling that Frank tolerated the way Lee affected people.

"Did Ruthie make things worse for Benjie by walking away?" she asked. "It wasn't clear if Lee was insulted."

"Ha," Frank either coughed or made a half-hearted attempt to chuckle. "She wouldn't be the first person to turn her back on him." But what if Lee was the vindictive type? Frank was too big-hearted.

"Don't worry about Lee," Frank continued. "All of us are under pressure and we've got a serious backlog."

"Okay, but Lee's easier to take when you're there," she said.

"Sorry, Alene," said Frank, hesitant, "but I'm wrapped up in another, related case. We found a second body dumped on another fire site in the neighborhood. Another young woman with a Whipped and Sipped carry-out bag crumpled in the front pocket of her jacket."

"Oh no," said Alene.

"The jacket was another discard of the Rosins," Frank added. "She was hidden under some bushes on another property slated as affordable housing and belonging to Benjie Rosin."

Chapter 9

"I don't want you to upset you, Dad, but Uncle Finn was at the café today," Alene said as she added tarragon to her chicken soup. She often brought vegan soups home from the café, and the kids loved them, but when her dad craved a classic chicken soup, she had to make it herself. He and the kids said they craved it, but Ruthie's stance on animals had rubbed off on Alene and she'd usually make herself a salad instead. Ruthie was strictly vegan and had made it clear that she could only work at the café if there were no animal products whatsoever. It was challenging sometimes, but Alene had never regretted hiring her best friend as pastry chef.

For the moment, she focused on her father—she didn't want this Uncle Finn business to stress him. Stress, she'd read, could trigger his myasthenia gravis. "He looks like your twin, Dad, and he charmed Edith Vanza. Can you imagine?" She checked whose turn it was to set the table. She just didn't have it in her to bug the kids about chores these days, but if Quinn didn't come in to set the table before dinner, she'd say something.

"Are you serious?" her dad asked. "Why would he bother you? Why wouldn't he come to see me the minute he got to Chicago?" Cal sighed. He was sitting across the counter from Alene. "I'm having trouble imagining Finn at all and we already know that there's something wrong with him, but I'm his brother."

"He said you'd stopped answering his texts, Dad," said Alene, which reminded her to check her cellphone. Frank had texted that he was home and completely wiped out. Alene texted back that he should take a long hot shower and get into comfy clothes, and she'd bring him a container of freshly made chicken soup. She turned it down to a simmer.

Cal said, "I didn't stop answering all his texts, just the whiny ones."

Alene decided not to respond to that. "Maybe he's lonely," she said, "and he chatted with Edith because she offered him something to eat and drink. We all crave human interaction." The pandemic had been especially hard on those who loved being with people like Cal did, but he had her and the kids trying to cheer him up every day. "Or maybe your brother is afraid you won't want to see him after everything he did."

"I do want to see him, but only if he's planning to explain himself." Cal made a peeved face that turned into a smile as Noah straggled in from his bedroom holding a deck of cards. Cal had a special fondness for his grandson. "I certainly don't want to sit around jawing about the weather or reminiscing about our childhood."

"Dad, I got the feeling that he wants to apologize and explain himself," said Alene. "We made a tentative plan to meet in the park after dinner before the sun goes down. The kids could walk over with us. What do you think, Noah? Want to walk over to the park after dinner? I'll get Kacey or Jocelyn to come with us." She didn't say it out loud, but that way she could fully focus on her father and whoever joined them could entertain the kids. Jocelyn would be able to help her father walk if he got tired. His autoimmune disease sometimes led to decreased muscle strength.

Noah sat cross-legged on the floor to set up a game of solitaire, and said, "Okay."

"We'll get eaten by mosquitos," said Cal.

"They're not that terrible this time of year, Dad. Not in the city." Alene had expected Cal to come up with an objection or two. "It's up to you," she said. "If it's not convenient, we can plan to meet with your brother another time."

Cal shook his head and pursed his lips, one of his countless ways of expressing disapproval. Alene flashed back to seeing that expression in seventh grade, when she'd gotten caught skipping school to go to the beach with a group of classmates.

"I don't know him anymore," said Cal. "I still don't understand why someone who knew how to

133

install electrical and plumbing systems would rob a bank. I admit that I'm curious to see him, but I don't have the warm feelings I used to have for him when we were growing up together."

"I know, Dad, and that's a shame," said Alene, hoping he wouldn't start repeating the list of all the things his brother had missed over the past twenty-two years.

"He doesn't even know that you have three awesome children."

"Awesome?" she asked. "You sound like them." The kids were usually third or fourth on her father's list of things Finn had missed out on, after her mother's cancer and her sister graduating from law school. "He might not know about my children, Dad, but he'd heard about my café."

"There were articles about that in both Chicago newspapers," said Cal, "whenever Whipped and Sipped was on one of those "Best of Lakeview" lists for vegan desserts and healthful breakfasts." He paused to watch Noah play solitaire and pointed out a ten of hearts that could go on top of the jack of spades. "Do you think Finn might have read about the kids on the internet?"

"I don't let anyone post about them," said Alene. "Remember how upset I was when Neal put their pictures on Instagram?" She'd been livid about it and worried that some shady internet troll now had a picture and name for each of her children. She'd come to the realization that Neal was going to make thoughtless decisions for eternity and warned him to never put the kids on social media again. But how did that warning help when he'd just come up with another careless move the next time?

Anyway, her job was to cheer Cal up, not push him deeper into despair. "I know this isn't easy," she said, turning down the soup and stirring it. "We can at least hear what your brother has to say, right, Dad? Didn't you ever think to yourself that he might have been coerced into participating in the robbery? Or that doing it was a stupid decision that escalated into something he'd never intended? And didn't you always tell Lydia and me that he'd made a mistake, but he paid for it?"

"That's because I didn't want you to think he was a total loggerhead, and I wanted you both to learn about consequences," said Cal, making a snorting sound. He had a hundred ways of describing people he thought of as idiotic. "But maybe I should just meet him for one conversation. Your mom and I used to imagine where he'd gone. She liked the idea that he'd had a change of heart and had taken a vow of silence in a monastery or something."

"I'm not sure those places still exist," said Alene.

Cal said, "I have no idea. Your mother was always looking for the positive side of things."

"Let's plan to go after dinner. I'll text Finn to confirm we're on for seven-thirty, okay?"

"If he decides to turn up," said Cal, shuffling into the living room. "And don't bring a purse or wear any good jewelry."

She followed right behind him. "Come on, Dad, why would you say that? And why haven't we had these conversations about Finn before?"

"Maybe because I'm like Ruthie," Cal said. "I don't like to gossip." He picked up his book about James Madison and refused to say another word. That was laughable—her father loved juicy stories about someone getting into trouble. Maybe he only enjoyed gossip about other people's families.

Alene went back to her room and called Frank to ask how he was and if he'd taken the long, hot shower she'd recommended."

He said, "It was a brilliant suggestion, thanks."

"What about Rhona?" Alene asked. "Did she come home?"

He yawned. "Maybe, but I'm already in bed, feeling under the weather. I hope it's nothing."

"Me too," she said, softly, thinking that there seemed to be only one illness making the rounds, and the possibility of Frank having it was horrifying. But he didn't need her to nag him about taking a Covid test. "I've got chicken soup with rice bubbling away as we speak." Why didn't his ex-wife take more of a role in caring for their daughter, especially on days when Frank couldn't manage?

"Thanks, my love," said Frank. She took a second to enjoy the feeling of being called that. Neal had never used endearments and she'd had to get used to Frank's romantic streak. In the beginning it was bizarre, as if she were a character in a movie. "I'm sorry I'm a little run down, Alene. I wanted to be there for you, help you deal with everything right now."

"I know," said Alene, mostly feeling sorry for herself at the thought of Frank being sick. They discussed what else she could bring, and Alene told him that her father was continuing to be melodramatic about his long-missing brother. She also told him about the café's long-hidden basement. It seemed like a fun diversion to take his mind off everything else.

"A visit from an uncle you haven't seen since the late 1990s and a speakeasy from the early 1920s," Frank said. "Your life is way more exciting than mine."

Just hearing Frank's voice, hoarse as it was, made her happy. Would it be the right time to tell him about Kofi seeing the body on Friday? Maybe she needed to wait until they could talk in person. "The basement is piled with newspapers and old furniture," she said instead. "It's not that thrilling."

"There's evidence of old speakeasies in buildings all over the city," Frank said, coughing this time. "Hope you'll wear gloves if you decide to look through anything. You never know what people save or how they save it."

Alene remembered a high school acquaintance whose mother was a hoarder. She'd filled their home with stacks of newspaper and piles of molding clothes. But the café's basement sounded like even more of a mess. Alene pulled herself up from her reading chair and headed back to the kitchen, phone in hand. She took the rice off the stove just as the timer beeped.

Frank added that they'd been able to identify the second body, a prostitute and meth addict. Her fingerprints were already on file. Her name was Juana Clemente. They hadn't yet found any family to notify.

"Poor woman," said Alene. She felt sick to her stomach and closed her eyes for a moment. Frank promised to call first thing the next morning.

Alene took a few deep breaths, thinking about the fragility of life. Had Juana Clemente just been in the wrong place, or had she been targeted? Alene adjusted her ear buds and skimmed the soup. She called Ruthie, Kacey, and Jocelyn to update them about Juana Clemente, the body found on the site of the second burned down building belonging to Benjie Rosin. "Also, Jocelyn, are you available to walk with us to meet my long-lost uncle near the park?" she asked.

"Absolutely," said Jocelyn. "I want to know more about this basement Olly's been blathering about. I also wish I could stop by and have dinner with you and your family. I miss that." Alene missed it too. Having friends over for dinner was one of those pre-pandemic things she'd taken for granted.

"You there?" Jocelyn asked when Alene didn't respond.

"Yeah, sorry," said Alene, "I'm still thinking about that woman. Nobody deserves to die like that."

"No, you're right," Jocelyn responded. "Creepy things have been happening and I wonder if any of it is connected. Do you think someone was fencing stolen goods in your building? Olly went on and on about the mobsters who must have spent time down there."

"I have no idea and I'm not sure it matters," said Alene, glad to think about something other than the second murdered woman. "Olly said there was a party area and a side room that he thinks might have been used by someone who was hiding from the police, but it could be all in his imagination."

Jocelyn chomped on something and said, "Olly told me that everything is smaller in the basement, like for a child, with a dresser and a washing bowl. And no closet."

"People were smaller a century ago," Alene said as she took the soup off the burner. It needed time to cool down before she could ladle it into separate containers. "And, they didn't have half as many clothes as we do today."

"Unlike me, because I hardly have any clothes," said Jocelyn with deadpan sarcasm. Her clothes were a long-standing joke between them. For weeks, she'd been waxing rhapsodic about the closet Olly had built for her in her father's old office. It had nine feet of double poles for hanging and four-foot-wide shelves going up to the ceiling for folded clothes and shoes. They talked a bit more before Alene said goodbye and removed her earbuds.

Quinn hadn't come out of her room to finish the table, but all that needed doing was setting out bowls, spoons, and napkins. One day, when Frank moved in, they'd make dinner together, or he'd come home from work just in time to sit down for the meal. When dinner was over, her dad would sit in his living room chair, the kids would go back to their bedrooms, so she and Frank could clean up together.

When she was younger, she'd thought she'd never stop traveling, going to concerts every weekend, or being out with friends, but now she'd be happy if she and Frank just sat at the kitchen table with cups of tea every evening, going over their days. She guessed that's how it was when a person got closer to forty.

She called the kids to come in for dinner after adding a cube of ice to each bowl of soup, just like her mother used to do. They put napkins on their laps without being reminded and Alene enjoyed a tiny sense of victory, small as it was. Cal started to retell some of his old stories about jumping onto trains and "borrowing" cars with his brother when they were kids, followed by derisive comments about Finn having disappeared. Alene doubted that her father had jumped on or off a moving train, although it was a thrilling tale for the kids. He didn't say anything else about Finn having made unscrupulous decisions involving banks.

"Do you kids want to join Mom and me to meet Uncle Finn after dinner?" Cal asked. "You know all about him already."

Sierra sighed dramatically and said, "It's not worth the risk, Grandpa." Since when was a walk in the park such a huge risk?

Alene was concerned about Sierra's growing negativity. But what if the only cure was for the schools to open back up and everything go back to normal? What raised her antennae was that Sierra, although she spent hours texting, had also been wandering aimlessly around the apartment for weeks. Or she sat staring out the window at the lake. She'd also started biting the ends of her hair and sleeping twelve hours a day—pandemic-related behaviors that needed attention, patience, and a solution.

Quinn and Noah were interested in Cal's tall tales because they made Finn sound like a swashbuckling pirate. "Of course, he might have slowed down in his old age," Cal added, gazing out the front window with that look on his face that told Alene he was about to launch into another story from back when.

He told the kids about being stuck in bed for weeks on end with pneumonia. It was in the 1950s, long before the internet was invented, and they'd had just one small black and white television in their house, he told the kids. There were only four channels available. He'd loved a show about a smart collie named Lassie and remembered how Lassie was a life-saving hero. Noah's eyes grew bigger, and Alene suspected that she'd be fending off renewed pleas for a dog.

Finn hadn't been allowed to go into the bedroom while Cal was contagious, but he'd stood outside the door every afternoon when he got home from school, telling funny stories. "That was before he decided to join his idiotic friends in robbing a bank," Cal concluded.

141

Alene frowned at him. Was he going to make it sound like just another glamorous adventure? "How about we talk about that later, Dad? For now, is there any chance you can find something positive to say about your brother?" she asked. Quinn and Noah talked about being glad not to have been born in the old days before cable television followed by a discussion about shows they liked.

"What exactly was Finn charged with?" Alene asked when it was just the two of them finishing up in the kitchen. It was already seven, so they'd have to leave soon if they were going to meet Finn in thirty minutes. "And how long was his sentence?"

"I don't remember the exact charge, but something like aiding and abetting. He was sentenced to six years, but got out early for good behavior or something," Cal told Alene.

Cal never participated in cleaning up from dinner when she was growing up, but Alene wanted the children to see that everyone in a family had to pitch in. They'd cleared the table and it was Cal's turn to help with the dishes, but he was tired and needed to sit down. She didn't believe that he couldn't remember the exact charge. That was the kind of thing he never forgot. He just didn't want her to know.

"But what exactly did he do during the robbery?" she asked as she dried the dishes and put them back in the cabinet. "Or what was he accused of having done?"

"He drove the getaway car," Cal said after a long pause. "He liked driving."

How had she never asked for the details before? "Why would he rob a bank, though, Dad? You've always said that he could fix plumbing and electrical systems."

"He said times were tough," said Cal, sighing, "but I think he had a gambling addiction. I heard that he started to owe money. Anyhow, they all got caught. Some got lengthier sentences, and two of them died in jail for one reason or another. Finn wasn't armed, he didn't go in the bank, and it was his first arrest, so he got off lighter than the other guys. I didn't know them well, but Galesburg was a small town, so I knew who they were. The guy who came up with the robbery idea was a tough nut. I heard that he started stealing cars before he got to high school."

Alene could have googled the robbery if she'd ever pondered it before, but it hadn't seemed all that interesting. She asked, "Why haven't you ever told me these details before, Dad?"

"I don't know. I talked about it a lot back then, but you and your sister were busy with other things," Cal continued. "You didn't like hearing about it. Don't you remember when Mom and I went down there for what I thought was a boring trial. I hated those slick lawyers, but your mother thought it was important to show family support."

"I agree with Mom," said Alene as she finished pouring leftover soup into containers, one of which she'd bring to Frank.

Cal said, "Yeah, well, you'd think Finn would have been grateful, wouldn't you? I mean, his wife

Winnie was the only one who thanked us for coming. I even helped him set up his business when he got out of the joint."

Alene set the pot in the sink to soak, and said, "We need to leave now if we're going to meet him, Dad. Do you want to bring a sweater? It might be cooler outside." Cal didn't move to get up out of the chair.

"I think it's too late," he said, shaking his head.

She didn't know if he meant that it was too late in the day, or too late for the relationship, but she let Jocelyn know and texted their regrets to Finn.

Chapter 10

"I just wanted to see Finn before one of us dies," Cal said the next morning.

On pre-pandemic Thursdays, Alene would have had to worry about juggling after-school driving and pickup for Noah's soccer practice, Quinn's guitar lesson, and Sierra's gymnastics. Now, their day was a blank canvas and she still had to work.

The kids were eating their pancakes with real maple syrup and didn't seem to be paying attention, but sometimes they homed in on adult conversations. She served her father fresh pancakes with fruit as he sat at the counter sipping his coffee.

Quinn asked, "What's an addicted felon, Grandpa?" Alene had to remember that at least one of her kids was always paying attention to conversations. Sometimes it was hard to remember what Quinn referred to, but Alene knew it was from last night's conversation.

Sierra snorted. "Convicted felon, genius," she said, turning to Cal. "You always make a face when you talk about Uncle Finn, Grandpa."

"Is that a fact?" Cal asked, grinning. He'd always encouraged the kids to notice those kinds of things, but they'd all taken it a step too far. Noah had recently pointed out that their father pinches his nose before making excuses when he's late to pick them up, Quinn had asked Neal's mom, their grandmother, why one side of her mouth wiggled, and Sierra had told Alene that her eyes used to only have creases when she laughed, but now they were there all the time. All three incidents had taken place in front of the whole family, and Alene had suggested that the children stop publicly announcing what they noticed.

"What makes Uncle Finn a felon?" Quinn asked after a few minutes of quiet pancake eating. She never let something go once her interest was piqued.

"He robbed a bank," Cal said, turning to Alene. "I'll tell you this much, if he starts lying about where he's been all these years, I'll push him out the door."

"No, you won't, Dad, because you shouldn't let him in the door in the first place," Alene said, reaching over with a napkin to wipe syrup dripping down Noah's chin. She loved sitting and eating breakfast with her father and children. So different from pre-pandemic days when she'd leave the house at five thirty in the morning, go for a run, come back, shower, and be gone before the children got out of bed. "Only because of Covid."

"Obviously, we'd both be cautious," Cal said. "In one of Finn's texts, he told me that he has one of those deluxe recreational vehicles," Cal said with a twinge of longing. Alene sensed that he was stalling again. Why was he so ambivalent about seeing his brother?

"You know who adores recreational vehicles?" Cal asked. "Mitzi Dunn. We could invite her to join us for a spin." Both Cal and Alene still loved Neal's mother. As lazy and inattentive as Neal had been with the kids, his mother had been loving and extraordinarily attentive.

"We should go see Grandma Mitzi," said Quinn. She'd already lost interest in her previous question. "You said it was safe if we were outside the whole time, Mom."

Noah said, "I want to see Grandma Mitzi too."

Alene said, "I'm sorry guys, I know you miss Grandma, but she's being very careful right now." The three of them spent a few minutes begging Alene for a sleepover at Mitzi's apartment. Mitzi indulged them, let them watch horror movies, told them exciting stories.

"Finn said he bought the best recreational vehicle available, probably with all the money he stole," said Cal. "I'd like to get a look at it."

"I want a look at it too," said Quinn. "Recreational vehicle is the same as motorhome, right? I love those. We should get one and take a vacation in it, Mom. You can go anywhere in a motorhome, and it's cheaper because you don't have to buy airplane tickets."

Alene remembered her father dreaming about renting a motorhome for a family vacation a few years before. He'd recently gotten diagnosed with MG though, and at the time, Alene couldn't imagine driving, sleeping, and eating in an RV with the kids but without her dad. She'd have had to spend hours discharging waste, grappling with a flat tire, and listening to fights about who sat where. "We can't go anywhere until this pandemic is over," said Alene, "but it's something to think about."

"When you say that, do you mean it's a real possibility, Mom?" Sierra asked.

"I said it's something to think about," said Alene.

"Right," said Sierra in her derisive adolescent voice. "That means nothing is actually going to happen, as usual, so forget about taking a vacation in a motorhome." She tossed her ponytail, deposited her plate and cup in the sink, and headed back to her bedroom. Noah followed, but Alene had to redirect Quinn's attention to clearing her plate before she skipped out of the room.

"We'll have to meet Finn outside, Dad, and not in his mobile home, no matter how luxurious it is," said Alene, washing the kids' breakfast dishes.

Cal took one last bite of pancake and sighed. Alene hoped he'd see his brother, but she wasn't going to force him. Cal headed into the living room to sit in his chair. Sierra came in to retrieve the book she'd left on the coffee table, and Cal asked her to bring him the family album, the one with "Baron" etched into brown leather. Alene was pleased to see that Sierra was willing to sit with Cal and look at it.

"Let me know what you decide, Dad," Alene said after he'd turned a few pages and had drawn Sierra's attention to pictures of his parents. He turned a page, pointed to a picture, and told Sierra about spilling Coke all over a girl's dress. She'd been so sweet about it that he'd fallen in love and ended up marrying her. It was of course Grandma Vivien, who'd died of cancer the same year that Alene graduated from college.

Sierra said, "I know, Grandpa, because my middle name is Vivien." She bounced out of the living room. Alene had heard the story at least a thousand times.

Just before she left for work, Cal said, "I'd like the kids and Lydia to meet Uncle Finn too." Alene knew Lydia wouldn't think of it. Her sister was too fearful about her pregnancy to risk being with them all.

"That might not work, Dad," she said. Maybe Alene's zeal about Cal rebuilding his relationship with Finn was more about reviving her own relationship with her sister. They'd gotten closer again since Lydia's pregnancy, but Lydia had continued to be guarded and rarely shared anything of importance. "But the kids and I will walk you over there," said Alene. "And Jocelyn, too. She'll come as your bodyguard."

"I hardly need a bodyguard, Alene," said Cal. "But right now, my eyes are fatigued and what I desperately need is someone to read to me." He looked beseechingly at Noah, who'd come back into the living room trailed by Quinn.

"I can read to you if you want, Grandpa," said Noah. He was always offering to help her father— they had a similar sweet nature, although Cal had gotten more acerbic over the years. Noah had Neal's dark complexion and high forehead, but Alene recognized her own smile, jawline, and ash brown hair.

"I'll read to you Grandpa," Quinn offered. "I have a louder voice than Noah, and he doesn't always know which words to emphasize."

Alene said, "You need to brush teeth and hair before school starts, Quinnie." Sierra had continued to dress as if her friends could see what she was wearing during Zoom classes, but Quinn couldn't care less. It wasn't worth arguing about it while school was taking place remotely. Alene hoped she'd stay a little girl as long as possible.

"Noah can help me this time," said Cal, handing Noah the newspaper, "but I'd be delighted if you'd read to me later." Quinn might forget to offer again, but Cal thought reading out loud was good for the kids. Zoom computer classes, he told Alene, weren't sufficient, and he wasn't going to let his grandchildren's education suffer.

"Read through the front page, will you?" said Cal. "Let's see if there's anything of interest."

Noah spent a moment searching, and said, "There's something about robbers who break windows and steal things, and something about a

150

fire, Grandpa. Let's start with the one about the fire, okay?"

Cal gave him a nod and Noah read that the fire destroyed a building slated for people who need affordable housing. Alene, looking over Noah's shoulder, recognized the fence, trees, and buildings surrounding the site where the skeleton of Benjie Rosin's building burned down. "The picture was taken last Friday, on May 22, 2020, and the police are seeking information from the public," Noah read, slow and choppy, but he was only in third grade. "Mom, they even put a phone number here because they want people to call if they saw something. Did we see anything?"

"Probably not," she said, troubled by the photo, "but that was excellent reading, Noah." Someone must have shot that picture from a neighboring window. She could make out Kofi's knit hat and the jacket he'd worn last Friday morning. His features were blurred, but the photo was him, scouring the site.

Sierra had come back in and was hovering near, dressed in jean shorts and a pink crop top. She'd spent twenty minutes straightening her hair. "Excellent might not have been the word I'd have chosen," she said. Alene flashed her a warning look, and Sierra focused on the ceiling all the way back to her room.

After she made sure lunch ingredients were ready for the kids to pull together and Cal was settled in his chair, prepared to supervise another day of online school, Alene left to walk to the café. When she got to the kitchen, she greeted her employees with a wave from the door. She'd been a hugger before, but nobody was hugging anymore. She worried about her employees who weren't in relationships and had no chance of touching another human for as long as the pandemic lasted.

Alene sat at her desk, checked the status of her coffee supply, and confirmed the week's orders before leaving her office to help in the kitchen. Everyone chit-chatted amiably whenever the blenders and mixers were being washed in between recipes, but Alene felt tension in the air. Kacey sneezed, and the rest of the staff looked ruffled. Alene understood. She was just as anxious about getting sick. She thought she heard a collective sigh when Kacey excused herself.

The hours sped by with chopping, grilling, and stirring, and as the lunch orders slowed, Alene found a moment to ask Ruthie about the clothes she'd donated.

"I put stuff in the giveaway bin all the time, Alene," said Ruthie. "It was a coincidence that both of those women wore our discarded jackets, and all it tells us is that they either searched our giveaway bin, or someone else did." She was standing behind a counter, whipping up a batch of pie dough that needed to rest in the refrigerator overnight. She'd put the pies together the next morning.

"Let's say someone was mad at Benjie for putting affordable apartments in their high-priced neighborhood," said Alene as she moved a pan of roasted and cooled onions, garlic, and cubed

152

potatoes into a container. They'd be tossed into tofu omelets and a bunch of other dishes first thing the next morning. "It could have been more than one person. So, they spend time searching for a way to slow him down or ruin his business. They find out that you're here, and they sift through the giveaway bin looking for something with your name on it, with the intention of framing Benjie for a murder."

Ruthie shook her head and said, "You're just guessing, Alene, and that's not the same as collecting evidence or showing proof. Too bad we don't know anyone who makes a living as a homicide detective who might be able to figure it all out."

"Maybe," said Alene, without acknowledging Ruthie's mild sarcasm, "but I wish you'd removed the name "Rosin" from your kids' jackets before you put them in the bin."

"To tell the truth, Alene, it never occurred to me," said Ruthie. "I was more troubled about people on the street being cold and wet." They should have whispered, but it was too hard to hear from six feet apart. Before the pandemic, they'd invited homeless people inside, and offered bowls of hot soup with warm bread. They'd sent unsold but beautifully wrapped pastry trays to a nearby shelter. Now, because of the coronavirus, people were unsure about anything touched by others.

"Listen, Six," Ruthie added, "They're going to find out what happened to those women."

"I hope so," said Alene. "Their families have no idea where they are."

Edith wandered back into the kitchen, and said, "I probably handed them their orders."

"It's not your job to hand out food and drink orders, Edith," said Alene. "And you know the rules about gossiping in this kitchen." She would have liked to add that if Edith's brother Gary hadn't taken care of her, she might have become one of those people living on the street.

Edith went on about how homeless people made their choices until LaTonya said, "Edith, just stop talking." LaTonya scraped dough from the sides of the large mixer while Edith headed back out to the café.

"I don't know about Ruthie's old clothes," LaTonya continued once Edith was gone, "but I'm pretty sure the Whipped and Sipped bags are coincidental, unless the thug distracted his victims with pastries before murdering them." Their smiles were grim.

For the next half hour, they were all quiet with their thoughts, baking or cleaning up after something went into the oven. Alene texted Frank to ask how he was feeling, and her father to ask if everything was okay with the kids. She texted each child a question that they were required to answer— now that the pandemic meant they needed cellphones, she wanted to make sure they understood the responsibility of being consistently available. The first time Sierra neglected to respond within an hour, Alene took her phone away for the evening. That had been a month before, and now the kids understood Alene's rules. Within ten minutes she received all three replies.

LaTonya, washing her hands, said, "I can't stop thinking about what's going to happen if the café closes. Nobody is hiring, but I'm going to have to look for a full-time job."

Alene had already been feeling miserable about the employees she'd had to let go. She went over and put a hand on LaTonya's shoulder. "I wish I could afford to give benefits," she said. In places that offered benefits, customers could spend over twenty dollars on a simple sandwich with a cup of coffee, plus tip. She couldn't imagine charging those prices. Most of her employees were part-time. Could she make it through the pandemic? Would she have to reach into her savings to keep the café going? The pandemic had changed everything, and no one was going to come out of it unscathed.

Edith appeared in the kitchen again, and responded with her usual tone-deafness, "If LaTonya leaves, I'll be able to get more hours."

There was no reason for Edith to be there. "Please stop coming into the kitchen, Edith," said Alene. "You're distracting everyone from doing their work."

"Well, there's so few orders being phoned in, and they're mostly online, so I don't have anything to do," she said, slighted.

"Really, Edith," said Alene before anyone else had a chance to weigh in. Edith was often too focused on her own misery to care about anyone else's. The carry-out business was just a fraction of what they'd made when people came in and sat down to eat and drink. "You need to be at your computer during work hours."

"Anyway, I'm only going to leave if I find something full-time," said LaTonya. Alene was sorry that the kitchen conversation kept coming around to survival.

Kacey said, "Sorry to change the subject, but why doesn't the CPD know anything about the first murder victim, Alene?"

"I still want to talk about my hours," Edith said, "and you're trying to change the subject."

"It's not the police department," said Alene, refusing to pay attention to Edith. "It's the city of Chicago that's six weeks behind on autopsies, according to Frank."

Ruthie said, "I hope everyone knows that it's a civic responsibility to help the police whenever they ask." Alene knew that was directed at her.

Edith piped up again. "If LaTonya is staying, you should keep in mind that Kacey doesn't pay rent and doesn't need to work. I don't think she even wants to be here. I could take some of her hours."

Kacey said, "You're not getting my hours, Edith. You don't bake or cook." Alene was happy to hear Kacey stand up for herself. Until Kofi had begun a concerted effort to build up her confidence, she'd been incapable of responding to her aunt Edith's acid-laced comments.

Ruthie was taking out the pans they'd need to make chocolate and cinnamon babkas, using a vegan version of her grandmother's recipe. "We don't need to speak like that to each other," she told Edith as she began rolling out the babka dough. "And LaTonya," she added, "One day, you're going to find a fantastic full-time job. As they say, this too shall pass." Ruthie liked summing things up with a good axiom.

Edith asked, "What about me?"

"You're needed in the café," said Ruthie. Edith left without another word. What she wanted, thought Alene as she headed to her office, was to be needed. Moments later, Olly passed her office door, and she heard him begging Ruthie for ginger or poppyseed cookies. She texted her father about meeting Finn near the now-closed grill at the Diversey Harbor. She recalled warm summer evenings sipping beers with Frank on the lawn surrounding the grill. They'd sat on Adirondack chairs encircled by people who were eating, talking, and laughing. Had anyone appreciated how free they were to enjoy themselves back then?

Texting done, Alene went back to the kitchen, where Olly was still nibbling something. "You planning to hang out in the kitchen all afternoon, Olly," she asked, "or is there still work for you to do in the basement?

Olly looked hurt. "I'm just waiting for Kofi to show up," he said.

"He's on his way," said Kacey. She'd covered a bowl of crushed walnuts with plastic wrap and was wiping down the nut counter that stood on the other side of the kitchen from where the rest of the baking was done. One of Ruthie's children had a tree nut allergy, so she was vigilant about not contaminating the nut-free pastries.

"Kofi's here," Kacey announced a minute later. She followed Alene out to the café. Kofi was outside the window locking his bicycle to the rack. Kacey held the front door open, her eyes sparkling through her glasses. Kofi made her happy. Her father had died the previous summer, and his widow, Kacey's stepmother, lived in a facility after having suffered injuries from being pushed down a staircase. She would never be able to live on her own again. Her son had worked for Alene until he found a job in a recording studio.

Alene greeted Kofi and asked if he'd seen the picture in the Chicago Tribune. "I don't think it's identifiable, Alene," he said. "And I want you to know that I appreciate your discretion."

Alene was about to respond when Edith, who'd been hovering, approached so close that Alene nearly had to push her away. "I don't want any of us to get sick, Edith." She looked over at Dori, who was busy on her laptop taking the last orders of the day. "That's why we're trying to be careful about staying six feet apart. It's so that we all stay healthy."

Edith was insulted. "I'm the healthiest person here," she said, hitting a chair like a defiant child.

Olly plopped himself down on the floor against the wall, legs sprawled in front of him, his orange curls in the usual disarray. Alene said, "Feel free to get back to the basement anytime." Olly made a production of getting himself up and moving slowly to the basement door.

"Anyway, I don't know if it's been proven that people have to stay six feet apart or even quarantine from each other," said Edith from her chair. She wasn't finished weighing in. Alene stared at her, speechless.

Kacey said, "People are dying from it, Edith."

"Maybe," said Edith, much to everyone's annoyance, "unless that's what they want us to think."

"Can we stop talking about this?" Dori asked. She rose from her seat at a table close to the wall. She'd been focused on final incoming orders while the rest of them had been talking, but now she was getting ready to leave. "Isn't there anything else happening in the world?"

She had a point, thought Alene as she returned to the kitchen. Dori had a musical-sounding lilt to her voice, and she wore bright-colored masks that matched her shirts. Also, until the pandemic forced everything to close, she'd started marketing both the café and connected bar as venues for everything from corporate events to bridal showers and birthday parties. She'd been surprisingly good at it.

After final clean-up, Ruthie and the rest of the kitchen staff headed out the back entrance. Kacey and Alene went out to the café, where Kofi and Olly were hauling garbage bags from the basement. Edith made another comment about how the virus might not be real, and Alene wondered if she'd have to break her promise to Edith's brother about letting her work for as long as she wanted to. What if she was pushing the rest of Alene's staff over the edge?

159

Dori had put away the laptop she used for orders, and now hurried towards the front door. "I'm out of here, but hope that old guy shows up again, Edith," she said just before she walked out the door. "I think he was interested in you."

Edith tsked and made noises about being friendly to strangers. "You can go home now, Edith," said Alene, waiting for Edith to leave. "Olly and Kofi," she turned to where they were still sitting, "is there anything you need before I leave?"

They shook their heads and asked if Alene wanted a quick look at the basement. "I thought you wanted to do a grand unveiling," Alene said. "And the important thing for me is that you set aside chairs and tables that can be refurbished. And throw out the junk."

"Have some faith and come this way," said Olly, pushing his unruly curls off his forehead and heading over to the crimson wall. He removed the poster that covered the staircase. "Watch your step, okay? Also, hold onto the banister, but don't lean on it because it needs work. And don't slip down the steps."

Alene thanked him, even though he was treating her like she was an old lady. Kofi went down and switched on a lamp whose cord was plugged in at the top of the stairs. Alene followed Olly, who got to the bottom of the stairs and swept his arm to indicate the whole space. "See that large area straight ahead?" he asked. "That's where the audience sat around the tables, listening to music from the band and drinking illegal booze."

"I see piles of crap everywhere," said Alene.

Olly growled. "You've got to use your imagination, Alene. That area against the back wall was once a bar. It's interesting from a historical perspective."

Kofi had turned on more lamps that illuminated the long unused space. Alene tried to imagine a stage, a bar, and an audience. She wouldn't get an audience these days even if she were to add cool lighting and purified, fresh air.

"It's kind of a mess," she said. "I think you should just throw everything out. Don't waste any more time sorting this junk."

"Are you kidding?" Olly turned and pointed to scattered piles of what looked like mangy old newspapers and faded magazines. "Those papers go back to the 1920s," he said. "They'd be worth something if they weren't moldy and disintegrating."

Alene didn't want to hurt their feelings, but she wasn't all that interested in a long-buried basement or ratty piles of old newspaper. And she could either buy cheap chairs online or ask Kofi to scavenge some.

"I'm not saying this is important," Olly said with a sweeping gesture, "but what I wanted you to see isn't NOT important." He loved being enigmatic.

"I'm looking at a lot of grime," she said. "Someone could get killed coming down those stairs, and the lighting is terrible." She was trying not to be brusque, but she wanted to finish up and get home.

"Unquestionably," Olly said with his theatrical presentation voice. "But a long-ago proprietor of this establishment devised an ingenious solution in case of a police raid." Kofi demonstrated how the sliding doors opened onto a bar, and another set opened to a doorway.

"Cool," she said, not enthusiastically enough for Olly. "And what's this on the counter?" She picked up the kind of metal box she used in the café to store tea.

"We found some old tins in one of the bedrooms," said Olly. "There are at least twenty of them, and some are hand painted and beautiful."

Kofi scooped one from the table behind him and presented it to Alene. "Plus, there's a surprise," he said. The tin was about eight inches tall and six inches in diameter, a dark golden color caked with dirt and etched with scenes of frolicking children.

"It's nice," said Alene, "In an old-piece-of-junk sort of way. What do you think they were used for and what possible use could they have for us now?"

"Glad you asked," said Olly, doing a two-step in his excitement. He must have been holding it in for several days. "They're in all different shapes and colors. I think they were used as decoration on shelves around the perimeter of the room, but who knows? Maybe the daughter of the owner kept her baubles in them." Who else used the word "bauble" these days?

"Kofi and I think that everything was running smoothly and then boom, the basement speakeasy operation came to a halt. It was like Mount Vesuvius erupting, except things weren't buried in ash. We found one table with a bottle and the remains of two glasses just sitting there like a couple of people were about to have a drink."

Kofi added, "It could have been a rival gang, or maybe the police came in and busted it all up, which would explain the broken furniture that we already got rid of. We also started cleaning up layers of dust and fallen ceiling, but we've got a way to go."

"I have ideas about turning some of these tins into something," said Olly. "I'm not sure what, but I like the colors and the patterns." He opened the tin he held with a sweeping motion and bowed down to offer it to Alene. "Some of them have stuff inside." He poked at what looked like bird feed.

"Could have been disintegrated old cigars," Kofi said.

"A century is too long for a cigar to hold its shape," said Alene, starting to move back towards the staircase. If they were ever going to use this space, that was the first thing that needed shoring up. They needed a sturdier banister and a real door with a lockable handle, not just an opening in the crimson wall. And there had to be running water if they were going to serve food and drinks, and a restroom that didn't require walking up the stairs. "You guys understand that there has to be a cure for Covid-19, and people have to be willing to go inside restaurants again before we do anything about this space, right?"

She thought she saw them nodding. "You'll never guess what else we found inside one of the tins," said Olly, gesticulating like he was on a stage. He slowly pulled a small, crusty-looking circular object out of the tin and said in a hushed voice, "This might be a real diamond ring."

"Or it's a real fake," said Kofi, ruining Olly's reveal. "It's too filthy to tell."

Chapter 11

"That's ridiculous. Who would hide a genuine diamond ring in a tin?" Cal asked. He was sitting at the kitchen counter, raising one eyebrow after Alene told him about her day and her visit to the basement she hadn't known existed.

"Olly wiped it a bit with a rag, and it looked like a real diamond ring," Alene said, "but it'll need to be cleaned, polished, and appraised. Also, it must have belonged to whoever started the restaurant way back in the 1920s."

"You can wear it when you and Frank get engaged," said Cal.

Alene sighed. "Really, Dad?" They were all wearing masks unless they were in their own rooms. She'd explained to her father and children that they were going to protect themselves for the next four or five days in case Frank had caught something, even if it wasn't Covid-19. So, no more hugging.

Quinn had burst into tears when Alene said they were taking a break from hugging. Noah had said, "Don't worry, Quinn. I'll still hug you." It had made Alene want to grab them both and never let them go.

Now Cal sat on the counter stool facing the kitchen, drinking a glass of water, and tapping his fingers on the counter while Alene finished shelving the dinner dishes. The kids were already in their rooms, hypnotized by their screens. "Maybe some timid guy bought that ring," he said, warming up to launch into it. "He might have spent three months of his salary and was building up the nerve to ask his girl to marry him. But right after buying it, he goes out to have a drink at his usual neighborhood speakeasy." Cal waved his hands for emphasis. "He hides the ring in the tin, maybe so he doesn't lose it, but on his way home, he gets hit by a bus, so nobody ever retrieves it and nobody else knows it's in the tin until Oliver Burns finds it a century later." Cal loved inventing a good yarn. "I hope the girl found someone else to marry her," he added wistfully.

"What a charming old-fashioned way to look at marriage," said Alene, "but we'll never know." Her dad used to encourage her and her sister to use their imaginations and he'd enjoyed both telling stories and listening to theirs. Lydia always wanted princesses who were smarter than all the princes. Alene had liked stories about true love. Her kids probably dreamed of going back to school and having their old lives back. They could play outside if they kept their distance from each other, but the parks were still closed. When would they ever get to let their imaginations go wild again?

Cal answered the cheery ring of his cellphone. After a few grouchy acknowledgements, he said goodbye and announced that his brother had canceled their plan to meet. Finn was turning out to be one more drain on Alene's energy.

"What'd he say?" she asked.

"He thinks he's a spy or something. He said he was being followed, and it wasn't safe to meet," Cal reported. "I could hardly understand him, but it sounded like more of his drama to me. You'll have to cancel with Jocelyn, but come on, Alene, I can walk over to Diversey without help."

"Yeah, I know, Dad, but Jocelyn loves hanging out with us and you two enjoy each other's company. I invited her for all our sakes." She didn't need to remind him that his muscles sometimes seized up and made it hard for him to walk. "But when we reschedule, maybe we should plan to meet elsewhere if he doesn't feel safe in the park. We could ask him to come to the café. We'd have the place to ourselves except for Olly and Kofi, but they won't bother us."

Cal shook his head and looked iffy about the venture. "Maybe, but if Finn thinks meeting me is dangerous today, why is it going to be safe tomorrow?" He used his forefinger to draw circles around his ear, the old-fashioned way of suggesting that someone was crazy. "Truthfully, I'm wondering why I wanted to see him again."

Alene said, "I'll do whatever you want, Dad." She was happy to have time to read through her mail, watch a sitcom about a ridiculous family, and get to bed early. It was a perfectly nice pandemic Thursday night. She called Frank, which reminded her of spending hours lying in bed on the phone when she was about Sierra's age, yakking with other girls until her mother would knock on the door and tell her to go to sleep.

Frank thought he had a severe cold. He sounded exhausted. "Rhona has one of her headaches," he said, "and I'm hoping she'll come with me to get tested in the morning."

It seemed like Rhona got one of her headaches every other week, but Alene thought Frank should have hightailed it over to get a test already, without waiting another day. She kept that to herself. "And," he continued, "she said that she's not actually dating this man, even though she seems to be with him all the time. I don't know what that's about. She told me I wouldn't like him for a bunch of reasons. His job is taking care of a family member, which doesn't sound like a job. On a positive note, she said he makes her feel good about herself."

"I respect that," said Alene. "It's a first step to growing up and figuring herself out."

Frank was quiet for a long moment and then admitted feeling defeated as a father. He'd asked Rhona to tell him more, and she said that this guy was a better person than Frank would ever be. Alene wanted to say that she'd come around one day, but it felt like a cliché. Frank said, "I hope to God she'll come around one day."

Alene was glad she'd held off on saying it, and they spent the next ten minutes whispering and dreaming about when he could move in with her, Cal, and the kids. They both repeated "goodnight" until there wasn't anything left to be said. It would have been a good time to tell him what Kofi had seen at the building site, but how could she interrupt a lovely conversation with something so serious? And how could she bother him when he was feeling so poorly?

Alene tossed and turned all night and had to drag herself out of bed on Friday morning. It was her fault, she knew, for keeping a secret from Frank, and she vowed to come out with it when she called him later. Until it was late enough to call, she stretched, showered, got her children up, and gave them breakfast. She patiently supervised them in making sandwiches for lunch and got them ready to zoom into their classes. Before calling Frank, she skimmed through the news on her phone. There were more stories about people breaking store windows and making off with armfuls of stolen goods. It was happening on Michigan Avenue and around the city, but it was also happening around the country.

It had been a full week since she drove Kacey and Kofi to that fire site, and Frank still didn't know. Alene started punching in his phone number, but then she stopped. People with Covid were reporting crazy symptoms, and some who'd survived described living with a "brain fog" for weeks. How could she bother Frank about work?

She called, and Frank answered the phone. He'd fallen asleep with the television on, he said, after speaking to Rhona through her bedroom door. Now he'd just gotten out of a long, hot shower, and he felt better, but last night, he'd felt congested and had been nearly out of his mind, worrying. He'd wanted to ask Rhona more questions about the guy she was seeing, but she couldn't stop coughing and sneezing.

"So, you're both going to get tested this morning?" asked Alene.

"I am. She's refusing to go," he said. "I was about to leave when you called." Alene begged him to stay as far as possible from his daughter, and to be vigilant. She tried not to think about what it would mean if Frank tested positive.

Olly was waiting for Alene at the kitchen entrance to the café, squatting against the wall in an uncomfortable-looking position that he quickly assured her was intentional. He rarely let a moment pass without strengthening muscles or working on his flexibility.

"What are you doing out here?" she asked when she was within hearing distance. "Haven't Ruthie and Kacey already opened?" She reached for her cellphone to check the schedule.

Olly shook out his limbs and said, "Rashid and Estrella are in the kitchen with Ruthie. I was waiting for Kofi and Kacey."

Alene quickly ran inside to help Ruthie, but it looked like the kitchen was under control. "Good morning," she said. Where was Kacey? She pulled out her cellphone and texted. It reminded her of all those times when Kacey disappeared, and nobody could reach her.

Olly lumbered in and walked directly into Alene. She turned to glare at him, and he held up his hands in a gesture of surrender. "You know I can't function well when I'm hungry," he said.

"If I give you something to eat, do you promise to get out of my hair?" Alene asked as she grabbed her apron and scarf off a hook.

"Absolutely," said Olly, tagging behind her out to the café after she tossed him a muffin. She walked back and forth in front of the windows. "What are you doing, Alene? What are you looking for?"

"I'm worried by Kacey being late, and I'm worried about people breaking the windows," she said. "Stories about it happening are all over the news, and on the way here, I passed a slew of boarded-up stores. Some are out of business, but others just have boards in the windows."

"I know," said Olly, pulling out a chair and making himself comfortable. "The downtown protests are serious, Alene, but the smash and grab attacks feel like some people are taking advantage of the chaos. Kofi and I can board up your windows."

Alene asked, "Won't that be a fortune since so many businesses are doing it?" She'd heard enough about these robberies to understand that it was time to do something proactive.

"I'll have to figure it out," said Olly. He followed her back into the kitchen, where she checked

Ruthie's list. Someone had already removed doughs and batters from the refrigerators and completed a few tasks. The next recipe on the list involved heating sunflower seed butter to make puffed rice treats.

"But aside from that," Olly continued, "I couldn't stop thinking about that diamond ring. I'm sure it's real, Alene. I soaked it in white vinegar, as per Mr. Google's directions, and it's a stunner. It might be a carat, and it's a square shape surrounded by diamond chips, with lovely filigree on the band."

"I love square diamonds. Where is it now?" Alene asked as she measured. "Could I see it?"

Olly shook his head. "It's back where I found it, hidden among the other tins. I'd love to have it appraised, but then you'd have to get it insured."

"It might have belonged to whichever of Kacey's great-grandmothers ran the restaurant, or the speakeasy," said Alene. "Sadly, there's nobody left to ask about it."

Alene always wore a simple gold necklace with a tiny diamond and small gold hoop earrings that she rarely removed, all from her mother. Lydia got the expensive stuff—the wedding ring, the pearls, and the tennis bracelet. She kept them in a safe deposit box and hardly ever enjoyed them. "I guess it'd be wise to get the ring appraised," she added. "Let's wait until the world is less dangerous but get back to me when you find the mother lode, Olly."

"Don't be surprised if I'm the one laughing," he said. "Also, when Kofi gets here, we're going to bring boatloads of garbage upstairs today."

"As long as you dispose of it legally," said Alene, now at the stove, warming the seed butter. "Have we updated the electricity situation down there yet? I'm worried about that old wiring."

"Not yet," said Olly, "but I'm planning to pull wires through and connect to an outlet on the crimson wall."

"Can you do electrical work?" she asked.

"I was hooking up electrical systems before you baked your first cardamom ginger cookie, Alene," he said. He'd pulled his orange curls into a ponytail on top of his head.

"That's interesting, Olly, because I'm more than a decade older than you." Now the nut butter was smooth. She took it off the heat while stirring in the coconut oil.

"I started my training when I was two," he said, folding his long arms across his chest. That was her clue that he wanted to be taken seriously. He seemed mesmerized by the circular motions of her spoon, but Alene knew he was simply waiting for a taste.

"Yeah," said Alene, "potty training." She winked. Olly was good at cheering her up, distracting her from brooding.

"Seriously, Alene, we've got this," he said.

"As long as you don't burn down the building," she said, thinking about the two fires and telling Frank about Kofi seeing the body. If Rhona had given him the virus, he'd have to quarantine at home, and Lee Bautista would take over.

"I will not encourage your negativity," said Olly, "and no offense, but you're not the only klutz in the house. Let's keep the poster attached when we're not here until we fix the stairs." Olly said, "no offense," whenever he was about to say something offensive.

Alene measured the puffed rice and poured it into the softened nut butter mixture. She wondered what was taking Kacey and Kofi so long to appear. Olly hovered. "Speaking of mobsters, he added, "Kofi told me he found the first body before the police discovered it, the one they haven't identified yet."

"Kofi told you," Alene repeated. Her stomach roiled again as she smoothed the mixture into a prepared pan, but maybe telling Olly was the first step Kofi needed to take. "I should have told Frank right after it happened," Alene said, mad at herself but relieved to say it out loud. "Now it's too late because he's sick. Lee is most likely going to take over."

Olly stared at her, but she checked her watch, wondering what had happened to Kacey. She worried whenever Kacey was late for anything. There'd been times during Kacey's tough years when she'd gone off somewhere to find a dealer, and Alene had helped search for her for hours. Kacey had often ended up lying unresponsive on her bed, but once, Alene found her passed out on the sidewalk several blocks away, and another time Alene's sister found her lying on the docks jutting out over the water. Alene hoped Kofi would notice and stop her if Kacey ever slid back into her old habits.

"Kofi's only mistake was sneaking under a construction fence," said Olly. "It's not like he murdered that woman. I think you should tell Frank, even though he's sick. He needs to know, and he can emphasize to Lee that seeing the body doesn't mean that Kofi was involved. You never know what tiny piece of information will help an investigation."

He was right, of course. Why had she thought protecting Kofi was more important? A reason she hadn't admitted to herself tumbled out. "Do you think it's possible that Kofi knows more about that body than he told either of us?"

Olly made the face he used when he thought that Alene was being ridiculous. The mask only barely covered it up. "Are we discussing the same Kofi Lloyd who repaints an entire wall if he sees a single flaw? Our Kofi concentrates on improving the world." He scurried into her office to turn on some music, and the Wedding Song from the Broadway show "Hadestown" came on.

What about that music hit her like a blast of wind? She and Frank would never be able to spend a lifetime together if she wasn't completely up front with him every single day. She said, "Olly, can you please open the refrigerator for me? And then please text Kofi and ask if he has Kacey with him. I'm getting worried."

"Always ready to help," he said, jumping up and heading out towards the café. "I suppose I should get started. Decide about the windows, though. We don't want any damage here."

Neither did she. Frank would call when he woke, and she'd tell him about Kofi. What had she been thinking? Alene was disgusted with herself. Would she feel any better after telling him, or was having kept this secret going to weigh on her for the rest of her life? She stopped to text Frank that she wanted to tell him something. Maybe Lee had already told him. Lee was a stickler about police matters except regarding his own conduct. Alene didn't want to join the accusatory bandwagon, but he was one of those cops known for treating some people as more equal than others. Alene could not fathom why Frank didn't put a stop to it.

Frank needed to stop smoothing things over when Lee screwed up. Instead of making excuses or apologizing for his partner, he should get Lee assigned to directing traffic or a desk job where he didn't have to talk to regular people. But Lee had once driven Kofi to a clinic after he'd scraped up his leg in a bike accident. Maybe Lee wasn't completely evil, and Kofi wasn't completely innocent.

She checked her messages—nothing yet from Kacey, and Olly hadn't come back in with an update from Kofi. Alene had to remember that they were both grownups, and she was neither of their mothers. She checked Ruthie's list for the next project needing attention. Kofi had been so wonderful for Kacey. He'd helped fill the hole that had opened after her father died. He'd inspired her to eat healthier, take better care of herself, and volunteer with troubled kids. They were the ones who struggled, and whose parents were ready to send them to the kinds of programs Kacey had endured, where they'd have to earn the right to sit in a chair or talk to anyone. The pandemic had put an end to her volunteering, but at least Kacey had aged out of those programs, and with Kofi's help, she'd been clean for nearly a year. It wasn't easy for her—Alene knew there were triggers everywhere.

She was about to start another recipe when Kofi and Kacey walked in. Kacey apologized for being late but didn't offer an excuse. Alene was so glad to see her, she nearly wept. Kacey put on her apron, washed her hands, scrolled through the to-do list, and went straight to work mashing bananas with peanut butter for one of Ruthie's banana breads. She never looked at Alene. Kofi went into Alene's office and changed the soundtrack from Broadway to country. He and Olly were constantly at odds about music. "It's Mickey Guyton," he said after Alene made a questioning face. The singer had a pleasing voice, but country songs all sounded the same to her.

Kacey, who was wringing the giant pile of grated zucchini, finally begged Alene's forgiveness. "I forgot how worried you get about me," she said.

Alene thought before answering so she'd get it right. "I do worry," she said, "but I shouldn't, because you're a grown-up, and also, you have Kofi to worry about you."

Kacey said, "I'm sorry, Alene." If Kacey can apologize like that, thought Alene, I can, too.

Everyone in the kitchen heard the exchange, but nobody interrupted until Kofi came back to the kitchen and said, "We wanted you to weigh in, Alene. Those round tables just need an intense cleaning, sanding, and varnish. Plus reinforcing with wood glue. We can refurbish at least six of the chairs. Is that good?"

177

Alene wiped her hands on her apron and followed Kofi out of the kitchen. "You've got my go-ahead," she said. "I prefer round tables, because unlike a four-top, if things ever get back to normal, each round can accommodate an additional couple of customers."

Olly was on the floor near the electrical outlet, slowly unravelling a spool of electrical wire through the opening in the wall. "Exactly my hypothesis," he said.

Edith and Dori came in and were getting ready to take online orders. Edith approached Olly and said, "I sure hope you're being careful." She was always quick to warn or scold. "You could fall down those stairs, Olly, and you don't know if the air down there is clean enough to breathe."

"I could have also fallen out of my crib when I was a baby, Edith," he said. "Isn't all of life fraught with danger?" Then he turned to follow Kofi down to the basement.

"One day, Olly," Alene said before his orange curls disappeared from view, "you're going to be bald and slow-moving, and then let's see if you're still laughing at other people." She turned and added, "Don't mind him, Edith."

"I try not to," said Edith, turning her back on the crimson wall. "On a more important subject, Alene, that homeless man sitting next to the door has been shouting since I got here. I think he's going to scare off customers."

Dori ran outside, and she must have said something to calm him down because the shouting stopped. When she returned a few minutes later, she said, "He's fine now, and there weren't any customers for him to scare."

Edith said, "Because they all ran away already." Vincent hadn't been there when Alene came in earlier. It was his third day in one week.

"He's probably a lonely old guy with nobody to take care of him, Edith," said Alene. "We all need to keep that in mind."

"Well, he's pitiful, and he's making me nervous," said Edith. "Just pitiful."

"Edith!" Ruthie had walked in from the kitchen and heard that. "He could be sick and confused, and you should call him by his name," she said as she headed behind the counter to make herself a coffee. "His name is Vincent."

Dori said, "He's not sick, but he's old."

Alene asked Edith to put on her apron and get started. Edith gave her a sullen glare and said, "I'm just saying that he's sitting too close to the door, and shouting. He's like those crazy people trying to destroy cities all over the country. They've already caused a ton of damage on Michigan Avenue, and they might come to Lakeview next. I'm just being cautious."

"Edith," said Alene, "please." She slipped back to the kitchen and into her office to change to a more soothing channel of female singers, starting with Brandi Carlile's "You and Me on the Rock." Some days she hardly paid attention to the music, and other days, it mattered.

While she was in her office, she called to reschedule the meeting with her father's brother. Finn picked up on the first ring. "I can't make another plan to meet if you're going to get my dad's hopes up, and then cancel at the last minute," said Alene.

"He canceled the first meeting," Finn responded in a truculent tone. She imagined the two brothers telling on each other to their parents when they were young, although Finn was five years older. He sighed and added, calmer, "I'm sorry for canceling last night, Alene, but I didn't want to put you or your father in danger."

That's nice, she thought, but totally irritating. "Why would we be in danger?"

"It's a long story," he said.

"I heard all about it." Alene cut him off. "You helped rob a bank in Galesburg and got sent to prison. Then you dug up the stolen money, and you left town. If meeting you in the park is going to be dangerous, Uncle Finn, why don't you just call my dad and tell him what you want to tell him instead of meeting in person?"

Finn cleared his throat, sounding weak and phlegmy. Alene wished she hadn't been so harsh—he'd probably been yelled at a lot when he was in prison. He said, "I guess it doesn't matter, but I've got a gift for him, and I wanted to give it to him in person. I feel like I owe him thanks for everything he did back then."

"That's thoughtful," said Alene. She knew her dad appreciated gratitude. "How about if, just for the sake of making this work, you give me the gift and I pass it along? Or we can send someone to pick it up from you, and you can tell my dad all about it over the phone. We can't keep making and breaking plans."

"I'd like to see him," said Finn. "It could be the last time we meet."

"I think my father would like to see you, also," said Alene. It'd be the last time because Finn was going to disappear again. That's how he operated. "But you cannot give him anything associated with the stolen money."

"I understand," he hesitated. "Look, Alene, I used my legitimate earnings to buy Bitcoin back in 2013," he said. "I was one of the early investors, and over the years, it's blown up in value."

Cal had once told Alene about the first cryptocurrency transaction in which a programmer had used Bitcoin, that would later be worth millions, to buy a couple of pizzas. "Just out of curiosity, where did you learn how to invest money like that?" she asked. Her dad said that Finn had never gone to college.

"I read up on it," he said. "You can find good information on the internet."

"Oh," said Alene, impressed that someone Finn's age was that tech savvy. It would have been her father's approach, too. She reminded Finn where they planned to meet, and after hanging up, called her dad to confirm. "He has a gift for you," she said.

"I don't want or need anything from him," Cal responded, as she'd expected, "especially if it's connected to a crime."

"I told him, and he assured me he bought it with money he'd earned." Alene explained about the Bitcoin and Cal expressed doubt about Finn's truthfulness. "Whatever it is, Dad, all you have to do is say thank you." She didn't mention Finn's anxiety about meeting the previous night.

Edith stopped Alene as she'd slipped her cellphone back in her pocket and headed back out to the café. "Have you read about that umbrella guy who goes around breaking windows at night, Alene?" she asked. "They've got police with their lights swirling on every block, but even upscale stores are closed. No one is shopping in Chicago anymore."

Dori was behind the counter making herself an Americano. "They're just not shopping at night," she said as she set the cup on the table and sat in front of her laptop. "Even stores in the Bloomingdale's building got their windows shattered and the police couldn't stop the people from stealing stuff."

The thought of it made Alene sick. She'd read in the *Sun-Times* about people getting seriously hurt and businesses being devastated. She couldn't afford anything happening to the café—she'd tell Olly and Kofi to board up the windows.

Lunch ordering had dwindled by the time they bounced up the stairs, Olly carrying a tin as if it was a toy he couldn't bear to leave behind. Edith kept looking at them, clearly wanting to be included and annoyed that Kacey and LaTonya had brought them snacks. "I didn't realize some people get to be served," Edith bellyached loud enough for them all to hear.

Suddenly, they all heard a whirring and the shattering of glass followed by a clunking sound. At first, Alene thought someone must have dropped something in the kitchen. It took a moment to realize that something had crashed through the front window. It had sounded like a missile and landed on the floor, narrowly missing Edith, who stood and screamed as if it had hit her.

Chapter 12

Alene punched in 911 while her staff streamed out of the kitchen and into the café. It was eerily quiet except for the sound of her heart pounding and Edith's crying. Ruthie usually left by two on Fridays, but now she pulled everyone away from the window and brought a hot drink to Edith. They all gaped at the brick. It seemed less like a torpedo now that it was on the floor.

Alene knew not to expect a quick response because several of Frank's colleagues were in quarantine. If he weren't sick, Frank would drop everything to run over. She called to tell him about the brick. "The police are on their way, so we don't need you to jump out of bed."

"That's a relief," Frank said in a still congested voice. "I'm sorry you have to deal with another problem, but you're good at it."

Frank always made her feel taller—or always had until now. Would he forgive her when he learned the truth? Alene told him she'd call back later and told herself that she'd come clean about Kofi during that call. She'd dragged this on way too long. She would have comforted Edith, who was still whimpering, but was relieved to see Dori pull her chair closer and put an arm around Edith's shoulders.

The brick looked like the standard rectangular red kind sold everywhere. Alene imagined running out to the sidewalk with a pistol in each hand. Whoever threw the brick might have whipped by on a bicycle, but she could envision shooting the tires off a fleeing car. Maybe she'd been inspired by the conversation about gangsters. Was that a car now screeching around the corner?

She hurried out the front door, but the street was nearly deserted. Where were the police? There was hardly anyone except for Vincent, in his usual spot leaning against the building, a young mom pushing a stroller up the block, and a couple strolling across the street. Stores weren't allowing in customers; the nail salon was closed, Jocelyn's Krav Maga studio was online only, and the bank on the corner was shuttered. Were even banks going out of business?

She turned to Vincent, who had the usual venomous expression on his face, and asked, "Did you see who threw that brick?"

Did he get bored sitting like that unmoving all day whenever he chose the ground outside the café, or was that all he was capable of? Where did he spend his days when he wasn't outside the café? Alene thought he'd have answered Ruthie, and said, "It would help Ruthie to know."

He spat on the ground and looked away, making her feel defeated. Kacey unlocked the door to let her back inside. "Any luck?" she asked.

Alene shook her head, pulled out the closest chair, and sat, holding her head in her hands. "How much is it going to cost to replace that window?" she asked no one in particular, staring at the mess of glass scattered across the floor. "I don't even know if it's worth fixing if it's just going to get smashed again."

Olly could come through in a crisis. "It's only one windowpane, Alene," he said, patting her back, which was oddly comforting. "It'll take us less than an hour to replace it." At least that was a relief. She assumed he meant he and Kofi could do it. "But I think our priority is going to be boarding up all the windows right now, before the weekend." Olly continued. "We can replace the broken windowpane afterwards."

"Thanks, Olly," said Alene. "You were right. I should have let you board up the windows before someone threw that brick." Olly responded by bowing to her.

LaTonya brought out a plate of cardamom ginger cookies, and they took a break to gather, nibble on cookies, and marvel that nobody had been hurt. Kofi and Olly finished whatever was left on the

187

plate. It was remarkable how they could eat after what just transpired. Alene had no appetite.

Kacey swept broken glass into a dustpan, but left it for the police to see, and LaTonya wiped the tops of the tables in case any shards had landed higher up. Dori closed the café account for the day, packed up, and left. Ruthie reminded Alene to contact the insurance agent before she went home, and everyone else went back to the kitchen to finish up and prepare for the next day. Olly programmed the sound system with a Bruno Mars channel and started dancing. He said Uptown Funk was just what they needed to cheer themselves up, but nobody else felt like dancing.

Alene went back to her office and called Frank to complain that the police hadn't yet turned up.

"They're doing their best," he said. "You didn't touch anything, did you?"

"Oops, should I have told them not to sweep? I was afraid someone would get hurt."

"Never mind," said Frank. "It's not going to change anything so forget about it. But listen, I got tested and it's just a cold."

"Oh, Frank," she said. "What a relief." She hadn't known it was possible to have just a cold these days. Then she took a deep breath and said, "Frank, I drove Kofi and Kacey to the fire site last Friday morning. I'm sorry, but I kept meaning to tell you. He was looking for art supplies like he always does, and he wanted a ride in case he found anything."

"You kept meaning to tell me?" Alene thought he'd get angry and say something, but he just breathed loudly. She knew he was angry and disappointed.

"I'm sorry, Frank," she said again. "He saw the body and ran back to the car. I promised Kacey that I wouldn't say anything, but I should have told you earlier."

Frank interrupted her to say, "Yes, you should have told me. We have to trust each other if we're going to have a life together."

That's exactly what she wanted, a life together. She understood, even without him saying a word, that he was disappointed. Maybe even hurt. Had she blown the relationship?

Olly spoke up just as she was putting her phone away. "I don't know how it happened, Alene, but remember that square diamond ring hidden in one of the tins?" he asked, his eyes wide with worry. "It's not there. Did I bring it upstairs at some point?"

Kofi was right behind him. "Maybe you did, and someone threw it back down the stairs."

"That doesn't seem possible," said Olly, unusually mopey. "I know I tossed it back in with all the other tins, but it's not there now."

If it was worth something, he should have taken it home with him, or at least set it aside. Alene could barely focus on something so meaningless. It would have been better if Frank had yelled at her, and then she could have cried, and they'd have made up. Instead, he'd thanked her as if she was a random stranger. "We don't know for sure that it's worth anything at all, Olly, but I'm sure you'll find it," she said calmly.

"I know it's worth something," said Olly with a theatrical sigh as he peeled himself up out of the chair. Alene thought costume jewelry could look expensive, like some of the things Blanca wore. She'd recently been accused of stealing someone's diamond studs, but it turned out she was wearing her own cheap earrings. Anyway, what did Olly know about appraising jewelry?

Kofi nudged him and said, "Easy come, easy go, Olly. Let's go get the plywood."

"Can't believe I'm such a bonehead," said Olly. Alene followed them out to the café, where the two of them spent a few minutes clowning around, as if Olly had already moved on from worrying about the misplaced ring.

"But you're *our* bonehead, Olly," Alene said, working hard to sound cheerful. "Isn't it sort of late in the day to find plywood? Isn't it in huge demand right now?"

"Set your mind at ease, Alene," Kofi called back to her from the sidewalk in front. "We're on it."

She couldn't leave before the police got there, so while her employees signed out for the day, Alene went into the kitchen to start prepping for Saturday. First, she whipped up a batch of salad dressings that she'd set overnight in the refrigerator. Someone would separate it into jars in the morning. Her dressings were better than anything sold commercially, and customers also used them as marinades.

It was well after three and the police hadn't yet shown up. Olly and Kofi returned, more quickly than she'd expected and proud to have procured enough materials. "We told you not to worry, didn't we?" asked Olly. He started chattering again, which was both soothing and maddening. Olly always said that being annoyed was the best cure for depression. "Why would someone break a window here?" he asked as he and Kofi brought in the plywood. "I mean, the bread is chewy and Ruthie's pastries rock, but really?"

Kofi said, "Is it just part of the general madness circulating around the city? Or has someone got something against the Whipped and Sipped Café?"

"And if that's the case," Olly speculated, pretending to hold a pipe like Sherlock Holmes, "could the miscreant have possibly been someone from the dairy or poultry industry trying to attack vegans? They're worried about a world in which butter and eggs no longer appeal to the masses."

"They're trying to stamp out the vegan ringleaders who bake without those key, moneymaking ingredients," said Kofi.

They kept going in that vein, trying to cheer her up, but Alene was too depressed to joke around. If Frank had accepted her apology and come over to comfort her after the brick ruined her window, she wouldn't be so nervous about someone trying to hurt her or the café. But he'd have brought Lee, who reminded her of Jon Burge, the crooked Chicago commander who'd been found guilty of torturing people into confessing to crimes they hadn't committed. Or like the previous mayor, who'd tried to cover up the case of a teenager shot in the back by a cop.

Frank had spoken about people needing the police more than ever; abusive husbands getting even more abusive and gang wars making the streets more perilous. Well, how was the public supposed to appreciate the police department when people like Lee were allowed in? Frank had also told Alene that crime was worse on the weekend, and here it was Friday afternoon.

Olly came inside to tell Alene that some cops were out in front. She greeted the two officers, one of whom carefully studied the scene inside the café while the other went outside to walk the perimeter. The first officer, a slim woman with long, wavy black hair tied in a ponytail, said that Whipped and Sipped had suffered less damage than some other stores. "A bicycle shop on Erie got almost totally cleaned out," she added.

The second police officer, a solidly built man with a thick neck and short-cropped brown hair, said, "I'm sorry there's nothing we can do except write it up for your insurance." Alene gave each of them a peach hand pie that would be easy to eat in the car, and they requested iced tea instead of coffee. Both officers said they'd stop by again to keep an eye on things. They gazed at the now-empty dessert counter as they left, and Alene assured them that they were welcome back. She knew they got hungry by late afternoon.

Olly and Kofi finished boarding up the windows while Alene watched them, pacing. "Go home,

Alene," Olly said. "we'll stay here and guard the place."

"The boards should protect the rest of the windowpanes," Kofi added, "but if you insist on staying, you can go down to the basement and take a nap."

"I've got a sofa in my office for that," Alene said, briefly thinking about moving to the café for the next few days. But what did she plan to do if someone tried to vandalize the place again? And who would take care of her children? Cal didn't have the energy to supervise, feed, and discipline them on his own. No, she'd go home, she thought.

Blanca called then. "I've been so worried about you," said Alene, sitting back down for a moment. "How do you feel? Where are you?" Finally, something positive.

"I'm in my home," said Blanca. "Those boys who rent my extra room, I told you about Marek and Ziggy, who gave me the Covid? While I go to the hospital, they took from me my hidden money and some of my earrings and my gold watch that my mother gave me. So, they disappear, and they leave a mess for me in the sink. So terrible."

"Oh Blanca, that is terrible," said Alene. She remembered Blanca showing her that watch; it had a delicate hammered-gold band. "Even after you gave them a place to live."

"Don't you worry, Alene." Blanca said, softer and scratchier than usual. "They gonna be sorry they pick the wrong person to steal from. I'm gonna find them. Especially because they pretend they're fine, but they're giving everyone sickness, like me. I'm okay now. The doctor says I should stay home five days, but I'm busy looking for those two on the computer. It's not so easy to hide from me."

Even when she'd been on vacations or gone home to Poland, Blanca would text updates and pictures, but she'd hardly communicated while she was sick. They'd all missed her. "Did you already call the police?" Alene asked.

"Are you crazy? They not gonna help find nothing. I have plan. Those boys gonna wish the Chicago police will save them from me." Blanca said. She sounded like herself again, her breathing unencumbered. "But it's bad this Covid, and I don't want you should get it. First, I think maybe I'm gonna die, but I'm tough like nails. How are you, and the children?"

Alene brought her up to date about Cal, the kids, Cal's brother, and Frank getting exposed to the virus. "We can't control everything what happens, but we can try," said Blanca. Alene had always admired her can-do attitude. "I'm fine now, but two people I know died, and I wish it was those two bums. It's worse for already sick people," she added. "But not everyone, Alene. My neighbor has very old father and that lady on the third floor with the singing bird. They're both fine."

"We're so glad you're back," said Alene. The family missed having Blanca around, especially Cal. He'd continued to pay her throughout her illness, and he'd set up a retirement fund for her, since he'd made his living as a financial advisor and knew how

194

vital it was to have what he called a "nest egg." He always said he'd ask Blanca to marry him if he wasn't such a sickly old geezer. But sixty-six wasn't that old, Alene thought.

"The doctors say everyone after Covid should have five more days alone," Blanca repeated. "But if you need help, Alene, I'm gonna take care of Cal and the kids."

"Thanks for offering," said Alene, "but we can wait five days. You need to be completely healthy."

Moments later, Alene called down to Olly and Kofi to say that she was leaving. She was inspired by Blanca to consider a plan for revenge against whoever threw the brick. If nothing else, it would make her feel better, although nothing could make her feel better about Frank.

Alene had just stepped into the alley and was about to close the door when she sensed someone hovering nearby. She nearly screamed before she saw that it was Lee Bautista.

"We're closed now," she said bit too harshly. But he'd scared her. Why was he slinking around the back? "Is this important or could you come back tomorrow when we're open?"

"I'm here to talk to Kofi Lloyd," he said, standing there as if he wanted her to invite him into the café. At least he was masked and six feet away, but she had the appalling thought of finding a way to give him the virus, followed by a wave of guilt.

"I'm sorry, Lee," Alene said. Had he recognized Kofi from that photo in the Tribune? She couldn't speak to him without a bubble of annoyance at the back of her throat. "But as you can see, I've already walked out the door."

"The sign on your front door says that you don't close until four." He continued to stand there and glower, probably thinking that he'd intimidate her enough to open the door and let him follow her in. Why did he think Kofi was there anyway?

"That was before the pandemic," said Alene trying to inch down the alley, away from the kitchen door. "Now we close earlier." She wasn't about to tell him anything specific. "Also, Kofi Lloyd doesn't work for me." His bike was locked on the street in front of the café, but she wasn't going to share that information.

She purposely avoided saying that there wasn't anyone there, or that business hours were flexible because of the pandemic. He shouldn't ever be able to claim that she lied, obstructed justice, or some other sneaky nonsense. He stood there as if his menacing stance was going to change her mind.

"You might want to try him at his apartment," she said in as chirpy a voice as she could muster. "Again, we're closed, and I need to go to the grocery store." She strode forward toward the street, away from his disapproving stare.

She honestly did need to stop at the grocery store. Her stomach roiled, but it was just from stress. Plus, she didn't have a way to warn Olly and Kofi until she was out of Lee's sight. She wasn't going to turn Kofi over for questioning of any kind. Frank thought people should respect the police despite their corrupt reputation, but Alene didn't agree.

"If Kofi Lloyd is in the café," Lee said, "you are lying to me. Is that what you're doing? Do you understand that two women were murdered?"

What happened to those women was awful, but what a jerk, she thought. The basement area is not part of the café, so she wasn't lying or obstructing anything. It was her right to leave at the end of the day. She'd say, if she had to testify in court, that Kofi had been brought into the café by Olly and was not one of her employees. Or maybe she was already coming down with the virus and she could say that her brain had been affected.

"Again, Kofi Lloyd doesn't work here," Alene said. It was hard to even be minimally polite to this guy, but nothing that she said wasn't technically true. She made a shooing-away gesture that provoked her when other people did it. "Now, if you'll excuse me," she added in a frosty tone to match his. The venomous look he gave her before walking away made her want to throw something at him, like that brick that had sailed through the café's window.

At least she knew her rights. She wouldn't have been so cocky had Lee not been so rude. Alene was grateful that Ruthie wasn't there to witness her behavior. She was ashamed of how she'd spoken to Frank's partner. One more thing to be ashamed of. She trudged toward the store feeling victorious but somewhat diminished.

Chapter 13

"Frank's partner just tried to scare the crap out of me," she told Olly, whispering into her cellphone. The sidewalk was empty, but just in case anyone was listening, she added, "If you happen to see our mutual colleague, could you please convey the message that Officer Lee Bautista wants to talk to him."

"What are you, a spy?" asked Olly. "Stop being suspicious of someone bugging your phone, Alene. Tell me what's going on. Who or what upset you?" She could hear Kofi say something in the background. She hoped Olly didn't say anything about being in the basement, finding jewelry, or stumbling across bodies. Just in case Lee was listening. Had she always been this distrustful?

"Turns out that someone was hovering outside the door," she said, "and I'm calling to suggest that you tell your friends to lock their bikes in safer locations." Frank would have recognized Kofi's bike locked up in front of the café, but Lee wasn't as thorough a detective, no matter what Frank said. Also, did the police have resources to waste money on searching for someone who was only a potential witness? Even if his picture had been in the paper, what had Kofi done except stumble across a body? There were evil people out there and plenty of unsolved murders to attend to. Not to mention bricks being thrown through the windows of people's businesses.

She didn't get a response, and asked, "Did you hear anything I just told you?"

"Yes, ma'am," said Olly. She could hear him whispering something unintelligible to Kofi. "And stop worrying about whatever it is, because I can move into your place and take care of your kids if you need me to. They love me."

Although that wasn't her current problem, it was true that the kids loved it when he babysat. He always brimmed with fun ideas, and she'd come home more than once to her children wearing makeup, dancing, or hunched over a table covered in cut-up magazines. It often involved a mess that she had to deal with. "Thanks, Olly, you're a good pal," she said. "I'm so grateful." Zuleyka, Kacey, and Jocelyn were also good babysitters, and they made sure Alene didn't come home to chaos, unlike Olly.

She walked quickly, and before going into the store, pulled on vinyl surgical gloves, grabbed a grocery cart, and wiped it down. She'd watched a medical news alert about protecting yourself by being extremely careful in the grocery store. Late afternoon was the worst time to shop—the stores were teeming with customers, she thought. She passed a neighbor from the sixth floor and a couple of longtime café customers, who greeted her warmly. She saw Peter and his sister in the peanut butter and jelly section, and waved, just in case they looked up, but they didn't. Taryn seemed extraordinarily patient. Even from all the way down the aisle, Alene could tell that she was explaining something, maybe telling Peter how peanut butter is made.

An hour later, Alene was back in her kitchen washing everything in the sink and wiping down the containers. She used a clean towel to dry and put everything away. Cal saw that she was jittery and asked if he could help, but she managed to blame her agitation on the brick that came through the window and mounting worries about the pandemic in general. Why should she give her father more cause for concern?

Alene made a salad, chopped and sauteed vegetables for the risotto, and set them aside. In the same pan, she heated olive oil, stirred in the rice, and slowly added cups of vegetable broth. Jocelyn called as she was stirring and asked, "Are we on for meeting your uncle at seven-thirty? It'll be too dark if we wait too long."

"Hope so," said Alene, "but I've told you about how uptight my dad has been. I'll call you if anything changes." She had to sign off when she saw an incoming call from Frank.

Frank's first words were, "My partner said you blew him off." He sounded more amused than upset, but he didn't sound warm.

"I'm sorry, Frank. I didn't mean to be rude," said Alene. She switched sides to stir the rice with her left hand. "How are you?"

"Nothing new," he said. "Meds helped and I'm better. What happened with Lee?""

"He doesn't like that he can't intimidate me," said Alene. "You do know that he can be a bully, right?"

Frank said, "So I've been told."

"I just told him we were closed, and I had to get to the grocery store. It was the truth. Can I call you back so we can talk after I drop off some vegetable risotto for you and Rhona?" Alene asked. "I don't want to come in and catch whatever it is you have."

"You're a sweetheart, but you don't have to bring food, Alene," said Frank. "I'm feeling better, and I don't have the virus."

"But you don't know for sure that Rhona's negative for it, Frank. Don't you think you should still quarantine?"

Frank said, "You're right as usual."

"It's going to be a drive-by delivery," she said, "so you won't see me." She set her cellphone down, tasted the risotto, and added a final shake of sea salt. Maybe he was still upset with her, so it was good that they weren't going to meet. But if Rhona had been exposed by her mystery man, she could still pass the virus to her father. Alene could have kicked herself for not thinking of that before now.

Cal said the risotto was the best he'd ever eaten, but he said that about everything, every time. Quinn said she loved how creamy it was. Sierra shrugged but kept eating. Noah picked out the mushrooms, as usual, but ate some of his salad and said he wished she'd make plain rice next time. At least they all got some nourishment, with minimal bickering.

"It's Sierra and Grandpa's turn to clean up," Alene announced after they'd finished eating. Quinn and Noah dumped their dishes in the sink and scampered out while Alene packed a container with food and a few other provisions that Frank would never think of requesting, like tissue and toilet paper.

She announced that she'd be back in twenty minutes, ran down to the garage, and drove over to leave the bags outside Frank's townhouse door in the Uptown neighborhood, about a ten-minute drive now that there was hardly any traffic. She called to tell him about the bags only after she was already back in the car, heading to Rhona's. He was grateful, and promised to use everything she'd brought, but he sounded distant, maybe from nerves, maybe because she'd ruined the relationship.

Driving home, after dropping a bag at Rhona's place, Alene listened to a newscaster announce another night of protests. Why were they so sure there was going to be more looting and violence? At the last second, she detoured to pass Benjie's burned-down building, feeling like she just had to see it again. The streets were mostly empty.

She passed it going slow, at ten miles per hour. Maybe the fire had been started by an owner of one of these beautiful old properties, who was upset about having an affordable housing project on the block. Some people didn't understand that those apartments were intended for regular people who had normal but necessary jobs like working in the shops, driving buses, or teaching preschool. They were just concerned about decreased real estate value, additional parking problems, and higher potential for crime.

Ruthie said that Benjie had been at a town hall meeting for the neighbors to weigh in before they started building in October. There'd been a lot of shouting. Some of the neighbors thought "affordable housing" meant busloads of drug dealers and violent criminals descending on the neighborhood. Benjie reminded them that they already had plenty of their own homegrown disreputable characters. He'd shown them a power-point and explained that his project was going to house people like caregivers, or elderly parents who couldn't afford expensive senior properties. Other organizations would provide social services to residents: exercise classes, after-school care for children, college prep evening sessions for teenagers.

Alene glanced at the buildings surrounding the burned property. Ruthie had told her that owners who lived near Benjie's affordable projects feared that their property values would go down, and their neighborhood would lose its desirability.

"Even though there's a moratorium on evictions right now, you can't argue with feelings," Ruthie had said. "In every fight about a property, it's often a few troublemakers trying to create a stink. It makes me sick when they try to drag Benjie's name through the mud."

Alene could hear that all the gossiping was tearing Ruthie apart. Benjie had been under pressure, and it had been giving him stomach problems even before the murders. Now that site didn't look like it would ever be a place where anyone would want to live.

Ruthie called as Alene pulled up to her own building. "How are you and what's going on?" she asked.

"Just dropped stuff off at both Frank's and Rhona's," said Alene. "I'm parking the car now and about to head to the elevator." She told Ruthie about Blanca being enraged that her two renters had stolen from her.

"Oy," Ruthie said. "What a shame."

It was nearing sundown on Friday afternoon, when Ruthie and her family usually started observing their day of rest. "Aren't you cutting it close by calling this late?" Alene asked as she turned off the car. "Is everything okay?" Ruthie would not have approved of how Alene had handled Lee's visit that afternoon, so it was better that she didn't have time to say anything about it.

"I've got over an hour until candle-lighting," said Ruthie, "and I wanted to tell you that we just learned something interesting. One of the neighbors who opposes Benjie's building has a police record for arson." She paused dramatically.

"Whoa," said Alene. "I wonder if Frank knows more than he's saying." She thanked Ruthie and wished her a good Sabbath the way Ruthie had taught her.

In the apartment, Cal and the two girls were sprawled on the couch, watching reruns of a show about school bullies. Quinn looked up and waved at Alene. "Does anyone remember when we used to go to school?"

Alene knew that it was a rhetorical question, but Sierra responded, "That was less than three months ago, Quinn." She'd been more combative than usual lately.

Alene decided not to respond. "It's after seven," she announced. "Are you all still planning to walk over to meet Uncle Finn with Grandpa and me?" She hoped the show they'd been watching had taught a lesson about how to be nicer, better people. Noah was sitting cross-legged under the dining room table, playing a video game he'd gotten from his father. She thought it was overly violent for a child, but Noah had told her that it was all pretend. He would never try to destroy enemy soldiers in real life.

Cal responded with a thumbs up. "I'm ready," he said.

"Shoes on, kids," said Alene. "And bring a sweater."

Alene called Frank while she waited. "My dad is going to meet Finn now," she said. "We're walking with him to the park. Did you and Rhona like the risotto??"

"Thanks for bringing all that dinner," he said. "I loved everything, but you know Rhona is beyond picky."

Alene said, "So you've told me." What if Sierra, who was already challenging, grew up to be that difficult? "On another note, Frank, I had a quick chat with Ruthie on the way home, and wanted to ask if those fires might have been started by people opposed to affordable housing? Could someone have purposely torched Benjie's building with the intention of slowing him down?"

"I guess we're talking about that again," Frank said with a loud, cranky sigh. "Anything is possible, Alene, but police work involves accumulating evidence, not just guessing likely scenarios. It looks like both women were murdered elsewhere. Their bodies were dumped on Benjie's properties that had burned down, but we don't know how many people were involved. There's a lot we don't know."

"I understand," said Alene. Was he getting annoyed that she wouldn't let it go? "Have they figured out if it was arson for either building? Ruthie told me about someone who's violently opposed to affordable housing and already has a conviction for arson. Don't you think he should be investigated?"

A moment passed before Frank said, "I promise we're looking into everything, Alene. You don't have to worry about it."

"I'm still concerned because of Kofi," she said, hurt that he was trying to placate her. "You didn't tell

Lee about Kofi seeing the body, did you? I love you and trust you, Frank, but I don't trust your partner."

Frank said, "I'm not sure I do either, Alene." She noticed that he didn't repeat that he loved her too. She'd screwed up. "But I'm still disappointed in you."

"I'm really, truly sorry, Frank." She knew she should stop talking, but that only lasted for a minute. "Can I ask you about the apartments on either side of the property—wasn't anyone looking out the window when the fire was started? And does anyone know how those women were murdered? If the first one was killed someplace else, how did someone sneak through a construction fence and deposit a body in the middle of the city, without anyone else seeing?"

"Alene, those are good questions, but again, this is not on your plate," Frank said in his gentle, soothing but still scratchy-sounding voice. Alene was way too stressed about everything—the fire, the dead women, the café, the pandemic, Uncle Finn, and even the ring Olly had found and lost. What if it had been stolen and somehow the café got involved in a lawsuit? What if there was a heap of jewelry hidden down there—was she responsible?

"But I can't stop myself from stewing," said Alene.

"It's not like you don't have anything else to worry about, Sweetheart," Frank said. She loved when he called her that—it was what her father used to call her mom. "But Alene, we need to talk some more about being honest with each other."

"I know," she said, feeling relieved that he wasn't going to break up with her over it. She was already so stressed. The pools and beach and parks were going to be closed, camp and summer school were canceled, and unless she was vigilant, they'd all end up sitting inside looking at screens all summer. "I'll call you back after we meet with my dad's brother."

She texted Jocelyn to say they were heading out, and Jocelyn said it would take her six minutes to run over. Then Alene texted Rhona with best wishes for her renewed health. Would they ever have a relationship?

Finally, Alene, her dad, and the kids made it out the door and down the elevator. There was a hazy light and clouds glided southward across the lake; she could feel a front moving in as they waited in the lobby for Jocelyn. Alene hoped the rain would hold off until later. It was Finn's last chance to meet with her dad. She was not going to keep making plans like this.

Jocelyn came bounding into the building's lobby after a few minutes and greeted everyone in her usual boisterous way. She hooked an arm through Cal's arm as they headed out the door. Cal told stories on the way, none of which were about Finn being a bank robber. That was a relief. Quinn and Noah stayed close enough to hear the stories, but Sierra dragged behind them all, focused on her phone. She'd wanted to stay home by herself, but Alene was troubled about all that time she was spending alone.

They hardly passed anyone on the way over, only a few dog walkers, but there were people hitting balls at the driving range—everything else was closed and it was one of the few activities anyone could do on the lakefront. Maybe the park district allowed it to continue because after waiting six feet apart on the sidewalk, each golfer was alone in his or her booth with a bucket and a couple of golf clubs.

"There's someone sitting on the concrete bench on the other side of the driving range," Jocelyn said, squinting as they got closer to the community garden. "I assume Finn is an old guy with silver hair and ears that stick out, kind of like yours, Cal."

"He was the good-looking one," said Cal, "and I was the smart one." Noah and Quinn had plunged into the bushes lining the driving range fence and were searching for stray golf balls. There were signs warning about the golf balls and Alene fretted about someone getting bonked in the head.

"It's too far for me to see details from here," said Alene, "but I'll know him when I see him." The previous summer, the lawn surrounding the restaurant just past the driving range had been dotted with Adirondack chairs. Families, couples, and groups of friends would sit outside on warm summer nights, sipping beer and enjoying the soft breeze. Now, the lawn was empty.

"I bet he looks like our father did at that age," said Cal. They'd started to walk past the hospital on the other side of the street. "St. Darius must be hemorrhaging money," he added as an aside. "Hospitals aren't doing any elective surgeries. Too bad for you if you need a tumor removed and too bad for them because that's where the big money is."

"I don't think the coronavirus has been a positive experience for anyone," said Alene.

Jocelyn stopped moving and held out an arm to stop Alene. "Two people just approached the older guy I thought was your brother, Cal," she said in a clipped voice. "One is hunched over and sitting in a wheelchair and the other is standing with the posture of a younger person. Did Finn say he was bringing some friends along?"

"No," Alene answered. "It was just supposed to be him."

Cal said, "I don't think Finn knows anyone else in Chicago. It's hard to keep friends when you disappear for two decades, so it might be someone asking him for the time."

"That's not a thing people do anymore, Dad," said Alene. "Everyone has cellphones. But Jocelyn is right. I can see a white-haired old guy in the wheelchair and the other one is standing to the side."

"I can't even see a bench," said Cal.

"Now the two of them are right in front of Finn," Jocelyn said, "and he's turned to face them. The wheelchair guy just stood up and is waving a stick in the air." She tried to hustle Cal along, her arm entwined with his.

"My guess is that lots of people have a reason to yell at him," said Cal.

"It's not a stick, it's a cane," said Jocelyn. "He leaned on it to get closer to Finn, but now he's smashing it on Finn's shoulder." Jocelyn signaled a halt to Alene. "The old guy just hit Finn again, and Finn collapsed on the bench. The old guy lowered his cane to the ground and now he's walking away. I don't want to leave you, Cal, but I should try to catch them. Can you walk the rest of the way?"

Cal refused to move. "I don't think you should get anywhere near them—you have no idea who they are or what they're capable of," he said. "Why should any of us put ourselves in danger just because of Finn? This is how it always was when he was around."

Alene stood frozen as they watched Finn crumple to the ground. "Are you saying that you want us all to watch your brother get pummeled, and not do something about it, Dad?"

"What is there to do? Anyway, I'm doing something about it," Cal said. "I'm hoping he isn't hurt too badly."

Alene didn't know how to respond so she turned to Jocelyn. "I'll walk with my dad if you want to run over there. Just don't get too close."

Jocelyn said, "They're already getting in their van so all I can do is memorize their license plate." And she was off.

Quinn and Noah saw Jocelyn sprint away and asked what was going on. Alene whispered that she'd pay them a dollar for each ball they found, so they got busy looking. Sierra was sitting cross-legged on one of the wood benches lining the path, totally immersed in her phone. There was nobody nearby to notice the white van speeding off or the moaning heap that was Finn Baron. It had taken less than three minutes. "I'm running over there, Dad," said Alene. "I'll see you in a minute. Don't rush."

She reached the bench in time to hear Finn wince as Jocelyn tried to make him more comfortable on the cement bench by bunching her sweater under his head. Alene touched him lightly on the arm and turned to see Cal still making his way over.

"It's Alene," she said to Finn, "Cal's daughter. We saw you get walloped from across the park, and we're sorry we couldn't get here in time to stop it. Can you talk?"

Finn opened his eyes and gazed at her with a confused expression, "No police," he whispered. His breathing was jagged, and the words came in spurts. "Cal?" he asked.

"I'm here, Finn," Cal said, stepping forward with a resigned sigh. "What'd you get yourself into now?"

All three kids were suddenly paying attention. It might have been the most exciting but appalling thing they'd ever seen. "Is that Uncle Finn, Mom? Did those two guys just try to beat up Grandpa's brother?" Quinn asked. Cal had been telling stories about Uncle Finn for a long time.

"Did you recognize those people who hurt you, Finn?" Jocelyn asked. It was the right question because it would be different if they'd randomly attacked him, but random attackers were rarely old guys who carried canes or got pushed in wheelchairs.

Finn moved his head, almost like a nod. "It's a long story," he said, his voice weak. "And I don't have much time to tell it."

Chapter 14

"It's always something with Finn," Cal said to Alene and Jocelyn. He turned to look at his brother and shook his head, oozing disapproval. "He's probably used to dealing with violent people who lose their patience with him."

"He's hurt, Dad," Alene said. She put her hand on Finn's forehead, hoping her touch comforted him. She didn't think of her father as heartless, but he was doing a solid job of acting like it. Finn took gulps of air. "Why did that guy hit you with his cane?" Alene asked. "Are you sure you don't want me to call the police, Uncle Finn?"

"I don't see any blood," said Cal, skeptical, as if it had been a performance and not a serious attack.

Jocelyn was on high alert, her eyes darting to all sides, scanning for enemy combatants even though she'd done coding in the navy and had never fought.

"That was horrifying to watch," she said, linking arms with Cal.

"Can you move, Finn?" Alene asked. "Do you need help getting up?" She studied his face for a reply, and when none came, added, "We should take you to the emergency room in case there's any internal damage." They didn't need to call an ambulance when they were this close to the hospital.

Finn wasn't moving, but they could hear him breathing hard. After a few minutes, he was able to speak a few words at a time. "I don't think ... they'll come back again," he said, his voice slurring. "They made ... their point."

"So, what was their point?" Cal asked. As soon as Jocelyn let go of his arm, he'd sat on the concrete bench perpendicular to where his brother was lying. "Something about not stealing?"

"Dad," said Alene, gritting her teeth. "Now's not the time."

Jocelyn introduced herself and said, "Sorry we didn't get here in time to stop them from hurting you, Finn."

Cal had lost any glimmer of patience. "So, are you going to tell us what you did that made those jokers beat you up? You're not making a great impression on my daughter and her children so far, Finn."

Alene turned to him. "Really, Dad? Can you give it a break?" She'd never seen him so unsympathetic, almost callous.

"That was Don Klavestedberg," Finn said, each syllable sounding labored. His eyes were closed, and

216

he was pressing a hand to his stomach. What kind of person would batter a frail, old man? "He waited years. To beat me up."

"That was Don Klavestedberg in the wheelchair?" asked Cal, "He was part of your gang, wasn't he? We're not going anywhere with you, Finn, and there's no 'we.' You can't come waltzing back into my life and think you're going to get my family involved in one of your nebulous schemes."

"I didn't mean ... for any of it ... to happen," said Finn. He was so quiet it was hard to make out what he was mumbling. "I explained ... in my letter. Edith ... was going ... to give it to you ... yesterday."

"I didn't get any letters from you, Finn," Cal said. "How about you, Alene?" She'd been checking on Quinn and Noah but turned back to shake her head. It was just like Edith to forget to pass along something important. "So much for your claim about sending me anything," he added.

"I wanted to email ... but didn't know ... anyone's address," said Finn.

"Why did Don whatever-his-name-is hit you with his cane?" Jocelyn asked. "It sounded painful. And who was the other person?"

When Finn didn't answer, Cal said, "I only know that Don was the genius who planned Finn's brilliant bank robbery. It's astounding that he's still alive, but my guess is that he refuses to die until he gets his money back."

Finn said, "I was going to give him money, and ... also I have something ... for you."

Alene saw the lines in her father's brow—he looked dismayed. "Well, thanks for the thought," Cal said. "Alene told me you didn't use stolen money to buy whatever it is, and thanks by the way for verifying that you stole that money, but truthfully, Finn, I don't want or need anything from you."

"I know," said Finn, his eyes still closed. After a moment, Alene thought he might have fallen asleep, until he jerked and moaned.

"Can we take you to the hospital now, Finn?" Alene asked. He didn't respond.

Jocelyn said, "I'll carry him over. He looks feather light."

Alene held up a hand to stop her. "I thought you're not supposed to move someone if you don't know what their injuries are."

"I'm assessing that now," said Jocelyn as she gently checked his pulse and moved his limbs. "I've had paramedic training Alene, and it doesn't seem like his neck or back were involved in that beating, but his pulse is racing, and his skin is cold. I'm afraid he's going into shock. He needs to get to the hospital now."

"It doesn't matter," said Sierra, upon being told about the detour. She was hunching over her phone. "It's not like I have any plans for tonight." Alene would have to call the pediatrician and ask for some suggestions regarding Sierra's growing depression.

"Uncle Finn needs to get to the hospital, Sierra," she said, "and afterwards, we'll head home." It wasn't as if being at home was going to make her any happier.

Cal's mouth was set in a determined frown, and he kept glancing at Finn, shaking his head with disapproval. "I wanted him to acknowledge that he let us all down. And to know what he did, aside from stealing all that loot, to earn a beating from Don Klavestedberg, that scumbag," said Cal. He looked impatiently at his brother. "You never paid attention when our parents said, 'You reap what you sow,' did you, Finn?"

Shadows were starting to fall now that the sun had descended behind one of the buildings across the street. "It's ... complicated," Finn said as Jocelyn carefully lifted him.

"Are you comfortable?" Jocelyn asked. "You hardly weigh anything."

Finn squinted at her and said, "I'm fine." He turned his head, looking for his brother. "Have some pity, Cal." Jocelyn carried him without breaking a sweat.

They followed Jocelyn across the street. "Last thing he gave me was, I don't know, sometime in the previous century," Cal told Alene, his arm entwined again with hers. "One time he replaced a light fixture in one of our bathrooms. Your mom asked him if he'd do it because she didn't trust me. As if it was such a production to replace a light fixture."

Cal groused when he was agitated. The hospital was just a few hundred feet away, but Jocelyn walked slowly so Finn wouldn't be jostled. Alene thought that at this rate it would take half an hour to get to the emergency entrance. When they got to the revolving doors, Cal said, "Jocelyn can bring him in while the rest of us go home. The mosquitos are out, as I predicted."

Jocelyn said, "I'll catch up with you later."

"Thank you, Alene," said Finn. He looked shrunken in Jocelyn's arms.

Alene and Cal started the walk home. Behind them, Quinn and Noah tried to push each other off the path onto the grass, giggling. Alene told them to stop because pushing often ended in tears. Sierra slumped farther back. "What do you think he wants to give you?" Alene asked her father.

"Who knows," said Cal. "He was a cheapskate, so it's either an old set of tools, or a second-hand minivan that needs new brakes."

"You've never had trouble making your disapproval clear," said Alene.

They'd walked past the hospital's parking garage when Jocelyn came running up from behind. "Only patients are allowed into the hospital," she said. "Before I left, your brother started babbling about cryptocurrency, Cal. He wanted me to tell you that he made a fortune."

"He always loved talking about making fortunes," said Cal, slapping a mosquito on his arm. "I bet they let old Don Klavestedberg out of prison because of the pandemic. You can see what he learned in there by the way he behaved this evening."

Jocelyn fell into stride with Alene and Cal. "I was nervous that they wouldn't let Finn into the emergency department without documents," she said, "but it turned out that he had his Medicare card and identification ready to go. I was relieved."

Cal interjected, "It was probably fake."

Jocelyn said, "I don't think it was, Cal. He wanted me to tell you he's giving you a motorhome. That's the gift. He said he bought it fair and square with his crypto earnings and hopes you're going to love it. It's all in the letter."

"Ah, the mythical letter," said Cal, slowing down even more. "And I don't even know what *'crypto earnings'* means."

Jocelyn hoisted Noah on her back. He'd gotten heftier over the year and wasn't the little sprite she might have remembered carrying. Alene said, "It could have been his own money, Dad. He told me that he bought Bitcoin in 2013 before it shot up through the ceiling."

Cal said, "That's about when they started buying and selling it." She heard a hint of acceptance. The streetlights turned on now that the sky was getting darker.

They were nearly at their building, but Quinn and Sierra were lagging, and Alene turned to urge them on.

"Maybe that's what he meant about making a fortune," said Jocelyn. "Why are you upset, Cal? Do you have something against the free market?" She loved ribbing him.

"No, but did his initial investment capital come out of thin air?" Cal turned to Jocelyn, swept his arm in the air in a gesture that meant he didn't want to talk about it.

"I guess my dad didn't tell you why his brother got sent to prison," said Alene. Quinn had caught up and was holding Alene's hand. Sierra was still behind, but they were all walking up the building's driveway.

Jocelyn said, "No, I've heard about the great bank robbery, but I'm more interested in the motorhome Finn mentioned."

"If it really exists," Cal muttered. "I'll believe it when I see it."

Quinn said, "I think that's the same as an RV, right, Grandpa?"

Noah was still on Jocelyn's shoulders. "I love RVs," he said. "We should take a vacation in one, Mom. But why are we talking about RVs?"

"I'm not completely sure, Noah," Cal said, "but I think Uncle Finn has one."

Sierra had caught up and weighed in about RVs. "It's probably old and smelly if he's been living in it," she said. "I only want to be in a new one that nobody else used before."

Alene flashed first her daughter and then her father disapproving looks as she helped Noah climb down off Jocelyn's back. She took her dad's arm and motioned the kids to go inside. Cal nodded at Jocelyn. "Thanks for helping us this evening, J," he said. "You're a good friend."

Alene also thanked Jocelyn. "Are you kidding?" Jocelyn said, giving Alene a quick hug. "I'm here for you. I love you guys."

Jocelyn ran off—she'd been staying in the back of her Krav Maga studio, which happened to be next door to Alene's café. Cal needed to sit down for a moment, so they stopped in the lobby. "If there is a motorhome," he said, "Galena, Illinois is one of the places I'd love to visit. No need to look for hotels and interact with other people during this pandemic. I'd also be interested in seeing a few national parks."

"So, you'd accept a gift from Finn if it was something you wanted?" asked Alene, not that surprised. Her father had always been filled with contradictions. "Lots of possibilities with a motorhome, right, Dad?"

"It's something to think about," Cal said, stroking his chin to prove that he was thinking. The children were already calling an elevator. "But if he has the motorhome here in Chicago, where did he park it? And who's going to pay that parking ticket?"

"Just like you to focus on that, Dad," said Alene.

She got everyone in the elevator and then into the apartment. The kids took turns showering and went to bed. Later, when she was in her pajamas and about to start reading, she called Frank to tell him what happened. "Should we have called the police? I mean, we were too far away to see exactly what happened, and he asked us not to."

"Alene honey," he said tenderly, "you respected your uncle's wishes."

"I suppose," she said. "But what about my wishes? I wish you'd come over."

"I'd love to," he said, "but I'm not leaving my apartment until I'm certain that Rhona didn't give me Covid."

"Wait, did she test positive?"

"She hasn't come home yet," he sighed, "so I have no idea."

At least he didn't say anything about their relationship and how Alene had disappointed him. And she was getting sick of hearing about Rhona's kookiness. He should force her to get tested or move out. As soon as Alene said goodnight to Frank, she called the hospital. She explained her connection to Finn, that she and her father were his only family. He'd been admitted, a man with a deep bass voice told her. She left her cellphone number as next of kin, and the man said they were short-staffed and weren't allowing visitors. Someone would call the next day if they found the time.

Chapter 15

Alene rose early Saturday morning, shuffled into the kitchen, and studied the refrigerator for a moment before deciding to make sweet potato waffles with ricotta and blueberries. Ruthie had inspired her to keep baked sweet potatoes on hand, always ready to slip into salads, stir-fries, and desserts. It was too early to call the hospital, but she made a note to call in a few hours—hopefully, Finn had come away bruised but not broken.

Before starting the recipe, she checked the café schedule and texted Rashid and Estrella to confirm that they were opening at six. Kacey and LaTonya were scheduled to get there by seven, and the four of them would handle all the baking and food prep before orders started to come in. Ruthie was always off on Saturdays, so Alene couldn't take the entire day off, but she'd go in later, after Neal picked up the children. The day always got off to a better start when they were ready for him and waiting outside.

Alene made a pot of coffee and texted Frank, who called back within moments. He felt marginally improved, he said, and it was still just a cold. Rhona had come home late again, and he hadn't slept well. Alene scraped bean paste from a vanilla pod and told him about how her uncle, the same one who'd been beaten the previous evening in the park, had driven the getaway car for a bank robbery thirty years before.

"I've heard a million stories about the robbery, but last night was the first time I'd ever seen one of Finn's co-conspirators," she said. "And that guy at the park was supposedly the ringleader."

"Why did you agree to meet Cal's brother in the park at night?" Frank asked. "That's never a good idea. Haven't you ever watched a crime film?"

She measured the dry ingredients and stirred them in a large glass bowl. "It was more like late afternoon, Frank. I told you that Jocelyn was coming along to help the kids and me accompany my dad to meet his brother. We certainly didn't expect Uncle Finn to get attacked."

"It must have been horrifying," Frank said.

"Yeah, it was." Alene shuddered as she added wet ingredients to the flour mixture. Sometimes all she needed was a little empathy.

"My dad thought that the old guy got out of prison early because of the pandemic. I couldn't believe that he attacked my uncle. My dad also said that Finn must have done something to deserve it."

Frank said, "It's not okay to beat someone with a weapon of any kind, Alene."

"I know," said Alene.

"The guy with the cane is still out there," said Frank. "You need to be vigilant until we pick him up."

"If I see someone following me in a wheelchair," Alene said with a giggle, "I'll run faster."

"I'm not joking," he said.

"You're not going to believe everything that's happened," Alene said later after she'd gone across the hall and Kacey pulled the door open. After telling Kacey about her uncle getting clobbered, she admitted that she told Frank about Kofi. "I think our relationship depends on me never keeping another secret from him," she said. "I don't know why I do things like that, when I know they're wrong."

"It's partly my fault," said Kacey.

Alene said, "No, this is on me."

"But I'm sorry I made you promise, Alene. Anyway, Kofi's not here. He went home." Kacey's hair was a mess, she hadn't put on her glasses, and she wore fuzzy socks and an old t-shirt from a 1972 Jethro Tull concert that must have been her father's. It was recognizable because Alene's mother's record collection, which Alene had kept, included two Jethro Tull albums. "I thought he might have told you he was leaving town," Kacey added.

"By home, do you mean where he grew up?" Alene asked, stepping inside. "Running away is about the worst thing he could have done, Kacey."

"He didn't think he was running away," said Kacey. "He was just going back to Galesburg. You know his cousin Umar, the one who lets him use the truck? That's who drove. They both grew up around there."

"Right, somewhere near where my father lived." Kofi had said Galesburg had changed quite a bit since Cal was a kid back in the fifties. "So, Kofi's with his family now?"

"I'm waiting for a text to let me know exactly where he is," said Kacey. "They were going to stop somewhere for breakfast on the way."

Alene said, "Keep me posted, okay?" She went back across the hall. Noah was up, heading to the television to watch cartoons. She was surprised to see that he was already wearing his bathing suit and a t-shirt.

"When's Dad coming to pick us up?" asked Noah.

Alene said, "Good morning, my love. I think he's coming at about nine-thirty, but it looks like you're ready to go jump into Grandma's pool right now." She gave him a hug and kissed the top of his head.

"I am," said Noah, already staring at pictures on the screen. "But I'm hungry."

Alene returned to the kitchen, turned on the electric waffle pan, and texted Kofi to tell him that Lee Bautista was looking for him. He was a grown man and didn't need her input about his decisions, but Kacey was fragile. Last thing she needed was to have Kofi accused of murder just because he'd been in the wrong place at the wrong time. Kofi didn't answer and she left a message.

Next, she texted Olly, who called back immediately. She'd thought he'd still be sleeping before eight on a Saturday morning, but where was there to go on Friday nights these days?

"Kofi's planning to hang out with his cousins," Olly said, longingly. "Wish I had someplace else to go and a bunch of cousins to hang out with outside. They're probably going fishing and building bonfires."

"He's not at camp, Olly," said Alene. "And we'd all love to go fishing and build bonfires but running away makes Kofi look guilty of something."

Olly responded, "We're all guilty of something in life." Just like him to get philosophical.

Alene was still baking a batch of waffles when Cal came into the kitchen, whistling as he poured himself a cup of coffee. Maybe that walk last night had been good for him, despite his brother being attacked and taken to the hospital. He didn't appear to be troubled, except that he started in on Finn stories as soon as Noah, Quinn, and Sierra straggled to the table.

"Did I ever tell you about the time I helped Uncle Finn deliver twin calves?" Cal asked. It was as if he were talking about a mythical character, and not the brother whose actions had been a source of embarrassment for years. The same brother who was now in the hospital after being battered with a cane.

Sierra glanced at her sister. "Why aren't you wearing a bathing suit, Quinn?" she asked. "Dad's picking us up to go to Grandma's in like an hour."

Quinn said, "I forgot."

"You can change later. Sit down and eat now," said Alene, plopping two waffles on each plate. She poured glasses of cold oat milk and made sure nobody drowned their waffles in syrup. Why had her father started changing his stories? When he used to reminisce about his childhood to her and Lydia, he'd been the leader in all the adventures. He'd saved people from floods, found lost animals, and confronted villains, with help from his older brother. When had he become Finn's sidekick? Quinn had recently noted that his name sounded like Huck Finn, which Cal had insisted on reading out loud to the kids when he learned that it wasn't being taught in school anymore.

"Tell the one about Finn stopping the robbers," said Noah. He was busy making sure that every bite of waffle included a blueberry. Alene suspected that was what her dad wished had happened, instead of Finn driving the getaway car for a bank robbery.

Cal said Finn was the one who'd stopped communicating, but Alene thought that people, even siblings, sometimes moved apart for any number of reasons. Until he got sent to prison, Finn had lived his whole life in the house where he and Cal grew up, except for that one time when he was running away or in prison. He'd somehow gotten out of the army because of his flat feet, but Cal thought he'd have been better off fighting in Vietnam than sitting around Galesburg with his low-life friends.

At least it was the weekend, and the kids would have a fabulous time at their grandmother's pool. Maybe they'd play tennis afterwards, or pickle ball. This was the end of what had turned into a rotten school year. Alene thought the kids hadn't learned a great deal since the pandemic forced them to stay home, bickering over whose turn it was to use the computer. She'd asked Neal to split the cost of two more laptops, so each of his children would have one for school, but he'd whined about business being slow because nobody was buying cars. As usual, Cal had stepped up and bought the new laptops.

The house phone rang then, and Quinn jumped to answer it. The contrast between her cheerful greeting to her father, and the look on her face when she handed the receiver to Alene, was striking. Alene knew immediately that Neal was calling to cancel on the kids again. "They've been looking forward to seeing you and your mom for two weeks," Alene told her ex-husband. "What's your excuse this time?"

Mitzi had caught the virus. Alene hung up on Neal feeling guilty for assuming the worst. She called his mother, who answered with a cough, and apologized.

"I hope it's going to be a mild case," said Mitzi. She had a terrible headache though, and Alene's stomach flipped. The virus could be vicious for older people. Alene promised to drop off soup later. Mitzi had always been a wonderful, supportive mother-in-law.

Cal, as usual, came up with a plan before the kids had a chance to start whining about their canceled plans. "How about a treasure hunt?" he asked. "It involves searching for hidden notes here in the building." The younger two looked interested. "Sierra's job will be to put the clues in the correct places, which means she'll have to be up and down on the elevators to set things up." Sierra had always loved riding the elevators. She'd been miserable about being stuck at home with nowhere to go. It was torture for a seventh grader. Alene remembered how vital her own friends had been in middle school, and how crucial it had been to see them every day.

"They're going to have to solve some math problems to decipher which floor to go to, and they'll need to look up some history to work out a few apartment numbers," Cal whispered to Alene. "Did you know that we have neighbors with names like Jefferson and Clinton? I've been planning this treasure hunt for a rainy day. I even have some questions about presidents ready."

Alene didn't know how she'd have survived the pandemic without her father. For the next twenty minutes she helped him set up his game, and then glanced at her watch. "Let's talk about Uncle Finn before I leave for work, Dad," she said. "You can probably reach him by about nine."

"He's probably fine. I bet he pretended to be unable to walk so Jocelyn had to carry him," said Cal. "Or he might have staged the whole event to have a place to sleep last night."

Alene gave him a look. "So, he got himself beaten half to death for a bed?" It wasn't worth arguing with her father when his mind was made up. She made sure the kids cleared the table, then she cleaned up breakfast, got ready, and left for work. On the way to the café, she walked under newly green trees, past mounds of purple phlox. The sun was weak, but it was doing its job, starting to warm things up.

"You're earlier than I thought you'd be," Kacey said when Alene walked in. She was in the middle of baking a cake. "Did Neal get the kids this time?"

"Guess," said Alene, shaking her head. "Not his fault though, because his mom has Covid."

"Oh, I'm sorry," Kacey said. In her case it had been her mother who hadn't been available after her parents divorced. Kacey had suffered through some rough years. "Everything is quiet here, but Olly's feeling sorry for himself because Kofi isn't here to entertain him." That sounded on brand to Alene. "Also, what are we going to tell Frank's partner if he shows up again looking for Kofi?"

Alene put her purse in her office and grabbed a clean apron. It was always a surprise when Kacey was talkative.

"We'll tell him what we know," said Alene, "which is that Kofi went home and that he has his cellphone with him."

"What if he asks for an address? I don't know where Kofi's staying," Kacey stopped measuring ingredients to push her glasses up with the back of her hand.

"Ask him next time you talk," said Alene. She took out her phone and showed Kacey the picture of Kofi searching through the rubble. It might have been taken just before he found the body. "This is the picture Frank's partner has."

"That could be anyone," Kacey whispered, squinting. "We only know it's Kofi because we were there."

Alene tried to sound like it didn't worry her, but she was shaken. "I wish it was that simple, Kacey," she said softly. She focused on adding flax meal, salt, and monkfruit sugar to the bowl. Estrella heated a pot of chocolate on the stove and Alene inhaled the swirling kitchen scents as she checked Ruthie's list.

LaTonya, who was kneading bread dough, said, "Hey, Alene, you know that tall, skinny guy who only tips a dollar?"

"That's the guy who presses his face against the window and stands there waving," Rashid said. He was chopping carrots so quickly that it looked dangerous. Alene could see the onions he'd caramelized cooling in a separate bowl.

"He's always holding hands with a blond woman," said LaTonya, "and Dori always talks to them."

"How do you know this?" Alene asked. "Are you out in the café instead of working here in the kitchen when the guy comes by with his sister?" They all focused on work for the next few minutes, trying to avoid eye contact. Alene added, "That's Peter and Taryn Berg. She holds his hand so that he doesn't wander off, and I think Dori is being friendly to customers, the way all my employees should act."

"He looks like a grown man," said Rashid. "Why would he wander off?"

"Because he's a kind-hearted guy but he doesn't function at his chronological age level," Alene answered. She always tried to enunciate to make it easier for Rashid. "We all have our limitations, right? Why do you ask, LaTonya? Remember Ruthie's rule about not gossiping in a sacred space like this kitchen?"

LaTonya said, "I only gossip on Ruthie's days off."

"Let's talk about something else," said Alene. She hadn't yet checked the schedule or task list.

Estrella, who continued stirring the chocolate, said, "What about the border situation?" She didn't often contribute to the conversation, but she was passionate about immigration. "Let's talk about that."

"I've seen Peter and Taryn a couple of times, and Peter reminds me of my stepbrother," said Kacey as she transferred batter into a muffin pan. "But Sandy can't have a conversation or go to a café by himself. Peter can probably even order on his own."

"I didn't realize he was intellectually challenged," said LaTonya, still kneading dough. "I don't know if being smarter leads to being nicer or better in any way. I know smart people who never help anyone, and not-so-smart people who are kind and generous."

Alene thought that there was often a temptation to hold forth while kneading dough because you could smack it down on the table to emphasize a point. "I like when we discuss why people do what they do," said Alene, "but I'm starting to feel the same way Ruthie does about gossip. It's boring."

Ruthie had left instructions for making vegan cannoli. Alene wasn't even strictly vegetarian, let alone vegan, but even she had been upset to learn that most cannoli were fried in lard. She thought Ruthie must be rubbing off on her after all these years.

"And none of this gossip matters in the grand scheme of things," Alene said. She'd taken out a bowl and began stirring dry ingredients together. After she added oil and water and kneaded it, the dough would need half an hour to rest before she divided it into balls, each of which she'd roll into the familiar tube shape of a cannoli.

"I was asking about Peter because he seems like a nice guy, but I think the sister looks at people to assess what she can get out of them," said LaTonya. She'd finished preparing the bread loaves and moved onto helping finish the vegetables. "I can always tell. That woman has privilege written all over her face, am I right?" She glanced sideways at Alene, who, on several occasions, had gently requested avoiding "us-against-them" conversations in the kitchen.

While Rashid chopped the parsnips, LaTonya worked the mandoline to make paper-thin slices of sweet potato. They'd be used in several ways; oven fried, baked into savory pies, or roasted in oval ramekins.

"Zuleyka texted me," said Kacey, looking up from her phone, her eyes wide. "She's got Covid."

Alene felt woozy. "Poor Zuleyka," she said. "She's on the schedule all this week. Can anyone take her place?"

"I can come in every day if necessary, and I'll find out what she needs and drop it off for her tonight," said LaTonya as she covered the mound of sliced sweet potatoes and rinsed the mandoline. "I feel so bad. She's one of my favorite people."

"I like her a lot too," said Rashid. Everyone turned to stare at him, and he quickly looked down at the floor, embarrassed. Alene thought they were both adorable but hadn't noticed that Rashid had a crush on her until that moment. "And I'm available to pitch in," he added.

"You know how Alene's dad used to come in with his caregiver before the pandemic?" LaTonya asked. They'd all stopped working and stood for a moment, absorbing the news that someone they worked with had caught the virus. "Blanca, right?"

Alene said, "Yes, Blanca is his caregiver."

"Remember how hilarious it was when she tried to talk to Zuleyka?" LaTonya laughed. "They couldn't understand each other's accents."

"Zuleyka doesn't think she has an accent," said Kacey.

"Blanca doesn't either," said Alene. She covered the dough with a cloth and set it aside while explaining that Blanca had rented out her extra bedroom to two men who stole her money and jewelry after giving her the virus. "Now she's home from the hospital and planning revenge," Alene added.

"I love revenge," said LaTonya. "What's she planning to do?"

"Why, LaTonya?" asked Rashid. "Are you asking for a friend?" They all laughed.

"I don't know," said Alene. It was eerie not to be able to communicate with a smile because half their faces were covered. Hopefully, scientists would quickly find a cure and the pandemic would end. "We can only hope that whatever Blanca is planning is legal."

Olly popped up at the kitchen door, the way he sometimes did. "Did I miss anything?" he asked. "Also, I'm starving to death."

"Zuleyka has Covid," said Alene as she prepared to stuff filling into rolls of dough. He'd been alone in the basement, and Alene couldn't blame him for wanting company. "So, we're all kind of freaked out."

Dori and Edith came in through the kitchen door one after the other, and pulled clean aprons off one of the hooks, even though they were handling orders and wouldn't be working in the kitchen. Everyone said a subdued hello, but only Dori responded. Edith was busy adjusting her sweater.

Olly leaned against a wall in the kitchen, gobbling a tahini cookie. "Seriously, Olly," Kacey said, "we've got enough to worry about. You knew that Kofi was going to leave town, didn't you? You could have warned me."

Olly didn't seem in a rush to leave the kitchen. "He's justifiably scared—he's afraid he'll be accused of arson, murder, and every other unsolved crime in Chicago," said Olly. "And why are they so focused on him? I know they identified the prostitute from her fingerprints, so why are they taking so long with the first victim? They should focus on that."

"Her name was Juana Clemente," said Kacey. "Don't call her a prostitute, Olly."

Olly rolled his eyes. "That's what she did for a living. I'm not judging her."

Alene said, "All I know is that if Lee Bautista shows up again asking for Kofi, I'm not going to lie."

"Just saying you don't have to volunteer information," Olly said before skulking out to the café.

Alene took a break in her office. She checked in with her father and learned that he hadn't yet called the hospital. "Send my regards to Uncle Finn when you do, Dad," she said. She switched to a Kenny Chesney soundtrack before heading back to the kitchen, where she spent the next forty minutes filling the cannoli and imagining a road trip out west with Frank and the kids. Maybe they'd hike the Grand Canyon or visit a couple of national parks. Most of the parks had closed because of the pandemic but they wouldn't stay closed forever.

Twenty minutes later, Olly came and asked her to follow him down to the basement. She was eager to see what Olly and Kofi had accomplished. "If you fall, you'll knock me out too, so please go slowly," Olly said as he led her down the rickety stairs. He got to the bottom and pulled another mask from his pocket. "Also, add this on top of yours because until we get an air filtration system going, it's going to be musty down here."

"How about fixing the banister so it doesn't wobble?" she asked." He'd set up a few lights and the broken furniture and piles of newspapers were gone. There were eight small tables, but they'd been pushed up against the walls. Some had chairs on top, upside down as if they'd put them there to wash the floors. Alene looked around the room, noting the raised alcove, visible from every corner of the room, where the band might have performed. The bar was at most eight feet, but the long space behind it might have had room for two or three bartenders.

"It must have been a gold mine when they packed sixty–seventy people in this space each night," Olly said.

It was hard to imagine. "It looks cleaner down here. You got rid of all those newspaper piles," she said.

"Lots of garbage bags had to be sacrificed," said Olly.

"But I don't see any pipes or a sink," said Alene. "How'd they wash their glassware?" Olly laughed about how on brand it was for her to worry about cleanliness and showed her the water hookup and drain a few feet to the left of the bar. "They used one bucket with soapy water to dip the glassware and another with clean water for rinsing," he said.

"I'd rather have gone without drinking for a decade," Alene admitted.

240

"More than a decade," said Olly, gesturing for Alene to follow him. "It went from 1920 to 1933, and most people stopped using these hidden bars the minute the Eighteenth Amendment was over turned."

Alene noticed nails on the walls that might have held pictures. "I think Kacey's dad bought this building from his friend Dennis, and it might have Dennis' grandparents who converted the place into a speakeasy."

As she followed Olly past the bar, he pointed out several doors. "We think they must have rented these small rooms out by the hour, if you get my drift." He made a show of winking.

"I know what that means, Olly," said Alene. He showed her the door to the tunnel he'd predicted earlier. It had once gone directly to the building next door, where Jocelyn now had her Krav Maga studio, and had been filled in at some point. Back in the 1920s, those who escaped a raid by the Prohibition police might have been able to lie low for a bit before later ambling away at their leisure.

Next, Olly led Alene into one of the bedrooms, where there was a small cot dwarfed by a chest of drawers. He pulled out a few of the drawers, pointed at the collection of tins, and said, "It's like they're having babies and multiplying."

The drawers were packed with tins. Alene reached for a red-and-blue striped tin with an intricate flower painted on each of the four sides. She turned it over, wishing she'd thought to wipe it down before she touched it. Olly plucked another one from

241

the drawer. "I randomly opened this one a while ago and look what I found." He stuck his hand in and pulled out what looked like another ring.

"Oh," she said, taking it from Olly and looking more closely at it. "I don't remember it being so sparkly – did you polish it?"

"No, this is a different ring," Olly said. "I'm sure that one'll turn up."

Alene continued to inspect the second ring. It was white gold with filigree on the band and tiny diamond chips surrounding a round, multi-faceted diamond. Lovely, but why wasn't it dirty and dulled by a century in a drawer? "I still like square diamonds better. How much jewelry have you found down here and what do you think was going on?" she asked.

"My first thought," said Olly, retrieving the ring Alene had been holding, "was that customers at this speakeasy walked out lighter than when they entered. Someone was lifting their jewelry back in the 1920s."

"It sounds plausible," Alene said, blinking in the dusty air. She considered all those drunken customers—they would have been easy targets for an unscrupulous employee or anyone who was there to enrich themselves.

"Even though I hate to think this way," said Olly, "I'm worried that someone has been sneaking down here since we opened the wall."

Alene couldn't imagine any of her employees doing that. "I don't think so," she said.

Olly's forehead was crumpled with worry, most unusual for him. "Don't say anything, okay, Alene? Kofi would never steal jewelry—that's not his thing—but who else would do it?"

"You don't know for sure that anyone is doing it, Olly," said Alene. "I'm sure there's an explanation." She headed back upstairs to wash her hands.

"I've been meaning to tell you, Alene," said Edith, waylaying her. "I got this letter yesterday and forgot all about it." She reached into the pockets of her long floral sweater and pulled out an envelope. "Your uncle gave it to me when I passed him on the sidewalk, but he was in a rush and didn't even stop to chat."

Chapter 16

Alene stomped into her office and slammed the door. After she finished reading it, she folded Finn's letter and put it in her back pocket. Her cellphone buzzed, and she recognized that it was from St. Darius.

"Is this Alene Baron?" It was a hospital person who was probably used to reaching voicemail and doubted that she was speaking to an actual person.

"Yes, it is," said Alene. "Are you calling with an update on my uncle, Phineas Baron?"

"Yes," she said. Her voice was thick and nasal, an ex-smoker. She said her name too quickly for Alene to hear it, followed by, "I'm sorry to inform you that your Uncle Phineas passed early this morning."

"He died?" The beating hadn't seemed that serious. "What was the cause of death?"

"According to his chart," the woman said, "he had stage four colon cancer, but the external beating caused hemorrhaging and hastened his death. He must have been in a lot of pain even before the beating, so in some ways, it was a blessing."

Saying that any death was a blessing seemed weird, and Alene's mouth went dry. "We had no idea," she replied. Poor Finn—why hadn't he told them about the cancer? The woman kept talking, telling Alene where to retrieve Finn's wallet and cellphone. Alene responded vaguely when she asked if the family needed guidance about funeral arrangements. Why would they have discussed funeral arrangements for Finn? She declined, anxious to get off the call.

"Your uncle asked his nurse to write a few last wishes that he wanted you to have. I could email it, or I'd be happy to read it to you now if that's more convenient."

Alene didn't think she needed to hear anything else, but if she'd realized Finn was dying, she'd have made sure to be nicer to him, less judgmental. She listened to the woman read Finn's last words—exactly what he'd written in the letter. She rubbed her temples and thanked the woman, who offered to email a list of funeral homes in the area. Alene dimly remembered the place where they held her mother's funeral, but she'd been at college and hadn't made any of the arrangements. Now it was up to her and her father. They were Finn's only family. Her sister wouldn't want anything to do with it.

Finn had hinted at not having time, but how were they to know what he'd meant? Maybe her father would have been less disapproving and more caring had he known. Alene would have invited Finn to a picnic or something, with Lydia and her husband, so he could have met the whole family. Or she'd have listened to him more. She was, as usual, disappointed in herself.

"I'm sorry to be the bearer of sad news, Dad," Alene said when he picked up her call. She repeated some of what the hospital person, whose name she'd never caught, had told her. She wasn't sure her father needed to hear all of it.

"I'm not surprised," Cal said with a sigh. "Damn," he swore under his breath, aggravated. "I wish we'd heard from him a few years earlier. And why didn't he ever get a colonoscopy? They do them all over the country and he knew it ran in the family. That's what killed our father."

Alene mentioned their need to discuss burial arrangements and told her father that Edith had ultimately delivered Finn's letter. "Great timing,' said Cal. "Did he say anything else about the motorhome?"

"Let's talk about it later, Dad," she answered. It was just like him to dwell on that.

Alene closed the café when orders stopped coming in and was home by two-thirty. She greeted her children and sat them down to talk about Finn's death. They were subdued for a few minutes before she needed to settle a petty argument involving pens. Then she handed Finn's letter to her father.

"Would you mind if we read it together after dinner?" Cal asked. "We can talk it through afterward."

"Of course, Dad," she said. She'd forgotten that he'd been having trouble with his eyes.

Dinner was homemade fish fingers and mashed potatoes with baby peas. Without prompting, Sierra had dredged the pieces of fish in an egg wash followed by a bowl of flour. She placed them on a prepared pan and set it in the preheated oven for ten minutes. Meanwhile, Quinn and Noah took turns mashing the boiled, cooled potatoes and Alene microwaved the bowl of peas. Cal set the table.

They sat down to an uncommonly subdued dinner. Cal barely lifted his fork, everyone else ate quickly, and there was no conversation. After they'd cleared the table, Alene excused the children to go to their rooms while she settled on the couch, a few feet away from where her father settled in his comfy chair.

"You ready?" she asked. Cal cleared his throat, and she began reading the letter from Finn. "*Dear Cal, I'm sorry for everything.*"

Cal muttered, "He damn well should be sorry."

Alene didn't look up. "*First, going back thirty years, I didn't know the guys planned an armed robbery.*"

"Really? So, he didn't notice that his cohorts were scumbags?" Cal interrupted. "The whole town knew who and what those guys were."

Alene waited until he finished. "*I was driving, and a couple of them said they needed cash from the bank, for lunch, but when we got there, they all went in. And when they came running out a bit*" *later, they were carrying garbage bags and guns. Then it was too late to back out.*"

Cal said, "So he never got lunch?" Alene didn't respond. "It doesn't sound at all convincing. My brother always wanted to know what restaurant we were headed to and where we were going after that. He'd never have picked those guys up in his van without knowing that they were going to rob a bank."

"Sometimes people are unpredictable, Dad," said Alene.

"Not Finn, though," said Cal. "He drove a minivan with sliding doors, and he had his electrical tools and equipment in the back. So, tell me, where did he put all that stuff to make room for the Stupid Squad? That's what we called that group of losers."

"I don't know, Dad, but how hard could it have been for Finn to remove a few things from the back of his van before he picked up the first guy?" she asked. "Any other questions or should I keep reading?"

Cal gestured for her to continue.

"*Afterwards, we moved the money to four metal briefcases. I already did a test run with dollar bills and knew that each briefcase could hold one million dollars.*"

Cal said, "That sounds like something he'd have done."

Alene gave her father a wary look. "Yeah?" she asked, rubbing her chin. "So, if Finn didn't know they were going to rob a bank, why did he do a test run to see how much money fit in each briefcase?"

Cal shook his head. "I have no idea," he said. "Maybe he explains it later in the letter."

"I'll continue then, "said Alene. "*I had a sizeable yard, with a garden and everything, so we buried the briefcases that night. You helped me the following Sunday, Cal. Remember how happy Winnie was when we planted all that hosta, salvia, and raspberries? We split up the peonies and hydrangea bushes and scattered lungwort all over the yard.*"

"I remember doing that," Cal interrupted again. "It was like when we were kids planting things for our mother. But let's go back to how they moved the money into briefcases. Did they do it in Finn's basement? And who bought those briefcases? Someone had them ready to be filled up with all that cash. I'm going to guess that Finn was that person."

Alene said, "You could be right about that, Dad, but we have no way of knowing at this point, so why bother asking these questions?" Cal had been sitting forward, but now he flung himself back against the cushions.

Alene continued reading. "*At the time, I was working for myself. I did electrical work in prison too, except it was mostly wiring problems and updates. You know they let me out before six years because the bank job was a first-time offense. Also, because I never stepped inside the bank, and I didn't have a weapon. Burgess, Klavestedberg, and Crow already had records. They also carried guns, and one of them shot a guard, so they got thirty years each. Stevens ended up with less time. I remember that he was having mental problems, maybe because of getting hit in the head a thousand times when he was boxing. We never liked each other anyway.*"

Cal looked off into space, his mouth half open in a bewildered expression. Alene asked if he wanted her to stop reading. "No," he said. "I was just remembering that Klavestedberg was married with kids. Stevens had a kid or two also, but he got divorced early. He boxed in high school—he was in one of the grades between Finn and me, and everyone used to say that he'd lose his mind one day if he kept getting clobbered."

Alene said, "It makes sense that you would know those men, Dad."

Cal twitched, as if he wanted to say something, but nothing came out of his mouth. He smacked himself in the forehead. "That's why that guy looked so familiar," he said.

"What guy?" asked Alene.

"That homeless guy I saw sitting on the sidewalk outside Whipped and Sipped last time I was there," said Cal. "I thought he looked familiar but couldn't remember how I knew him. It's Stevens. Vincent Stevens. He was such a bully in school."

Alene dropped her jaw. "Vincent? He's been sitting outside the café once or twice a week for months. Dori and Ruthie always bring him food."

"You should warn them not to get too close, Alene. He must have been the one who got sick and was moved to a different prison. Like I said, he suffered from severe concussions when he was

251

younger. And he used to have a violent temper—I wonder if he's calmed down with age."

Alene stared at her father. "He shouts at everyone. He's nearly impossible to understand, though, and he can't stand me."

"I wonder if someone told him that you're related to Finn," said Cal. "Finn screwed all those guys when he stole all that money. Or maybe Vincent recognized me one of the times I came over to the café. Maybe he remembered that I was Finn's brother, or he thought I was Finn."

"He wouldn't tell me who threw that brick through the window," said Alene.

"I wouldn't be surprised if he threw it himself," said Cal. "Will he still be there if we go now?"

"I never know when he's going to be there," said Alene.

"Let's call Frank," said Cal. "Vincent could have killed someone with that brick."

"But he didn't." There was no way she'd let Noah play any sports that caused head injuries. "Let's just call the police non-emergency number."

Cal looked at her as if she were reciting dreadful poetry. "No, Alene, I think you need to call Frank. Vincent is not right in the head, and he knows how to inflict pain. There's no telling what he's capable of doing."

"He seems kind of old and infirm," she said, punching in Frank's number. "He doesn't look strong enough to even lift a brick, let alone throw it like a missile, Dad, but maybe I'm wrong.

"Hi Sweetheart," said Frank. "How are you?"

"You're not going to believe what I'm about to tell you, Frank," Alene began. He breathed loudly but listened until she finished the story.

"Vincent Stevens," said Frank. "I'll make sure the guy gets picked up. Let me call you back later." Alene felt lighter as they said their goodbyes. She set her cellphone on the table. Ruthie and Dori had been so friendly to the guy—what if they'd been putting their lives at risk whenever they handed him a sandwich?

"Can we get back to Finn's letter?" Cal asked, startling her. She leaned back into the couch and continued reading.

"*After I was paroled, I went back and dug up the briefcases. It was in the middle of the night when I knew Winnie was sleeping. Each case can hold ten thousand one-hundred-dollar bills. I already told you that I researched it. That was one million in each case, as I mentioned earlier. It wasn't a problem to either bury the briefcases or dig them up, but it took me years to invest the money. I did it the same way I sent those money orders to Winnie. They let you move ten thousand at a time.*"

Cal held up his hand and Alene stopped reading. "Can you imagine walking out of a bank with that much cash?" he asked. "And after he dug it up, where did he store it all this time? The one thing I know for sure is that he learned a lot about how to sneak around the law."

Alene hesitated before continuing. It did seem strange to imagine the cash being stuffed into garbage bags. Had they been the heavy-duty kind?

"You should know they killed my son Jimmy on purpose. They got someone on the outside to do it. I think Klavestedberg arranged it from prison. He's still alive—Burgess and Crow died in prison, but I heard they let Klavestedberg go early because of the pandemic, and he's in Chicago. I know he's after me. If I disappear this time, it's because of him."

Cal interrupted to say, "You can't spend your life disappearing and tell your family that this time is going to be different."

Alene continued. *"Stevens got out early too, but I don't know if he survived."*

"Well," said Cal, "at least we know the answer to that one."

Alene gave her father a chance to continue, but he sat there shaking his head, so she went back to reading. *"I've been in Chicago for a month, but I haven't been well, Cal, and it took some time to build up my courage to reach out. I really do have a gift for you. My RV is parked at the McCormick Place Marshaling Yard. There's no electrical hookup or dumping, but there's a generator. It's only thirty dollars a night, about half what it costs to park a car a few blocks away."*

Cal said, "He stole four million dollars, but he's saving money on parking."

"You'd have done the same thing, Dad," said Alene. "Don't you usually respect people who find ways around paying full price for things?"

"Not this time," he said.

"Fine," said Alene, exhaling. *"It's yours, Cal. The motorhome is yours, and the title is inside (hidden in the toaster on the counter). You have to register it at your address and find a place to park it when you're not traveling. I put the keys in the empty tip jar in your daughter's restaurant. It's a fabulous motorhome and I think you're going to love it."*

Cal said, "It's probably going to be repossessed as stolen property."

Alene didn't even look at him. *"I'm at stage four colon cancer, Cal,"* she read. *"I know, I'm an imbecile for not having colonoscopies. I've got what killed Dad in 1974."*

Cal interrupted again, "I remember we went fishing after our dad's funeral because neither of us felt like talking to other people. I can't believe he's got the exact same thing our father had." Alene waited a moment before resuming.

"They'd have taken care of the cancer had I stayed in prison, but I needed fake identification when I got out. I knew the guys were going to come after me. I couldn't get health insurance so I couldn't get treatment. That's all there is to it."

"Wait a minute," said Cal. "So, he's sitting on all that money, but he doesn't get his colon tested because he doesn't have insurance to pay for it." Cal seethed, his pointer finger jabbing in the air. "A few thousand dollars wouldn't have ruined him. Our father was a stickler like that, he did whatever he could to avoid spending money."

Alene bit her tongue. Didn't he recognize himself? He'd become generous in his old age, but

Alene remembered having to beg for money before she was old enough to earn her own. Sometimes it was to buy new clothes, but often it was for a school outing, or to buy a birthday present for a friend. He'd probably forgotten about those days.

"That's it for the letter, Dad," she said, "but he also gives instructions about how to find the motorhome after you retrieve the keys. He signs it, '*Your Loving Brother, Finn*.' And there's a postscript that says, "*Alene has created a friendly, home-like place in that café and her employees adore her*."

They sat for a moment, and Alene handed the letter to her dad even though he couldn't see it well enough to read. It was a connection to the brother he'd just lost, the brother he'd once shared a room with, spent his childhood with, and loved. Although if she asked him, he'd say that he lost Finn decades ago.

She got up to wash the dinner dishes.

Chapter 17

First thing on Sunday morning, Alene roasted a tray of tomatoes, red peppers, and onions to blend into a soup. She'd serve it with grilled cheese sandwiches for dinner later that day. She whipped up a batch of fluffy scrambled eggs and set out fruit salad and muffins from the café for her family to take when they wandered into the kitchen.

Later, after they'd cleared the table and she finished washing the breakfast dishes, Alene helped the kids with their Sunday cleaning. She was still thinking about Finn's motorhome, imagining trips they could take. Would it turn out to be luxurious and comfortable, or stuffy and damp? Finn might have shared her father's tendency to exaggerate. She helped Quinn and Noah remove bed linens and remake their beds with clean sheets. Noah liked superheroes, Quinn's were covered in purple flowers, and Sierra, whose bed was across the room from Quinn's, had chosen white so that it didn't clash with her sister's bedding.

It was another misty morning, but it looked like the sun was struggling to come through. After they completed their chores, Noah and Quinn wanted to ride bikes with Alene. Sierra usually loved being outside, but that was when she was with her friends—last summer she'd been part of a gaggle of girls sitting on the rocks overlooking the water, walking along the lake path, or hanging out in the park. This summer, nobody was hanging out anywhere. "I already risked my life walking to the park with you on Friday night," Sierra said with a disgusted expression. "I'll stay home, again."

Cal advised Alene to stop worrying and suggested a game of backgammon to Sierra while Alene went riding with Quinn and Noah. "She could use some time away from her younger siblings," he said with the expression that meant he was about to convey some wisdom. "She needs some grandpa time."

Someone had knocked down the fence again—it had been set up to keep people out of the park and discourage gatherings, but Alene was glad to see that they'd be able to ride on the wide gravel bike path. It was more fun than riding on the sidewalk across the street. They stepped over the downed fence and rode south on the nearly empty path towards the bench where they'd found Finn, close to Diversey Harbor. Hardly anyone was out, and the only noise was an occasional car, runners, the rustling of trees, and the sound of their bicycle tires on the gravel.

Quinn and Noah dashed on and off the path, chasing each other around tree trunks. They'd pulled ahead of Alene and momentarily vanished in the greenery. It was typical of them not to respond when she called their names, but she sensed movement to her right. She thought that the kids were about to circle in front of her, so she stopped her bike.

That's when something bashed her in the head. Was it a tree branch, weakened by the rain? She felt she was collapsing and hoped the kids were okay, that it hadn't been one of them running into her. Now, someone was carrying her. Had Quinn and Noah called an ambulance?

Alene opened her eyes in a dimly lit room, lying on a hard surface, like a hospital gurney, her head pounding and her tongue dry. She could move her arms, so she was able to sweep her hair out of her face, but she couldn't move her legs. Was she in a cast? She hoped she hadn't fractured a bone. The air felt cool and musty, like in the café's basement. After a moment she got accustomed to the low light and gazed around. It didn't look anything like a hospital room. Someone was sitting in a chair a few yards away.

It was Peter Berg, hunched over his phone. He wore a mask, which was comforting, but hers was missing. His cheeks looked smooth, and Alene randomly wondered if he shaved himself or if his sister helped him every morning. Maybe he was able to use an electric razor. But where were Quinn and

Noah? Did someone take them home after Alene got hurt? How long had she been knocked out? And where was she?

"Hi Alene," Peter said, smiling and happy to see that she was awake. "How are you?" he asked, as if they'd just passed each other on the sidewalk. He looked skeletal in the blue light of his cellphone.

"I'm dizzy, Peter, and I need a drink," she said, trying to see him more clearly, "Thank you for asking. Where are we? What happened and where are my kids?"

Peter didn't look up from his phone. "We're in my basement," he said, with a hint of pride. "Taryn thinks it's spooky, but I like that it's quiet and nobody yells at me or hits me."

It was a weird conversation to be having. She tsked. "Where are my children, Peter?" she asked again. "Nobody should ever yell at you or hit you." Peter let his large head fall forward. How could anyone get mad at someone so open and naive? Alene rubbed the back of her neck. She had to figure out what was going on.

Peter sighed and lifted his head. "My dad hits me sometimes, but Taryn says it's because he had a very hard life. And he's very old but she says he loves me anyway." Peter returned to his game.

"But why are we here?" Alene asked, trying to get a sense of where the door was. "And where are Quinn and Noah? Are they alright? Did something fall on my head, Peter?"

"I didn't do it," he said as if she'd insulted him. "Taryn hit you and you fell down. I picked you up

260

and carried you to the car because I'm stronger than Taryn, and then I carried you into the basement and tied your legs like Taryn told me to." He bent over his phone and continued playing, although he glanced up long enough to add, "She isn't strong enough to carry you."

"Thank you for explaining," said Alene, still confused. "But I'm worried about my children, Peter. Do you know where they are?"

He shook his head like he didn't understand why she was asking the question. What did she need to know in this situation aside from how to get out of it? Alene tried to keep her voice gentle. Peter was guileless, like her children had been when they were younger. Even when she'd been upset about something they'd done, she'd had to explain herself calmly, or they'd burst into tears. "I'm thirsty and my head hurts, Peter, and I'd like to go home now. Quinn and Noah were riding bikes with me. Can you untie me, please, so I can go look for them?"

"I can't, Alene, even though you said please," Peter replied earnestly. "Taryn said you should wait here because we need your help."

Alene started to simmer, but how could she be upset with Peter? Did he understand what it meant to keep someone tied up against their will, or did he think they were playing some sort of game?

"I'll be happy to help you," she said, trying to sound perky. On television people got hit in the head and bounced up afterward as if nothing had happened, but she'd started feeling nauseated and her head was pounding. "First, I need to know what happened to my kids. Did you see them? And I need water and some medicine to help me feel better." She couldn't feel her cellphone in her back pocket. Would Peter have taken it, or had it dropped? "Also, do you have my cellphone, Peter?"

"I saw a boy and a girl on bicycles, and I waved to them," he said, "but I didn't see them after I put you in the car." Had Quinn and Noah seen what happened? Had they called the police or told her father that someone knocked her out, carried her to a car, and left her bike on the sidewalk?

"My head hurts and I'm thirsty, Peter." How many times would she have to say it? She'd have to remember to speak clearly and ask one question at a time. Had Taryn and Peter been lying in wait, or did they just happen to pass by? She'd passed them during her runs, so they knew she was usually outside in the morning, but they couldn't have known when, or which route she'd take.

"We have medicine for headaches," Peter said, "but Taryn told me not to leave you alone and not to untie you, so I don't know how you can get it. It's upstairs."

Alene could hardly think. "I'd feel better if I could have some water." Only her legs were tied, and she'd managed to sit up as she spoke, but her head did ache. They could have knocked her out and put her in the car in less than thirty seconds.

"I'll share my water with you, Alene," he said, holding out a water bottle. Should she risk taking a sip or should she remind him about the coronavirus? She didn't know how much time had passed, but maybe Quinn and Noah had seen her bike lying there. Maybe they'd seen Peter put her in the back of the car. They must have turned around and gone home to tell her father what had happened. Peter said he'd carried her to the car. Hadn't anyone else been close enough to question what was going on? They'd hardly seen any people on their ride, maybe a few dog walkers and runners. And unless someone stole her bicycle, it might still be there.

"That's very sweet of you," she said, "but you need your water. Taryn told you not to untie me, Peter, but would it be alright if I untied myself?"

He nodded and she felt like it was a small victory. "Thank you, Peter," said Alene as she unwound the rope. It wasn't knotted, but he must have used enough rope to tie several boats to a dock. It took a long time to unwind. "I'll feel better after I splash some water on my face. Will you show me where the bathroom is?" She hoped it was upstairs where she might be able to look out a window or get to a door.

"It's right through there." He pointed vaguely towards the back of the dark space, where the bathroom was also located in the café's basement.

"Okay," said Alene, continuing to unwind the rope. "Did your sister tell you how I can help?"

"Taryn said that you have something that belongs to us," he said, mesmerized by his phone, "because your uncle took some money and now you have to give it back." She abruptly realized that she'd recognized the man who'd beat Finn with a cane—the same man she'd seen Peter pushing in a wheelchair. That was their father! Had Peter been waiting in the minivan? The second person must have been Taryn. Alene thought it had been two men.

"Does your dad walk with a cane?" she asked.

"Yes," he said. "Mostly I push him in a wheelchair but sometimes he walks. And he hits me with his cane when he's mad."

"I'm sorry," she said, as she freed her feet. His father was responsible for hastening Finn's death. She stood and tried to get her balance but fell back down. "Can you help me find my cellphone, Peter, so I can call and—she thought fast—"ask my uncle what he took?" He didn't need to know that Finn was dead.

"I know what it is," he said. "It's a key, Alene. You took a special key."

Couldn't they have asked for it instead of bashing her in the head? What kind of people were they? "Maybe we can go look for my cellphone near where I left my bicycle," she said, this time managing to stand. "I can call and ask my uncle for the key."

Peter shook his head. "You shouldn't lose your phone, Alene. You should be very careful with your cellphone." The game on his phone involved brightly colored balls. "I only have one job, to tie you with the rope and watch you until Taryn comes home."

Alene said, "That's two jobs."

His eyes widened. "I'm going to tell Taryn that's two jobs. She's getting me a tomato sandwich on pumpernickel from that place where you work. That's my favorite bread. Do you want a sandwich too? I could call and tell her because I have my cellphone right here." He repeated, with a dismayed look at her, "You shouldn't lose your cellphone, Alene."

"I know, you are one hundred percent right about that," she said, walking the perimeter of the room until her feet were back to normal. "Thank you for offering a sandwich, Peter, but I need to go home to make lunch for my family." She passed several closed doors that reminded her of the doors in the café's basement. She wondered if there'd been a speakeasy here as well.

"They can get sandwiches from the Whipped and Sipped Café too," Peter said, as if that solved every problem. "And after we eat lunch, we'll go get the key and pick up my motorhome."

She let her mouth fall open. Finn said he'd left the keys in the tip jar, but the title was in her father's name. She could give them one of the keys, and then report it as a robbery, but right now she had to get out of this basement. "How will we find the motorhome if I've never even seen it?"

Peter stopped playing with his cellphone and looked at Alene, his eyes flashing and his arms gesturing with excitement. "It's a Palazzo, which is the best kind, Alene, and it has a forty-nine-inch mounted television and a ten-thousand-pound hitch." His fingers were extended, and his mouth was wide open in a huge smile that was visible through his mask. He entwined his fingers, watching them in wonderment. "Taryn says you have to come with us because you have the key. There's a man who found your uncle and took pictures of my motorhome and that's how we know all about it."

Alene tried to show him that her pockets were empty. "I don't have the key, Peter, but it sounds like you like motorhomes," she said, as perkily as possible. It wouldn't be as easy to distract Taryn. She suddenly realized that Peter had just told her someone had been following Finn. "So, someone followed my uncle and took pictures?"

"Yup, and I love motorhomes," said Peter, taking off his mask and smiling. "And also pictures of motorhomes."

"No, please keep your mask on," said Alene. "Do you have another mask for me? I don't want you to get sick."

He frowned but complied with her request. "You shouldn't lose your mask or your phone, Alene," he said, probably in the same tone his sister used with him. Alene's immediate problem had nothing to do with Covid. "You know what else about motorhomes?" he continued. "They're also called RVs and they have gigantic wheels."

Alene had started worrying about what Taryn was going to do to her and couldn't respond. She wiped her tears with the back of her hand. Peter looked troubled, as if he might cry too. "You should go to the bathroom and clean up, Alene," he said. "That's what Taryn says when I cry. You can drink some water too, but there's no towel in the bathroom so you have to dry your hands on your pants."

Alene found the correct door and turned on the light. There was a filthy toilet, a cracked sink, and a

266

moldy old bathtub. She washed her hands and cupped them to drink handfuls of water, drying them as Peter had suggested, on her pants. She left the door ajar on her way out, so the bathroom light illuminated some of the walls. "Do you want to try a new game, Peter? My son has a fun game with different candies. Do you like candy?" If she had his phone, she could contact Frank. Or dial 9-1-1.

"No, I like bread, especially pumpernickel. But don't worry, I've got something else to play with." He set his phone down and pulled a paper clip from his pocket. "When I was waiting in the van one day, I saw you and your dad walking with a very tall girl," he said, sounding unexpectedly shy as he twisted the clip. "I like very tall girls. What's her name?"

It took Alene a moment. "That's my friend Jocelyn," she said, casually picking up his cellphone. It wasn't password protected, which might have been too confusing for Peter. She texted Frank. It took less than ten seconds to write "help." Next, she called Jocelyn. "Would you like to say hello to her? She's going to answer any second."

He made a delighted face. "I already have one girlfriend, but I only get to see her sometimes." Had Taryn arranged for someone to take care of Peter's physical needs? What did he mean exactly? Was it a prostitute? Or was that too dramatic—maybe just a caregiver?

"I bet Jocelyn would love to talk to you," she said, putting the phone on speaker and inching towards the stairs. Maybe she'd get a head start and run. But that wouldn't help. It was hard to think clearly. "She likes men who are tall, like you."

She prayed for Jocelyn to pick up, but of course she never answered numbers she didn't recognize. Neither did Cal or the children. Or Ruthie. Alene cursed robocalls. Would Frank understand what was happening? Her text had been too vague. She punched in his number again. She wasn't thinking straight—should she have dialed 9-1-1 instead? It went to voicemail. She tried one more time.

"I'm way taller than my dad," Peter said, never taking his eyes off the paperclip. "He had to go to jail and now he's shorter. Sometimes Taryn goes to jail too, and I have to live in a bad place where they hit and yell. And they burn their toast."

Alene's head ached, and she was getting tired of talking to Peter. Hadn't someone mentioned that Peter and Taryn lived close to Zuleyka? And Blanca lived west on Diversey too. Her apartment might also be close by. If Alene got out the door and got her bearings, she could find one of their buildings. She'd have to tell Ruthie how listening to gossip might have saved her life. She said, "But now you live here."

Frank answered on the fifth ring, "Frank Shaw." Had she ever been this happy to hear his voice? She put the phone on speaker. Peter waved at it as if Frank could see him.

"Hi, Frank. This is Alene and I'm with Peter Berg," she said, "but I'm not sure exactly where we are. I have a terrible headache because Peter's sister hit me in the head."

"I told you, we're in my basement, Alene," said Peter. "Hi Frank, this is Peter Berg. I'm sorry Taryn hit Alene in the head. I don't like when she hits."

"I don't know where Peter lives," Alene continued, speaking quickly. "And I'm worried about Quinn and Noah." Could Frank hear the panic in her voice?

"We're waiting for Taryn to bring me lunch," Peter shouted.

"I hear you, Peter," Frank said. "Can you tell me more about the basement where you live?" Did that mean he was going to try to pinpoint the location via GPS?

"Tell him that I don't live in the basement, Alene," Peter said. "My bedroom is upstairs, and it's painted different colors. And there are lamps and colored pencils, and little airplanes hanging from the ceiling, and pretty rocks that I found at the beach. Also, I have books and other stuff."

"Frank," said Alene, trying to hold herself together. "I need to go home now, and I'm worried about my kids."

Frank started to respond, but Peter took the phone and said, "Bye Frank, see you later."

Alene said, "That wasn't nice. Why did you hang up on Frank?"

"I told you," said Peter, smiling at her as if nothing was wrong, "that you can't go home yet because we have to wait for Taryn. Don't worry, though, because my house is close to that place where you work, that has everything I like. I go there all the time. Is the problem that you're hungry?"

269

Alene wished she'd studied psychology. What was the correct way to speak to someone like Peter? "That's my restaurant, the Whipped and Sipped Café," she said. "I sell fresh bread and pastries and cookies every day, but I can't do that when I'm stuck here in your basement."

"I love fresh bread," Peter said. Now, he seemed mesmerized by a thread on his shirt. "My dad had to eat stale bread in the jail. Then they let him go home, and he wanted to find his money, but your uncle took it, which was not nice. Taryn told me to play on my phone in the car, but I looked out the window and I saw my dad hitting a man and the man fell on the ground." He wiped his nose with the back of his hand. "That made me cry and my dad said I'd be next if I didn't quit blubbering, but Taryn told him he shouldn't hit me with his cane."

"I'm glad she stood up for you," said Alene. So, Peter had waited in the van while Taryn helped their father try to kill Finn. "Taryn's a good sister, right?" He bobbed his head up and down. In the movies, the police could zero in on an address almost immediately. Had Frank been able to do that from his home?

"And she said if I do my job today, I get to see my motorhome. That's why you can't go home yet." He beamed, proud to have explained the situation. "Remember I told you about it? It's a Class A and Alene, can I please have the key to my motorhome now? I just want to look at it," he added. Alene heard footsteps on the stairs and her breath caught. She backed up against the wall and tried not to cry.

It was Rhona Shaw. Hadn't she been sick all week? At least she wore a mask over her mouth. Alene said the first thing that came to her: "What are you doing here?"

Peter said, "Hi, Rhona. Alene and I are waiting for Taryn to come home with my lunch." He looked worried. "I'm not sure there's enough to share though. I'm sorry, Rhona."

Rhona looked around as if she'd never been there. "This place has a basement? Don't worry about lunch, Peter," she said. "I'm not hungry." Her head snapped back to Alene. "How do you know Peter and Taryn, and more importantly, what are you doing here?"

"I don't know," said Alene, anger creeping into her voice. "You'll have to ask Taryn why she smashed me in the head, knocked me out, and told her brother to tie me up and not let me leave." Rhona looked back and forth between them. She clearly had no idea what was going on.

"Are you okay, Rhona?" Alene asked, concern winning over her own discomfort and fear. "You had that horrible headache and we thought it might be the virus."

Rhona shook her head, walking over to Peter and placing a hand on his shoulder. "I have severe allergies and that migraine headache has plagued me for nearly a decade. It's not an uncommon hormonal reaction, but every single month, my father panics that something is horribly wrong." She sighed, and Peter mimicked her, as if he too was disturbed.

"Why are you here, Alene?" Rhona asked as she gazed around the dim space. "I didn't even know this place had a basement, but I saw the open door and heard voices coming from down here."

Rhona was the last person Alene had expected to see. "I don't know why I'm here," she said. "Is Peter the guy you wouldn't tell your father about?" Peter didn't seem capable of functioning as a dealer or a boyfriend. Maybe Taryn was the dealer.

"It's complicated," said Rhona. "I'm Peter's caregiver. It started as a job, but it turns out that he is a sweetheart and I like taking care of him." She reached down to rub his shoulders.

Peter hummed happily. "Rhona takes care of me and she's my girlfriend," he said, reaching up to pat Rhona on the back, which sent her plunging forward. Peter looked worried until Rhona told him that she was fine and reminded him to be gentle.

"Maybe you can help me with this current situation, Rhona," said Alene in a bouncy voice. "I don't have the key that interests them." Drinking water had helped, but she'd give anything for some ibuprofen.

"It's a key to my motorhome, Rhona," Peter added helpfully, "and I'll take you for a ride in it, but right now it's my job to watch Alene until Taryn comes home with my sandwich. It's from the Whipped and Sipped Café. Did you know that Alene works there?"

"I love that place," Rhona said. "Alene is my friend, too, Peter, so we need to be nice to her, right?"

"I am," he said.

Rhona took his hand, "I have an idea," she said. "It's pretty outside and we can look for birds and squirrels while we walk Alene home."

"Okay." He looked at her anxiously, his brow furrowed. "But Taryn told me to stay here. Will you still be my girlfriend if I can't go for a walk?"

Rhona looked at Alene before answering. "I can't be your girlfriend if you're mean to Alene," she said, digging in her back pocket and pulling out an extra mask for Alene

"I'm trying to do my job," Peter said, louder now that he was panicked, his hand covering his mouth as though he couldn't imagine such a horrific consequence. "Taryn told me that Alene has our key."

Alene was surprised that Rhona had picked up on the situation so quickly. "No harm done, Peter. Let's just go for our walk," Rhona said as she pulled him towards the stairs. He held back like Noah did when it was time to go to the dentist, dragging his feet. "We'll text Taryn, so she won't worry about where you are."

It was like watching a movie. Frank had complained about Rhona not being able to make friends or have relationships. He had no idea.

Heels snapping against the concrete stairs sent shivers up Alene's spine. Taryn's shrill voice filled the basement as she got to the bottom of the stairs, holding a Whipped and Sipped carry-out bag. "What are you doing here, Rhona?"

Rhona froze. Taryn marched over to Peter and struck his face, shouting, "You didn't listen to me." Peter cried out, and Rhona rushed over to him. He'd fallen out of his chair and huddled on the floor with his arms over his head as if expecting more blows.

"She had to go to the bathroom," he wailed as Rhona stroked his large head, trying to comfort him.

Taryn shook her head and pulled a gun from her pocket. She directed Alene to sit and offered a hand to pull Peter off the floor. He refused, and Taryn kept the gun on Rhona. "I don't think you understand what's going on here, Rhona," she said.

Rhona said, "I don't need to know."

Taryn said, "Yeah, you do. Alene's uncle let our father languish in prison for nearly thirty years, and now it's time to get back what should have been ours. I'll ask you again. What are you doing here?"

Rhona stiffened and her eyes narrowed, like her father when he was angry. "Peter sits home all day unless I come over, and I thought it would be fun for him to go for a walk to see the baby geese and ducks in the park. I tried to reach you, Taryn, but you didn't answer your phone, so I came over. I didn't know it would be such an immense problem."

Alene was proud of Rhona for responding like that. Was Taryn crazy enough to shoot one of them in her basement? Was it just about the motorhome, or was Taryn trying to get revenge for what her father had endured? And why would she take her anger out on Alene, who had barely known Finn?

"Well, it is a problem. I hired you to take care of my brother when it's convenient for me," Taryn told

Rhona. "I didn't invite you to drop by whenever you want." Alene couldn't process fast enough, but had Rhona just been admonished for trying to do something considerate? All this time Frank thought she was selfish. If only he could see her now.

Peter got up off the floor and hopped on one foot, already over being smacked in the face. "I want to go see the baby geese, Taryn, can I go to the park with Rhona?" Why didn't adults keep that ability to move seamlessly from devastation to ecstasy?

"Shut up, Peter," said Taryn, pushing him away.

Peter gasped as he got his footing back. "We don't say that word, Taryn." he said, frantic and appalled. "You're supposed to say, 'Please be quiet.'"

Taryn paid him no attention. "I hired you for one reason, Rhona, and I can replace you in a heartbeat." She stopped to rub her forehead—was she deciding whether to shoot? Alene had no idea what to do. She tried to catch Rhona's eye, but Rhona was glaring at Taryn.

At that moment Peter pulled himself up to his full height and towered over his sister. "No, you can't replace Rhona," he shouted. "She's my girlfriend."

Peter tore off his mask and gulped air. "You are not being a nice person right now, Taryn Berg," he said, letting out a wail, his mouth opened in a tortured sob as he pushed her back with all his strength.

Taryn smashed into the wall. She dropped the gun and crumpled to the floor. Alene held her breath, scared that the gun would fire randomly, but it fell and slid away. All she had to do was lean over and pick it up. Rhona ran to Peter, now howling, and put her arms around him so he could cry on her shoulder. Alene gaped at the gun in her hand. Frank had mentioned once, in passing, that the first thing you do when you pick up a gun is to verify what's in the barrel. If it's loaded, he'd said, you aim it away from yourself. She aimed it at Taryn, who lay motionless on the floor.

Frank burst in then, followed by two uniformed officers, all masked, with their guns drawn. "Breathe, Alene," he said quietly, stepping towards her, "and relax your grip."

She hadn't realized how tense she'd been, but as she exhaled, she lowered the gun to her side, and Frank took it from her with his free hand. She wished he could hug her to stop the shaking, but all he could do was nod at her, because at that moment there was a loud explosion to her left. Someone yelled, "Get down. Someone's shooting from upstairs."

Peter screamed hysterically, and Frank told Alene to get down in as gruff a voice as she'd ever heard. The next shot fired sounded like it was farther away, and then everything went quiet.

The next voice sounded like Frank's partner, calling down, "All clear."

Chapter 18

Lee Bautista walked over to the crimson wall and stood next to the café's new basement door. He gawked at Dori, sitting by herself at a corner table, as if she were a sheep and he the wolf. Alene felt sorry for her. Dori had tried to leave at closing time, but Frank wanted Alene's entire staff to stay for a few minutes, so now Dori fidgeted uncomfortably in her seat, probably worried that Lee was planning to ask her out as soon as the meeting ended.

It was July, and the coronavirus was still hopping across the globe, so everyone was masked, although they were still eating and drinking. People were being careful, taking quick bites and sips and pulling their masks back up. To be extra safe, the tables were scattered.

It had been several weeks since Alene spent a fraught afternoon in Peter and Taryn's basement.

Alene had never thought of Lee as a hero, but he'd been the one to stop Don Klavestedberg from getting off another shot. Taryn and Peter's father couldn't walk down the stairs and had risked his own kids' lives by shooting randomly into their basement. Lee had shot Klavestedberg with a single, justified bullet, but had still been placed on leave. Frank said that was police department protocol.

The paramedics hadn't been able to calm Peter after the gunshot. He'd cried hysterically as the police paramedics carried his still unconscious sister up the stairs, and as two of them led him outside to their waiting car. Alene calmed Peter's anguish by giving him the Whipped and Sipped bag that Taryn brought home for him.

"Thank you, Alene," he'd said, still sobbing. "I thought the policemen weren't going to let me have my sandwich because I pushed Taryn." Both Alene and Frank had promised him that nobody was mad and assured him that sometimes pushing was the right thing to do.

Now, Cal leaned closer to whisper to Alene, "Not sure I have patience to listen to Frank's partner tell the whole story from start to finish." They were sitting at one of the café's newly refurbished Prohibition-era tables.

Frank, on Alene's other side, leaned forward and said, "I think it'll be worth your while, Cal."

Blanca, back at work after a week in the hospital and ten days of quarantine, sat to the left of Cal, sipping an iced tea, and staring at the other police officers off to the side. "Why they need to be here? Are they guarding us?" she asked.

Frank shrugged and said, "They probably came for the cookies and free drinks." Blanca looked satisfied with Frank's answer.

"Nobody's forcing you to stay, Dad," Alene whispered. "Blanca can walk you home and I can fill you in later."

"Never mind," said Cal, taking a sip of his iced coffee. "I'll stay. Maybe we'll learn something interesting."

Cal and Blanca sat with Alene and Frank, whose chairs were pulled close. Kacey and Kofi sat next to Benjie and Ruthie Rosin, both of whom looked less exhausted than they'd been in the weeks after Benjie's building burned down. They still hadn't started rebuilding.

Sierra, Quinn, and Noah shared a table in the far corner of the café and were nibbling strawberry-rhubarb crisp and assorted tahini, chocolate chip, pistachio, and ginger cookies. Their grandmother, Neal's mother, Mitzi, was with them, still without a sense of smell after her Covid battle, but otherwise healthy. She'd been disappointed that neither Cal nor Alene had told her everything as it unfolded, and she wanted to hear every detail about what had happened. Alene had even invited the kids' father, but Neal had declined.

Some of Alene's staff members hovered near the counter and others sat around, waiting for Frank and Lee to tell them the entire story. They were all healthy for the moment, although Zuleyka hadn't yet gotten back her sense of taste and needed a nap every afternoon. Frank's daughter leaned against the wall near Frank and Alene. Olly, who stood admiring the improvements he'd made, had propped open the front door to get more air circulation, which was good for everyone because the sun was shining, and it was finally summer.

LaTonya called out, "Let's get this going, Lee. Are you going to finally tell us who the first victim was? You told us about the second woman, Juana Clemente, but who was the first one? What was her name and where was she from?" It was disturbing that it had taken so long to identify her, and the city's excuses weren't cutting it anymore.

"Also," asked Ruthie, "why were those two women dumped on my husband's properties? And why were they wearing my kids' discarded jackets?"

"And who murdered them?" Kacey asked. "We all want to know what that was all about."

"What happened was that they were both snatched off the street and strangled by the same person," said Lee Bautista, scratching his head and shuffling as if he couldn't find a comfortable standing position. Frank preferred to stay seated.

"Who it was?" Blanca asked. "You arrested the person who killed those ladies?"

Frank said, "It was Vincent Stevens, the man who sat outside the door pretending to be homeless." The room broke out into small conversations as they all swallowed that piece of news.

"What did Ruthie or I do to upset Vincent Stevens?" asked Benjie Rosin. "Did they figure out that he was the one who started those fires that destroyed the two buildings?"

Frank nodded. "They did, Benjie. They found lighter fluid in his car, and other evidence that tied him to both fires."

"But why?" Ruthie asked.

"We might never know," said Frank.

"Go back to the women he murdered," said LaTonya.

"All right," Lee said. "You already know about the second victim. The first victim was a thirty-four-year-old Bulgarian immigrant named Rada Kochev. She worked as a caregiver in a Lakeview nursing home. We couldn't find any connections, and it looks as though Vincent Stevens chose both women randomly.

"Why did it take so long to identify her?" asked Rhona Shaw, who was considerably improved, but still sounded demanding to Alene. Frank kept his eyes on Lee.

Lee said, "The pandemic has slowed everything down and made everything more difficult, but we're all doing the best we can."

"Let's go back to Taryn and Peter Berg's father, Don Klavestedberg," said Frank. There's a lot of moving parts to this story."

"Peter and Taryn's mother legally shortened their name from Klavestedberg to Berg after their father got sent to prison," Lee said.

"Taryn wasn't a bad person," Frank continued, "but Don Klavestedberg badgered her into helping him get revenge on Finn Baron, Alene's uncle. The plan was to steal whatever Finn had and kill him. Then Klavestedberg ran out of patience."

There was murmuring as if everyone had something to say about it, the way people do in a crowd. Frank and Lee had worked on solving the murders of the two women, but there'd also been other crimes—arson, destruction of property, identity theft, interstate gambling, kidnapping, and tax evasion—the cases had gotten convoluted, and it took time to connect them. Alene had lots of reasons to be grateful that the drama was over.

She was glad Frank had invited colleagues who knew about Whipped and Sipped, like the cop with long, wavy black hair and her partner, the one with a thick neck and short brown hair. They'd come after the brick sailed through the café window. The third officer was tall, dark, and muscled. He'd made his way over to LaTonya, who seemed atypically flustered. Alene enjoyed watching the police officer trying to flirt with her.

Frank cleared his throat. "This won't take long, folks," he said, waiting until they quieted down. "Taryn Berg's lawyer plea-bargained for community service and supervision."

"She was dealing prescription drugs and meth," Lee added in a way that made it clear he disapproved of her plea bargain. "She was also responsible for abducting Alene, so I think she should have paid the price, but she's apparently the brother's primary caregiver."

According to Frank, Lee had helped connect and tie up all the loose ends, from the fires to the murders of the two women, to the broken window. Alene agreed that Taryn deserved to be in prison but that having her at home would be less disruptive for Peter. Peter had probably already forgotten that Taryn slapped him, and that he'd given her a concussion when he pushed her into the wall. Did he remember that she'd had to spend a few days in the hospital afterwards?

Rhona had admitted that Taryn Berg had offered her Oxycontin in exchange for taking care of Peter. They'd met in front of the café, waiting to pick up their orders. Rhona had been ashamed of having become addicted and couldn't bring herself to tell Frank all those months, but she'd discovered, to her surprise, that she liked caregiving. At least she'd apologized for all the secrets she'd kept, like her drug problem. She had work to do, but she'd made a start.

Frank was astonished—now Rhona was talking about going back to school. She wanted to work with special needs adults, like Peter. Although she'd agreed to see an allergist about her sensitivities to foods and smells, she was still a hypochondriac. She came by it honestly, Frank said, and Alene knew enough about divorce not to respond.

"We're all sorry that the department isn't as healthy as we'd like it to be," Lee said, defensive in front of Alene's staff. "Let's go back to the Galesburg bank robbery in 1990. Although the crimes we're discussing were not connected, the perpetrators were." He kept stealing glances at Dori, who never once looked his way. That's exactly the way Alene would have handled someone like Lee Bautista.

"They all know that my brother robbed that bank with those goons," said Cal. People started chattering again, and Alene thought it would take all day to get to the end.

"With all due respect, Mr. Baron," Lee said, "the facts do not align with your version." Alene thought it was a sinister way of calling her father a liar.

"All I know is what my brother told me," Cal said. Alene didn't think he'd properly grieved Finn's death, but he'd insisted that he'd gotten used to his brother's absence years before. "Finn thought they were going to lunch that day, they stopped to get cash at the bank while he stayed in the car, and they came out with guns and money."

"We'll get back to that," said Lee, "because it's not true." Cal made a face indicating disgust, and at least got a consoling look from Blanca.

"Here's what we learned," said Frank, always more diplomatic than Lee. "A few weeks before he died, Finn Baron wrote a letter to the bank that he and his pals robbed back in 1990 and gave directions to a locker that contained all the money they'd taken, plus twenty-five percent interest."

"That's one million dollars in interest," Cal whistled. "Does that sound overly generous to anyone else here?" Alene gave him another disapproving look.

Blanca gave Cal a soothing pat on the back and whispered loudly enough for Alene to hear that people should always stand up for their families. "What about my stolen money and my jewelry, Frank?" she asked in her booming voice. "Alene told me I should ask from the police for help, but you didn't do a single thing."

Alene realized she should have made it clear that this meeting was specifically connected to the bank robbery, the murders, and Finn. Frank reminded Blanca that he and Lee solved homicides, and Blanca said, "So if I killed both of those boys, you'd be interested?"

There was some laughter and more chattering. Alene said, "Come on, Blanca. Frank and Lee are here as a favor to me. Can we wait until after they're done to talk about your burglary?"

Blanca grudgingly agreed. Alene turned to Frank and said, "Keep going, Frank. Sorry about that."

"You all probably know that Don Klavestedberg died of a gunshot wound before we could charge him with attempted murder," said Frank. "Vincent Stevens, however, should not be on the streets, and has been charged with two counts of murder and a few other crimes. He'll be sent to a psychiatric correctional institution."

Edith, who hadn't said anything yet called out in her nasal twang, "I warned everyone that there was something wrong with him."

Kacey hugged Kofi, who furtively wiped his eyes. Frank had already spoken to him, so he knew he was off the hook. As an apology to Frank, he'd offered to donate a sculpture to the police department, but Frank told him that CPD had to be extremely careful about receiving gifts.

"Why did Vincent murder those poor women?" Kofi asked. "Did you get any answers from him?"

Lee said, "No, we didn't, because he's incapable of speaking coherently about anything."

"But if any of you ever stumble across another dead body, you're going to contact the department right away, right?" Frank asked. "And if you ever have an issue with a Chicago police officer, you're going to call me, right? And if you're too shy to call me," he stopped to point at each of them, "Alene will do it for you." He pulled her close and the café erupted in applause.

Frank hadn't let her off easy. He'd been so upset that she'd kept Kofi's secret, he'd insisted on couples' therapy. They'd had to do it online and were still meeting with a therapist every week. It had taken a lot of talking for Alene to understand the depth of Frank's disappointment in her.

"That's not the kind of relationship I want for us," he'd said. Alene had known that all along.

"I don't get why Vincent Stevens killed those women," Jocelyn said then. "Don't victims usually know their assailants?"

"Usually, but not always," said Frank, "and Vincent Stevens was not in his right mind. He had a history of erratic behavior and aggression."

"Did he set the fires?" Benjie asked.

"He threw the brick, didn't he?" asked Olly. "Where is he now?"

"We think he set the fires and threw the brick, but we might never know for sure. He's currently in a lockdown psychiatric facility," said Lee. "But he's not admitting anything. And we learned that he owns a townhouse, not far from here. He had a daughter living with him, who was overheard saying that he'd been disturbed about property values going down in the neighborhood. He also ranted about Benjie Rosin."

Vincent had a daughter. Alene looked at Frank, who caressed her hair and said, for the benefit of everyone, "Thanks to Alene Baron for pointing us in the direction of neighbors who oppose Benjie Rosin's buildings." This time, Alene bowed as they applauded. She thought the police would have found the information without her help, but it was nice of Frank to acknowledge that she'd made some valid suggestions. It meant her far-fetched suspicions were sometimes correct, and it meant that being honest with Frank brought them closer.

Everyone waited for Lee to continue except for Dori, who'd gotten up and was heading towards the door. She probably didn't care about the stories, so Alene understood her wanting to leave. Lee gazed after her, but Dori didn't give him the satisfaction of turning around. The three extra cops also took their leave, probably because they'd finished their snacks.

Frank said, "We have a couple of other points." He waited until the front door closed again.

"As I was saying," he said, "we've learned a few other new things that I haven't even gotten a chance to share with Alene yet."

Alene looked up—she thought she'd heard the entire story. She'd organized the meeting so she wouldn't have to keep explaining the trajectory of events, but it was good to hear it all clearly explained. Now she glanced at Rhona, who was watching her father with an almost admiring look. That was new.

"The first thing is about Phineas Baron," said Frank, "and forgive me if this is a shocker for you, Cal."

Cal snickered. "Don't worry, Frank," he said. "At this point, nothing you say about Finn is going to surprise me. He's gone, and I've made my peace with it." The funeral had been perfunctory, and they'd cremated him, but at least Lydia and her husband came so Cal got to be surrounded by family. Alene reached over to squeeze Cal's arm. Finn had been his only brother. Even though she wasn't as close to her sister as they'd once been, Alene couldn't imagine losing her.

"As it happened, Don Klavestedberg did not mastermind the 1990 bank robbery," said Frank. "It was Finn Baron." Cal raised both his hands in the air and dropped his jaw. Alene was surprised too.

"We now know that Finn directed the operation," Frank continued, "from start to finish. He bought the metal briefcases, he convened the team, he made sure that the bank suffered a propitious blackout on the day of the robbery, and he bought the bags to carry the stolen cash. That's why all the money was buried in his backyard, and that's why both Klavestedberg and Stevens were after him. That's also why these cases are linked. Finn Baron didn't deserve to get out of prison before the others, but he was cunning."

Edith sat there shaking her head. "I don't believe any of this. Finn was one of the sweetest men I've ever met," she said. "He came to visit me at home, twice." Alene didn't even know what to say. Maybe it had been a long time since a man expressed interest. She wondered if they'd slept together but quickly brushed that thought aside.

Cal had recovered and said, "It doesn't matter anymore. Finn is dead."

But Alene realized that Finn had lied to her face. He'd lied to everyone. "How did you figure out that Finn was the mastermind?" Alene asked. He should have gotten at least thirty years, like the others.

"We followed the paper trail," Lee said. "And Phineas made the mistake of bragging when he was in prison, so we had corroborating evidence."

"You mean from jailhouse snitches?" Cal asked. "Finn got out twenty-two years ago—what took you so long? And what about ..." Alene suspected he'd ask about the motorhome and shot him a warning glance. Instead, he asked, "What about the cryptocurrency, was that a lie too?"

"No, he really did start investing when Bitcoin was first available, and he made a substantial amount of money," Frank said. "We brought in specialists to unravel that part of the case because it was on the federal level, but the upshot is that Finn made a bundle. He moved around a lot, never got close to anyone, and frequently changed his identity."

Lee jumped in, "We've found at least twenty fake Social Security numbers that he used. And he gambled, but not in mob-controlled houses. Also, never more than ten thousand at a time."

Frank took over again, "We know that he moved at most ten thousand dollars from each account, every month. When an account fell in value, he didn't take anything."

"Do you know how many accounts he had?" Cal asked.

"We've identified about twenty of them so far," said Frank. "I suspect there are more."

Cal, who'd worked as a financial planner for thirty years, whistled through his teeth again. "So, let me get this straight. Ten thousand dollars times twenty different accounts add up to two hundred thousand dollars." He'd gotten louder and more dramatic. "You're saying he pulled that in every month?"

Lee shook his head. "It wasn't every month."

Alene mulled over the money Finn stole. Had it been worth losing his family and being alone all those years? She didn't think so. She looked over at her children, who'd finished eating and seemed to have lost interest in all the talk. Sierra was playing on her cellphone and the other two were starting to bounce around. Alene hoped they'd last another few minutes.

"What else did you learn, Frank?" Jocelyn asked. "You said there were a few things."

"Yeah, so this might also come as a surprise," Frank said, pausing. "Dori Stevens is the daughter of Vincent Stevens. She was arrested when she left here a few minutes ago. We didn't want to embarrass her in front of all of you." Alene was surprised that Frank and Lee had been so sensitive. She couldn't believe that Dori was Vincent's daughter.

Lee added, "She'll be charged with aiding and abetting. She helped her father with the two bodies."

Nobody moved for a full moment, stunned. Alene realized that Lee hadn't been leering—he'd been keeping tabs on Dori. She'd totally missed the boat on that one. "I hired Dori in November, before the Christmas season started," said Alene, "and Vincent started sitting outside around Christmas. I wonder if she mentioned my name, and he recognized that we were related to Finn."

Frank said, "Could be. He might have encouraged her to take this job. The one thing Vincent kept rambling about was that Finn Baron screwed him over. What I don't understand is why Dori went along with his craziness. She's not mentally ill."

"In any case, we've got her in custody," Lee said. "Maybe her father threatened her. Who knows?" He sounded wistful. Perhaps Alene hadn't been completely wrong about Lee liking Dori.

"But Dori was so good at marketing," said Ruthie. "And she was so considerate." Alene thought Ruthie was an angel, but maybe angels are incapable of suspecting malevolence.

"Are you guessing, or do you have proof about Dori?" Kacey asked.

"We don't arrest people based on guesswork," Lee answered, a bit more harshly than needed. "We found evidence in her car. Dead bodies leave clues."

"I bet Vincent made her do it," Olly said. He'd thought Dori was all right.

Edith turned red. "Dori is my friend. She would never allow dead bodies in her car." Maybe it was too much simultaneous bad news. She started sobbing and Alene worried that it was unsafe to breathe near her. Luckily, Jocelyn was there to wrap an arm around Edith's shoulders and gently guide her out. They all started gathering their things and heading to the door.

"Tell everyone about the diamond rings before they leave, Frank." Olly called out. Alene wondered why jewelry kept playing a role in the dramas of her life. There was a collective groan because Olly hadn't stopped referencing those rings since he found them. The lost one had turned up in his backpack, which was always a disorganized mess.

"We'll never know who they belonged to," said Frank, his arm around Alene. "So, there was no crime committed, much to Alene's relief."

"I wouldn't wear them no matter what," Kacey interrupted. "I don't like wearing dead people's things."

Olly said, "Otherwise known as antiques. You don't like antiques, Kacey."

"Yes, I do," she said, giving him a look. "Just not rings."

Frank said, "And since all of you are here, I thought it would be a good time to ask Alene something." He got down on one knee and Alene's heart felt like it was about to burst. There was a collective intake of air, and the room hushed except her son, who asked, "What is Frank doing?"

"I'm asking your mother to marry me," said Frank, looking up at Noah. His voice choked before he turned back to Alene. "I want to spend the rest of my life with you."

Noah's voice rang out, "And us, too. Right, Frank?"

"Absolutely," said Frank, still gazing in Alene's eyes.

"Wow, Dad, I can't believe it," said Rhona, clapping. "You're doing it." Everyone joined in the applause as Alene turned back to Frank.

"I've had the square diamond cleaned and appraised," Frank continued, "and it's going to look beautiful on you if you accept it." He pulled the box from his pocket. "It might need to be sized."

Alene was uncharacteristically speechless. Frank kissed her forehead, opened the box, removed the ring, and slid it onto her finger. She closed her eyes and wished her mother was alive to witness this moment.

That only lasted a second, because Blanca stood up and tapped on her glass until it was quiet again. "Congratulations to the happy couple. We're all so delighted for Alene, but I knew Frank wouldn't find those two boys who stole my things. Don't worry, I took care of it, and nobody got murdered." She lifted her arm in the air and said, "This is my gold watch that they gave me back."

Frank and Lee exchanged glances, and both turned to Blanca, unsure if she was admitting to a crime of some sort.

"You're not going to believe how she handled it," said Cal. "She called her grandmother in Poland, who then called the mothers of those two men. That's what I call justice." Everyone laughed.

Blanca interrupted, "They gave me Covid so now I can't smell anything, but they came to Cal's apartment, they returned what they took from me, and they tell me they're sorry."

Cal chuckled. "I wish you could have been there, Frank. It was beautiful."

Frank was looking at Alene, one arm around the back of her chair. "Cal?" he said, "We're okay."

Alene smiled, even though she was masked, and nobody else could tell.

Recipes

V = Vegan
GF = Gluten Free

Cardamom Ginger Cookies
V, GF

2 TBSP vegetable, avocado, or light olive oil
1 TBSP unfiltered apple cider vinegar
1 tsp pure vanilla extract
½ cup dark brown sugar, brown rice syrup, or
    maple syrup
2 cups almond flour, gluten-free flour (I use
    Namaste from Costco)
1 tsp baking powder
1 TBSP ground ginger powder
1 tsp ground cardamom powder
1 tsp ground cinnamon powder
¼ tsp fine sea or table salt
Option 1: 3 TBSPs turbinado, demerara, or maple
    sugar (large sugar crystals) for topping
Option 2: add zest from a small orange to the batter

In a large bowl, stir together olive oil, vinegar, vanilla, and brown sugar. In a small bowl, stir together flour, baking powder, ginger, cardamom, cinnamon, and salt. Stir the wet ingredients into the dry ingredients until combined. Refrigerate for 20 minutes (or so). Preheat the oven to 350°F/180°C and spray or line 2 cookie sheets. Remove batter from fridge and form into 1- or 2-inch balls. Press the cookie balls a bit and dip into the sugar if desired. Bake for about 10-12 minutes until golden (faster if you prefer soft cookies, slower if you prefer crispy cookies). Remove from the oven and let the cookies cool for about 15 minutes before transferring to a serving plate.

Chocolate Babka

V

2 tsp instant active dry yeast (1 package)
1 ½ to 2 cups plant-based milk (like oat, coconut, or nut)
¾ cup cane or monk fruit sugar (divided into ¼ and ½ cup)
4-5 cups all-purpose flour
1 tsp sea salt
¼ cup vegetable or olive oil
1/3 cup margarine like Smart Balance, Earth Balance, or another 'vegan butter'
¼ cup unsweetened cocoa powder (Hershey's Extra Dark works well)
2 tsp ground cinnamon
1 tsp pure vanilla extract
½ cup semi-sweet chocolate chips, divided (I use vegan mini chips)
Optional Glaze: microwave ½ cup dark brown sugar with ¼ cup water for one minute

In a large bowl, stir the yeast into the plant milk and ¼ cup of the sugar with one cup of flour. Let it bubble for a few minutes while you gather your other ingredients. With a large spoon, stir in the rest of the flour with salt and oil, until it all comes together in a loose ball. Knead the dough until it's no longer sticky and put it back into the bowl to rest, covered with a dishtowel, until it doubles in bulk (an hour or two, depending on where you live).

In a small bowl, stir together the softened margarine or vegan butter, the rest of the sugar (½ cup), cocoa powder, cinnamon, and vanilla extract. It will look like a paste.

While the dough is rising, line two standard loaf pans with parchment or baking paper. Divide the dough in half and roll each half to ½ inch thick. Spread ½ of the cocoa-cinnamon mix, and sprinkle with ½ of the chocolate chips. Leave a space, don't spread the filling to the edges. Carefully roll the dough over the filling and use a bit of water to glue down the edge. Repeat with the other half.

Now, with a sharp knife, slice each half lengthwise. You should be able to see the filling and the layers. Gently twist the first two halves so that you can still see the filling. It doesn't matter how you stuff it into the prepared loaf pan because it's going to look beautiful after it's baked, so it's up to you. Repeat with the other half.

Cover with the dishtowel and let the dough rise again until doubled, at least an hour. Preheat the oven to 350°F/180°C and bake for about 30-35 minutes. Optional: A few minutes before the loaves are ready to remove, microwave the glaze listed above (this is optional) and drizzle it over the top of each babka.

I learned how to bake Babka from my sister's mother-in-law when we were both young brides. Savta Leah was from Rumania and called them 'roladas,' and I used to bake them at least once a month. We'd eat one and freeze the other so that when we needed a rolada/babka, I could take it out of the freezer, heat it up in the oven, and serve it for dessert, a snack, or breakfast.

Lemon Poppyseed Cookies

V, GF

½ cup light brown sugar
¼ cup cane or monk fruit sugar
½ cup vegetable or light olive oil
1 tsp pure vanilla extract
Zest and juice of one large, fresh lemon (do not use
    bottled lemon juice)
2 cups gluten-free flour (I use Namaste Perfect
    Blend from Costco)
1 tsp baking soda
½ tsp baking powder
½ tsp fine sea salt
1 TBSP poppyseeds

Preheat the oven to 350°F/180°C. Line and spray 2
baking pans. In a large bowl, stir sugars, oil, vanilla,
lemon zest and juice (get every last drop). In a small
bowl, stir together flour, baking soda, baking
powder, salt, and poppyseeds. Mix the dry
ingredients into the wet ingredients. Use a
tablespoon to scoop 12 glops of batter onto each
baking pan (it'll be thick) for 24 big cookies. Bake for
12 -13 minutes until they start to brown around the
edges. Remove from the oven and let them cool
down. These cookies are soft and pillowy.

Meyer Lemon Rosemary Cake
V, GF

Zest and juice of 2 large, fresh Meyer lemons (or 3 small, but do not use bottled juice)
½ cup avocado, vegetable, or light olive oil
¾ cup agave or maple syrup (agave will be sweeter)
½ cup unsweetened applesauce, or blend (until smooth) a small, seeded apple with the liquids
1 teaspoon pure vanilla extract
2 ¼ cups all-purpose or gluten-free flour (like Namaste flour)
2 tsp baking powder
1 tsp baking soda
½ tsp fine salt
1 ½ tsp chopped rosemary (fresh is better, but dried will work)
Optional: powdered sugar to dust on top

Preheat oven to 350°F/180°C, line and spray a 9" round or a standard loaf pan. Into a large bowl, stir lemon zest and juice, olive oil, agave, applesauce, and vanilla.

Into a small bowl, sift the flour, baking powder, soda, and salt. Pour dry ingredients into the lemon mixture, add rosemary, and stir gently together just until mixed. Bake 35-45 minutes until the top bounces back. Cool in the pan for about 30 minutes until you can easily remove the cake to a serving platter. Dust with powdered sugar if desired.

"Very nicely lemony, very moist, very versatile - dessert or breakfast treat or great with afternoon

tea! I checked at 30 minutes (first pic) and put back in for 5 minutes - used the toothpick test the second time. It came out of pan easily and I had a piece after it 20 minutes out if pan - still slightly warm - YUM!!! I thought it was easy and I will def make again!!" Tami Olsen (Northbrook, Illinois)

Peanut Butter Banana Bread

V, GF

3 very ripe large bananas
½ cup soft, natural peanut butter
¼ cup dark brown sugar
2 TBSP unfiltered apple cider vinegar or lemon juice
½ cup plant milk (like almond or another nut, oat, coconut etc.)
1 tsp pure vanilla extract
2 cups gluten-free flour (I use Namaste from Costco. You can also use all-purpose flour)
1 tsp baking soda
½ tsp baking powder
1 tsp cinnamon
1 tsp coriander
½ tsp ground ginger
½ tsp fine salt
Option: ½ cup semi-sweet chocolate chips or chopped nuts

Preheat oven to 350°F/180°C. Line and spray a standard loaf pan. In a large bowl, mash wet ingredients. In a small bowl, stir together dry ingredients. Add flour mixture to the banana mixture and stir just until blended. Fold in the chocolate chips or chopped nuts, or some of each (if desired). Transfer to the loaf pan and bake for 50-55 minutes until the top springs bake when pressed. Allow it to cool before removing it from the pan.

Pumpernickel Bread

V

2½ tsp active dry yeast (1 package) OR: ¼ cup
    sourdough starter (Start the previous night if
    using starter, and after the first knead, let the
    dough rest covered in the refrigerator
    overnight)
1 ½ cup strong coffee, room temperature
2 TBSP unsweetened cocoa
2 TBSP dark brown sugar
¼ cup olive oil
3+cups bread or high-gluten flour
1 cup rye flour
1 tsp salt
Optional: 3 tsp caraway seeds

In a large bowl, combine the dry yeast (or ¼ cup of
starter) with the coffee, cocoa, sugar, and 1 cup of
bread flour. As soon as you see bubbles, add the rest
of the ingredients, slowly folding it over until it's a
big, sticky ball. Use a scraper to get it all out of the
bowl and onto a floured surface. Knead, adding a
little more flour if needed, until the dough is smooth.
Rinse out the bowl, lightly oil it, then turn the dough
to coat it on all sides. Cover the bowl and let dough
rise until it's nearly double in size (1 to 2 hours).

If you used a sourdough starter and began the
previous night, remove it from the refrigerator first
thing in the morning, and let it get to room
temperature before punching it down and kneading
it.

Knead both kinds of dough for 5-10 minutes until it
has the feel of an earlobe (I know that sounds yucky,

but it's true). Return it to the bowl, covered, to rise again, and let it rise until it's nearly doubled (this will depend on moisture and altitude). Now, mold it into a round or oval loaf and with a sharp knife, make a few slashes on the top.

If it's a yeast dough, transfer it to a lined baking pan and preheat the oven to 400°. Bake for about 45+ minutes until it's golden brown and when you tap it, the sound is hollow. Remove from the oven.

If it's a sourdough, put the bottom of a Dutch Oven (an enameled, thick-walled cooking pot with a tight lid) inside and preheat the oven to 400°. Carefully place the slashed round of sourdough inside the Dutch Oven and cover it. Bake about 40+ minutes covered, then remove the cover and bake an additional 10 minutes until the crust is browned.

Remove from oven.

Let your bread cool down a bit before slicing. Enjoy!

Radish-Top Pesto
V, GF

1 bunch green radish tops, washed and drained
    (use the radishes for something else)
1 handful of fresh Italian parsley
⅓ cup extra-virgin olive oil plus more as needed
¼ cup fresh lemon juice (one medium lemon)
3 cloves raw garlic
½ to ¾ cup unsalted, roasted almonds,
    pistachios, or walnuts
Salt (at least ½ tsp) and freshly ground black
    pepper, to taste

In a food processor, pulse until everything is
uniform. Stop processing before it becomes
mushy. Serve with cut-up vegetables (like the
radishes) or crackers.

Sweet Potato Quinoa Salad
V

2 medium sweet potatoes, unpeeled and cubed or diced
1 tsp sea salt
3 tablespoons extra virgin olive oil
1 cup uncooked quinoa
2 cups water or vegetable broth
1 can (15oz) reduced salt black beans, rinsed and drained
1 large red pepper, cored and diced
1 small red onion, diced
¼ cup (2 or 3 sprigs) chopped fresh parsley
½ tsp smoked or regular paprika
½ tsp chili powder
½ tsp garlic powder
¼ tsp ground pepper
Zest and juice of two fresh limes (not bottled)

Preheat oven to 400°F/204°C. Pour the olive oil over the sweet potatoes, sprinkle with salt, and mix well. Place on a baking pan and roast for 40-45 minutes until slightly browned, flipping the potatoes at least once. After removing them from the oven, let them come to room temperature.

Meanwhile, in a large microwave-safe serving bowl, microwave the quinoa in water or broth for 10 minutes (or cook as directed in a pot on the stove and then move to a bowl). Stir lightly. Add the black beans, diced red pepper, diced red onion, chopped parsley, and spices. Add the cubed sweet potatoes.

Add the zest and juice of 2 limes and stir lightly until the salad is blended. Add an additional tablespoon (or two) of olive oil if it's too dry, and more salt and pepper to taste. Add an additional protein if desired, but quinoa is packed with protein!

Tahini Chocolate Chip Cookies
V, GF

3 cups old-fashioned gluten-free oats (I use the Trader Joe kind)
2 TBSP flax meal
1 tsp baking powder
1 tsp ground cinnamon
¼ tsp fine sea salt
½ cup packed brown sugar (light or dark)
½ cup canola, light olive, or avocado oil
¼ cup plain tahini
¼ cup water
1 tsp pure vanilla extract
½ cup semi-sweet chocolate chips

Preheat oven to 350°F/180°C. Line and spray two cookie sheets. In a food processor, blend oats, flax meal, baking powder, cinnamon, and salt - until uniform. Add brown sugar, oil, tahini, water, and vanilla. Blend just until it's smooth, then stop. Stir in the chocolate chips (pulsing will break apart the chips). Transfer to a bowl and refrigerate for about 15 minutes while you clean up. With wet hands, form 24 balls and space them on the two cookie sheets. Bake for about 13-15 minutes until slightly golden. Cool for at least 10 minutes. If you try to nab one before it's cool, it will fall apart!!

Acknowledgements

Thanks to DX Varos Publishing for waiting patiently even though I haven't come through with a new Whipped and Sipped novel each year. I'm grateful to Sandi Wisenberg; teacher and editor extraordinaire, who, with her trusty pencil, edited draft after draft of three Whipped and Sipped books so far, and to "The Squad," she convened. The four of us, including poet and Professor Emerita Natania Rosenfeld and essayist/soon-to-be-novelist Thalia Mostow Bruehl, meet every week to listen, encourage, and make suggestions to each other from a place of love and admiration.

Thanks to my brilliant sister-in-law Annie Gottlieb, who turned her laser-focused copy-editing skills from science to culinary mystery and cleaned up flaws both big and small. Thanks to Tracey Phillips for inviting me to join the Blackbird Writers — a fabulous group of authors that read each other's books and support each other's marketing efforts. And thanks to Sisters in Crime — I'm honored to do be on the Chicago board and have learned an immense amount about writing, publishing, and marketing from our monthly programs.

Thanks to my close friend and first reader, Arna Yastrow. Thanks to Valerie Biel for her PR and Marketing work and author friends Anne Louis Bannon and Karen Odden (whose superb historical mysteries are among my favorites) for giving me the feedback I needed to finish Charred. Thanks to everyone who tested my recipes, which usually start out with silly mistakes (because I assume that everyone knows exactly what my shorthand instructions mean): Ann Leviton, Arna Yastrow, Claire Quinn, Debbie Schy, Diane Halivni, Eric Vollrath, Linda Kupfer, Lucy Shirrell, Marla Levie Craven, Rachael Siegelman, Sherrill Joseph, and Tami Olsen.

For ongoing love and support, I thank my mother, Helen Pinsky, my siblings, and their spouses: Janet and Gadi Cohen, Elizabeth and Milton Pinsky, Cindy Berryman and Martin Pinsky, and my cherished children: Danielle Sassower and Scottie Thomas (who were kind enough to provide me with a grandchild), Rebecca and Drew Willert, Gabriel Gottlieb, and Annie Beckman. Unending thanks to my beloved husband David, my first and best critic, who provides near constant love and support.

About the Author

G.P. Gottlieb holds undergraduate and graduate degrees in piano and voice. During her career as a cantor, a high school music teacher, and the administrator of the law center at DePaul University College of Law, she has also written stories, songs, and several unwieldy manuscripts. She is a graduate of the French Pastry School's Bread Boot Camp. Furthermore, she is the host of New Books in Literature, a podcast of the New Books Network and partner of LitHub. After recovering from breast cancer, she turned to writing in earnest, melding her two loves, nourishment for mind and body in recipe-laced murder mysteries.

If you enjoyed reading Charred...
Please leave a review!

AMAZON, BARNES & NOBLE,

GOODREADS, and BOOKSHOP.ORG

Visit the website (https://gpgottlieb.com) to read
more about the Whipped and Sipped Mystery series,
more of the author's recipes,
her list of all-time-favorite mystery authors,
and her New Books Network podcast interviews
with authors of literary fiction!

Stay in touch!

Facebook: authorgottlieb

Twitter: GottliebGP

Instagram: WhippedSipped

Alene Baron's life is never dull!

First she solved the murder of a friend in

Battered

Then, the mysterious death of the local bully in

Smothered

And two more local bodies were found in

Charred

Now, Alene and her staff host a memorial for the father of one of her employees, who died while hiking in Colorado with a few friends. Alene knows one of the friends' wives from her kids' school. When that woman's husband is found dead a month later, Alene finds herself drawn into another mystery in

Pounded

Coming soon to a bookstore near you!